FORBIDDEN ORIGINS PRESENTS

I0665600

echoes of
the old
UNIVERSE

A COLLECTION OF SHORT STORIES FROM THE WAR FOR THE UNIVERSE

JAY LAWSON
ANGEL ROMERO
DYLAN GORDON
NOAH ALMAZAN
DOMINIC DEVITO
SETH PHOTOPOULOS

FOREWORD

After the schism between Corrin and The All Father, all out war broke out across the universe. Homes were set ablaze, planets were turned into battlefields. Children became soldiers and mothers became murderers. These letters, retellings, and first hand accounts have been compiled together to show that Corrin's split from The Black Palace not only affected his life, but everyone else's as well.

"EVEN THE SMALLEST PERSON
CAN MAKE THE BIGGEST
RIPPLE ACROSS THE STARS."

-ZAMAN

TABLE OF CONTENTS

Table of Contents

ECHOES OF
THE OLD
UNIVERSE

TALES

The sun rose over the horizon, casting a blanket of golden light across the valley. The hum of Black Palace aircraft sounded in the distance. It smelled of morning dew and smoke from the campfire. Heleyna liked to wake up early to watch the sunrise while she ate her breakfast. She sat uncomfortably against a tree, her old joints aching from having to sleep on the hard ground.

Her entire village had fled into the forest when they heard reports of Black Palace troops marching on the nearby towns. Heleyna stared down at her breakfast; a couple of unripe Skal fruits and some stale bread stared back. Their food supplies were running low, she hoped the soldiers were only passing through so they could return home soon.

As Heleyna finished up her breakfast, the rest of the townsfolk were waking up and each going about their day. She saw a group of kids who would normally be running around playing or telling jokes and laughing. Instead they were just sitting, staring into the fire or huddling next to their parents while they handed out food. She couldn't bear to watch the once lively kids in this state.

"Gather around children," she said, waving them all over to where she was sitting, "I want to tell you all a story."

The kids reluctantly made their way over to her and sat. Her own granddaughter sat at her feet. She thought for a second, deciding which story would be good for the kids to hear right now.

Finally she picked one and began. "Long ago, on another planet far away from here. There were people known as the Halvodis, they were peaceful people who lived in nomadic tribes."

"What is nomadic?" asked one of the children.

"Nomadic means they traveled around and camped out wherever they found themselves, never really settling down and building towns."

"So like we're doing right now?" the kid asked.

"Exactly," said Heleyna, "The tribes of Halvodon all traveled around their planet, foraging for food and living amongst nature."

She began to braid her granddaughter's hair while she continued the story.

"Once a year all the different tribes from around the land would come together and hold a huge beautiful festival. They would lay out a huge feast with different foods from each tribe. Music of all different types would play throughout the night. People dressed in vibrant colors danced and laughed while kids ran around and played."

She told the kids of all the different cultures that existed in Halvodon and how each tribe had their own way of living.

The kids listened happily. She looked around at all their faces while she talked, happy to be giving these kids some hope for their own lives. Heleyna explained how the Halvodi festival was the biggest gathering anyone had ever seen and how people would plan for it all year long until the day finally came.

Her granddaughter looked up. "Can we have a party like that Grandma?"

"Maybe someday," Heleyna replied, "But for now we need to stay here until the bad people go away. The Halvodis, however, had this festival to celebrate life. Entire valleys and meadows filled with people having a great time. The children swam and played in the rivers while the adults danced and told stories from around the planet."

Another child spoke up. "Do they still have the festival each year?"

Heleyna thought of the Halvodi people and their sad history. The Itarian Empire had invaded Halvodon in the Seventh Cycle and since they had no standing military, the Halvodi tribes stood no chance. After that, when The All Father awoke, he tried to get them to submit and when they refused he wiped out the entire planet.

"Sadly, the Halvodi people are no longer around," she said, silently wondering if her people might suffer the same fate.

Heleyna looked around at the children wondering if they would get to reach adulthood. She quickly shut that thought out of her head and thought of another story to tell.

"Have you kids heard the story of Doren's Rebellion?"

The children shook their heads. Heleyna cleared her throat and began her story.

"The Itarians used to make men fight each other for their entertainment. Doren had special powers and because of that he was taken from his family as a young boy around your age. He was trained to fight as a gladiator in giant arenas full of people. Doren was one of the best fighters the Itarian Empire had ever seen. People from all across the universe would travel across galaxies to see him fight. These fights, however, took advantage of people with special powers. They were forced to fight against their will and would be punished or killed if they refused. Doren did not like this and neither did the other fighters, so they all banded together under the leadership of Doren and fought against the Itarians. For an entire year they fought, and although Doren lost his life for the cause, the Itarian Empress put a stop to the enslavement of these people and stopped the gladiatorial matches all together."

"Wait, if he was such a great warrior," one of the little kids started to ask, "Then how did he die?"

"Well…"

She thought for a moment.

"The Itarians were very powerful, but what matters is that he died for a reason. He completed his mission of getting the fighting matches to end and he freed all his fellow warriors. On his home planet of Scav, the people built a statue to honor him, his life, and his death. Sometimes sacrifices need to be made for a good cause."

Heleyna spent the rest of the day telling the kids stories, some from her life when she was younger, some tall tales her own grandmother had told her when she was a child, and some histories from across the universe.

By the time she wrapped up her last story, the sun had begun to set and the kids were all being called back by their parents. Only her granddaughter stayed behind watching the sunset with her. They split a piece of bread and ate in silence until her granddaughter spoke up.

"Grandma?" she asked without looking away from the pink light the setting sun painted across the darkening sky, "Have you ever been to space?" She took another bite of her bread.

"No,' Heleyna answered honestly, "I've always wanted to go, honey. Sadly I'm too old now."

The sky was quickly getting darker and hundreds of specks of light sprinkled the darkness like freckles across the universe's face.

"I'm gonna go up there someday," said the little girl, pointing up at the stars, "I'm gonna go see all the stars up close."

Heleyna chuckled at her granddaughter's enthusiasm.

"Well, you ever see them, tell them I said 'Hi'."

As the sun faded and the moons and stars were the only light left in the sky, Heleyna and her granddaughter laid down to sleep. She watched as the child fell asleep. Heleyna closed her own eyes and slipped into a slumber. She dreamed that her granddaughter would one day fulfill her wish of seeing the stars.

ALLEGIANCE COMMUNICATION

Message from: Scout Leader Odarus Med

To: Allegiance General Jargus

Location: The connected worlds of LweeVeer

Recruitment failed. After arriving to the liberated city of Xharcos Bay, zero civilians joined our ranks. The morale here seems low after Black Palace loyalists attempted to destroy the land bridge that connects both planets. Many of our fighters are urging to return home. Has word been sent out to Corrin and Allegiance command about the men and women being able to rotate out? We lost communication with our supply route two weeks ago. Food is low. Blasters for the company are deteriorating. Immediate response is requested.

Scout Leader Odarus Med

THE PIT

The planet Hanroh is a difficult environment to live on unless you are a Hanran. The Hanran people are practically the same as every other humanoid species throughout the universe, except they have large digging claws instead of hands and have eyes able to see even in pitch black settings. The claws allowed the Hanran society to evade the dusty and dry conditions of their planet by tunneling and living in the mountains high in the sky where life could survive.

That is at least what I have been told. My name is Bi-Zo. Well actually, my name, or rather my identification number, is 25913. We are no longer allowed to truly have names and must only address ourselves, and each other, by our ID numbers. But my parents thought it was important to give me and my brothers names, even if they had to be kept secret.

I am a fifth generation pit dweller. We have lived in the darkness and cold, surviving off only nutritional pills since the second generation.

The days of living in the mountains for the Hanrans is over, if it was ever really true. The Hanran people are now slaves to The Black Palace, myself included.

The surface of Hanroh may be harsh, but The Black Palace only has interest in what lies beneath it.

Ironium Metal is scattered all throughout the dirt, going deep into the planet. With our ability to tunnel in and out of the planet so well, our entire population was enlisted into The Black Palace. We were forced to harvest Ironium to be used as second protective plating of the Black Palace fleet.

Every day is the same. We are alive only to serve and aid The Black Palace. Yet there are whispers, whispers about the surface, about something called the sun. A ball of fire in the sky, that lights up the whole world. It doesn't sound believable. No one alive has ever seen such a thing. There is nothing but darkness. It is all we have ever known, and to believe that there is something better is foolish.

People say that the pit is open, that sunlight enters only to be swallowed up by the vastness of the pit so it does not reach us. My parents believe these words and hold out hope. They heard stories from their grandparents about a time before the pit. But I think it's all made up.

There is no room for teaching or hoping in our lives, only surviving and mining. The pit is split up into four quadrants. One for living and the other three for digging. Each quadrant is so large that you can stand at the highest level and even our eyes are unable to see the bottom. I do not believe in the sun, but I do believe that the surface exists, and that our pit spans under the entire surface of the planet.

No one has ever escaped the pit, how could they? The Black Palace has guards positioned everywhere, and there are more people like me, who believe only in survival, than the dreamers who hold onto hope of one day seeing the sun. At least until just now.

A small group of Hanrans, including my parents, apparently have been plotting a rebellion this whole time. They attacked the Black Palace guards at the top of the first quadrant and caused an explosion that shook the whole quadrant. This started a whole uprising, and chaos ensued in a mad dash to try and escape through a rumored opening to the surface caused by the explosion. I don't believe in the sun, but I won't miss an opportunity to escape this life of bondage.

I ran through the levels of the quadrant, lost in a sea of my fellow people, as The Black Palace began to gun down every Hanran they saw. I inched closer and closer to the highest level. The gunfire was increasing but I finally thought I saw it.

A light brighter than anything I have ever seen was right there, but standing in the way was an armada of soldiers firing upon us. My fellow Hanrans charged aimlessly toward the light and I got caught up inside them. Bodies fell left and right, but eventually our numbers overwhelmed the soldiers and we started to climb out toward the surface.

As the struggle for freedom raged on behind, I climbed out to the surface. It was bright. I turned around to see the pit spanning out over the entire horizon. Then, I looked up. The sun, it's true. A ball of fire in the sky. It warmed my skin.

I basked in its light, but only for a moment. The Black Palace soldiers regained control of my people behind me. As they opened fire on me, all I could think about was how nice the sun felt, and how foolish I was for not believing.

BLACK PALACE CORRESPONDENCE

Lieutenant Sei'yd to Commander Gydian:

Our forces have taken heavy losses on Telamor. We need reinforcements or we will lose strategical positions in both the North and the East. We need Overseeing General Kartov to approve troop deployment from the fleet stationed in the Davos System in order for The Black Palace to retain control of the planet. Radio communications have been taken out by Allegiance Insurgents across Telamor. I fear this message will not make it to you in time commander. If not, I Lieutenant Sei'yd, Officer of The Black Palace, recite my oath:

For the Spear. For the Father. For the Universe.

Lt. Sei'yd
3rd Infantry- Telamor

LOVE THROUGH FEAR

Would you rather love someone through manipulation or love someone through fear? That's what my sister always asked me. She had a way of turning philosophical moments into annoying lectures. To be honest, it's what I miss the most about her.

She was conscripted into the Black Palace Military four years ago. My father couldn't handle it, so he left. My mother has been a shell of herself ever since. I remember watching The Black Palace appointed Governor of our town address us all that day. He told us that "The Creator" called for all boys and girls between the ages of fifteen and twenty-five to join the military. I was thirteen at the time. Two years too young. I remember all the mothers and fathers screaming and crying as soldiers snatched their children away. Why didn't we fight back? It wasn't until later I heard parents talking about Halvodon and the massacre that took place there. If Halvodon couldn't do anything, how could we on Gorkon.

I basically raised myself after that. I was the only daughter left of a broken family so I looked for a job and found solace in my work. I got a job in the mines. I met a boy. I expected to be conscripted but it never happened. Everything seemed normal. I mean, as normal as it could be. Then, news started to come in about a battle between Corrin and The Black Palace.

I had just finished my last shift and was on my way home when I saw a bunch of workers gathered around an old Itarian transmitter. The message being received was weak but we all heard the words.

"Freedom is here! Take up arms now!"

Many of the guys I worked with were older men. Fathers whose children were conscripted into The Black Palace. Many couldn't fight. Some were mumbling amongst themselves about what to do. I pushed my way closer to the radio and turned up the volume.

"This is General Dalire of Kaasiar. Corrin and a few warriors from Wan-Ri have made the first blow towards The Black Palace."

Corrin? The son of The All Father? I saw everyone's eyes widen. More people gathered around now. The General's voice continued.

"No matter where you are, no matter what planet you reside on, this war includes you. No more sons, daughters, sisters, and brothers will be at the mercy of The All Father!"

I gripped the table.

"This is the fight of our lives. Join us! If you are able-bodied, meet us on Vaxlier four days from now. This is General Dalire of Kaasiar. Out!"

People were chattering loudly now. Many were confused. Corrin is the son of The All Father and he's fighting against him? All out war? I didn't know exactly what was going on, but I knew what I needed to do.

I pushed past the large crowd that had gathered around and raced home. My mother was sitting on the porch looking up to the stars. I could have told her what was going on. But there was no time.

I packed a bag and darted out of the house. I stopped momentarily and looked back. My mother was still staring up at the stars. I became a ghost when my sister was taken. But maybe now, maybe if I fight, I can find her and bring her back.

At the edge of Paradin, traders were loading up their ships to head off world. I looked for anyone heading to the Rayon Prime System. Luckily, a woman was heading there. I told her I had money. I mentioned I worked in the mines and could help around the ship for free. I made it clear I needed to be on Vaxlier in four days.

She looked me up and down. I was bigger for my age. Had dark hair like my father. She looked into my brown eyes and I guess she could tell how determined I was. She didn't ask any questions. All she did was take my money and said we'd be on Vaxlier within three days.

Her ship was a speeder, used mostly for quick trading deposits to different star systems. She looked a little older and rough around the edges. I didn't care though. I needed to get to Vaxlier. I knew this was dangerous. I knew if this war was real, I could possibly die. But I figured that if I did see battle, maybe there was a chance I'd find my sister. Maybe she'd shoot at me on some planet out there. Maybe we'd come across each other on the battle field. I didn't know. One thing I knew for sure was that I figured out what she meant all those years ago.

I would rather love someone through fear. Not fear of them, but fear of never seeing them again. I would rather die knowing I did everything I could to find my sister, despite knowing how scary this journey was about to be.

I don't care about the war. I don't know Corrin or The All Father. My sister is out there somewhere. And if I have to be afraid and alone to find her, then that's what I'm going to do.

"LOVE ENOUGH TO ENDURE"

They asked me if I would die for him
I said for him I would live.
They told me that meant nothing
That I would live all the same.
I reminded them, in times like these,
That death is a sacrifice easily made
And living is the greater testament.

-JONLI WIRBUSING

ASSAULT ON KYROS VI

For six months, war had engulfed the galaxy. The armies of The Black Palace clashed with the ragtag coalition of militias and planetary defense forces that composed The Allegiance. Planets and star systems traded hands. Fleets of starships collided in the blackness of space. Death and destruction was the rule of law, and the Anrachi were eager to finally get in on the bloody action.

When Corrin initiated the war against his father, entire star systems flocked to his banner, and the Anrachi were no different. Decades of rule under The All Father were peaceful, but it was an Imperial peace. If any planet, any star system, any civilization, dared to step out of line, The All Father would bring to bear the Black Palace and its immense weight down on any disruptor.

Before The All Father's conquest, the Anrachi were said to potentially rival the Itarians; if given enough time to build and develop. But when The All Father began his reconquest of the galaxy, the Anrachi gladly folded their forces into those of The Black Palace.

And for a time, it was good. The universe thrived, Anrach expanded and influenced its neighbors. But as the centuries passed, things changed. Trade deals were exploited, taxes levied, and more and more Anrachi boys were demanded as cannon fodder for The All Father's war machine.

When word came back that over a million Anrachi sons had died during a particularly bloody battle on the other side of the galaxy, they decided enough was enough. Articles of Separation were drafted, and independence agreed upon. However, The All Father has eyes and ears everywhere, and he brought his might down on the Anrachi.

For over a year, the Anrachi held out, but The All Father was too much. The Anrachi Chancellor was executed, their military neutered, and Kyros IV, Anrach's sister world, taken as a stronghold for The Black Palace.

For decades, The Anrachi suffered more and more under the yoke of The All Father's oppression, but then Corrin came along, and things changed. His single act of defiance inspired and emboldened the galaxy. His victory proved that The All Father wasn't infallible. He could be defeated.

Anrach sent emissaries to Arcadia, Lord Corrin's capital world, and quickly committed their forces to The Allegiance. That presented a problem. The Anrachi military was small, but their industrial capacity had grown over time. With that in mind, General Roan

Vallick, current head of the Anrachi Defense Force, was tasked with bringing up the fledgling military to a wartime footing.

For six months, Vallick rebuilt the Anrachi military. The rearmament project involved retooling the planet's industry. Shipyards were federalized, and warships of all types were churned out at breakneck speed. Modernized and updated ships of the line fought small engagements against probing Black Palace battle groups just outside of Anrach's moon, Jotuun.

The navy's mission was to hold off The Black Palace while the army was rebuilt, and in the time that he was given, Vallick reformed the Defense Force. Over twelve million soldiers were recruited, and all were trained in record time.

Divided into the Army, Planetary Guard, Starfighter Corp, and Marines Corp, the Anrachi Republic Combined Forces rivaled that of their ancient counterparts.

Vallick was proud of the men and women now under his command, and quickly turned his attention towards their first military operation in centuries. Both the military high command and civilian leadership agreed on their first target: Kyros VI.

Losing their sister world had remained a sore point for Anrach. Knowing how dangerous this battle could be, Vallick reformed the famous Anrachi Rangers; once feared throughout the galaxy, disbanded after The All Father's reconquest. Amassing over four hundred ships, and an army of over three million, Operation: Iron Dawn was under way. The assault on Kyros IV had begun.

Onboard the Anrachi troop transport *Obrah Silentum*

One hour before Kyros VI space fold

Corporal Niles walked in lockstep with the rest of his Ranger company. They were making their way to the ship's central hangar, where preparations were underway for the Kyros invasion. Rangers, Marines, and Infantry mulled about, prepping drop ships and munitions.

Tanks and APCs were driven onto armor and infantry transports; supplies checked and double checked. His unit, Alpha company, was apart of the 45th Anrachi Rangers, one of six regiments that had been chosen to participate in the first wave of Iron Dawn.

Alpha Company marched into the middle of the massive hangar, paused and stood at attention.

Their commanding officer, Colonel Andros, hopped onto a crate of ammunition, and cleared his throat.

"Ladies and gentlemen, welcome."

He looked around at the Rangers standing in front of him.

"While I understand you've all been briefed beforehand on our mission here, it won't hurt for us to go over it one more time."

He took out a holo projector from a pouch on his breastplate, and turned it on. A projection of snow covered Kyros popped on, and zoomed in on a massive Anti-Capital Ship cannon that rested on a ridge-line planet-side. The cannon was stationed dead center of a Black Palace stronghold.

"As you know, the 45th and our sister regiments have been tasked with seizing the six guns scattered around Kyros from the hands of the Palace. Command figures they'd be put to better use under our control."

Niles and his fellow rangers chuckled.

"We'll be inserting via drop pods. It's going to be a hot drop; air support will be limited until we can take those guns, and we won't get any armor until we've secured them. So that means we have to move fast."

Andros shut the projector off, and looked back at his men.

"However, command thought wisely, and sent ahead the Raiders to set up the battlefield for us."

That caught Alpha's attention. The Raiders were a unit within the Rangers. They were trained for sabotage incursions. They were dangerous, ruthless, and methodical.

"If they did their jobs right, while we come down in our pods, the Palace will be in for an explosive surprise." Andros hopped down from his perch. "We are thirty minutes out Rangers, let's get that last minute prep done, move!"

Bridge of Anrachi Battleship *HawkMoon*

Ten Minutes before Kyros VI space fold

Supreme Commander Vallick stood on the bridge of his flagship, the HawkMoon. Considered to be the most powerful warship ever built by Sabo Industries, the premiere Anrachi shipyard; it was only fitting it would be the flagship for the invasion.

Vallick looked down at his personal computer screen.

"Ensign, put us on yellow alert."

"Aye aye sir."

Alarm klaxons began to softly wail, an automated female voice spoke over the ships PA system:

"All hands yellow alert, all hands yellow alert."

Two holo emitters lit up in front of Vallick's station. On the left, Admiral Reya, her Navy uniform neat and pressed. On the right, Marshal Venrum stood at attention, his cap held cooly under his armpit. They both saluted in unison.

"At ease."

They both lowered their hands.

Reya spoke first. " Commander, all ships are accounted for. Starfighter squadrons prepped and ready for launch the moment we space-fold into Kyrosi orbit."

Vallick nodded.

"Good."

He turned his attention to Venrum, who picked up on the unspoken signal to speak.

"Sir, my Rangers and Marines are at their launch bays. Once their goals have been accomplished, our Infantry and Armored units will be able to land and push out of the beachheads. And if our intelligence is correct, the Palace forces arrayed against us are understrength, lacking morale. Should be a quick campaign." He put on his cap, and placed his arms behind his back.

Vallick mused over what Venrum had told him. He fiddled with the watch his grandfather had given him when he was child. It was still in good condition, something Vallick always held a sense of personal pride over.

"Venrum, remember what we learned in the Academy: quick campaigns are ideal, but are hardly ever fought."

He sat back down in his command chair, and let out a sigh.

"I admire your optimism, but even if The Black Palace is outmanned, they still have home field advantage. They've had time to map out every corner of Kyros. Our own maps are out of date, and they know that."

He took another glance at the battle plans for Operation Iron Dawn.

"Reya, can we spare any more fighter-bomber squadrons for close air support for the first wave of the invasion?"

Reya looked at someone off screen, and nodded.

"Yes we can."

"Good. Let's get to it then."

Central hangar bay
the *Obrah Silentum*

Less than five minutes until Kyros jump

The Silentum was on red alert status. The alarm klaxons blasted throughout the transport. Within the hangar bay itself, the 45th scrambled into their assigned drop pods. Orbital Insertion Pods were always used by the Anrachi, and these current, updated designs were state of the art. In ancient times, they only carried three troopers, and they were incredibly flimsy. Even the slightest touch from anti-air fire could destroy a pod, making their usage high risk.

But with new designs courtesy of Maven Manufactorum, OIP's were made of sturdier material, that came with energy shielding and allowed allowed for six soldier capacity, a full fireteam, to use them. Niles strapped himself in, checking to make sure he was safely secured in his seat.

His teammates did the same. Andros spoke to Niles and the rest of the 45th over their universal communication channel in their helmets, "Looks like advance elements of the strike group have engaged the Palace fleet."

"We have our window, be ready for the space fold!"

A thirty second countdown showed up in the top right corner of his helmet's heads up display.

Adrenaline shot through Niles's system. He felt the Silentum space fold into Kyrosi orbit. The Navy technician banged on the outside of the OIP.

"You're good. Give em hell boys!"

Hundreds of OIP's were disgorged from the bellies of the Obrah Silentum and other troop transports. Given the range of the planetary guns, it was a fast drop; the transports quickly folded out of range. As they dropped into Kyrosi atmosphere, the Anrachi battle group grappled with the Palace fleet stationed above Kyros.

Destroyers and frigates harassed the much larger Palace ships, while Anrachi Battleships directly engaged the Spearcraft carriers one on one.

Starships traded energy fire, missiles left contrails in space, and fighter craft flew in between their motherships like gnats. It was pure chaos.

The Ranger's drop pods hurtled down from the planet's upper atmosphere, with Skyclaw fighters providing escort. Niles opened up a video feed in his heads up display; a camera attached to the underside of the OIP allowing him to watch their descent onto Kyros.

The 45th Rangers were tasked with securing the gun tower stationed on the planet's northwest sector. Dubbed "Tower Delta", it was situated in the center of a Palace stronghold; itself surrounded by a network of trenches. The 45th's designated landing site was about a click out from the stronghold, which would put them in the snow covered forest that encircled the enemy base.

And if the Raiders did their job correctly-

He was interrupted from his musings as dozens, and then hundreds of explosions began to appear on the planet's surface below them.

"Looks like the Raiders did their job!"

The Raiders had gone ahead of the invasion force, and had planted small, powerful, undetectable explosives in vital parts of the Palace strongpoints scattered around the planet.

Everything from munition dumps to air bases were fair game. And from what Niles could tell, Tower Delta's defenses weren't spared from the Raider's meticulous and thorough planning.

After a ten minute free fall, the OIPs activated small thrusters that would slow their decent, preventing the pods from slamming into the planet's surface at terminal velocity.

Niles watched the altitude counter get smaller and smaller, and the surface getting closer and closer.

"Get ready boys!"

The pod slammed down hard, and the entrance panels burst open. Niles and his teammates jumped out, weapons up and ready. A few other pods landed near them, and a rendezvous marker appeared on the compass of Niles's HUD.

The now platoon sized unit made their way to the muster location that Andros had set for the company. Anrachi Friend or Foe tags highlighted their fellow Rangers, preventing any friendly fire incidents from occurring as they all trooped their way slowly through the snow. It was slow going, but eventually Alpha Company had gathered in a loose defensive perimeter at the assigned coordinates.

Andros took a few seconds to take stock of the situation at hand. For their first combat drop, the 45th had taken no casualties on the way down. A few firefights had erupted against some. Palace patrols, but they sustained light casualties, and had wiped out the opposition.

Niles was busy gathering extra magazines for his assault rifle when Andros began relaying orders over the coms.

"Alright, Dog, Kando, and Sorin Companies have engaged the tower's garrison. We have a few trenches to navigate before we can join the party but it's nothing we can't handle."

Niles slammed a magazine home into his weapon; bringing his full attention to Andros.

"Everybody ready?!"

The Rangers belted out a "Hoorah" in response.

"Alright, I want light repeaters laying down suppressive fire as we push the trenches."

He pointed at a Ranger armed with a heat seeking rocket launcher.

"I want heat seekers targeting enemy pillboxes and their auto turret defenses."

As he relayed orders the company quickly took up positions at the edge of the forest.

A pair of Skyclaw fighter-bombers screamed overhead, strafing the Palace trenches with Fusion missiles and plasma fire.

"That's our cue gentleman, let's move!"

With a battle cry, Alpha company ran across the clearing. Light repeaters laid down covering fire, and heat seeking missiles streaked past the charging rangers, impacting against their targets.

Niles and his fireteam were amongst the first of the company to reach the trench line. They hopped in, sweeping their weapons around the trench, scanning for enemy movement.

But it appeared to be for nothing. Dead Black Palace soldiers littered the trench, body parts scattered everywhere. More rangers jumped in, and pushed deeper into the network; clearing out any dugouts they came across.

Niles stepped over a dead Palace trooper, a piece of shrapnel penetrating his helmet; the metal going through his lower jaw and out the back of his head. His body couldn't help itself, the sight sent a shiver down his spine.

"Contact!"

Over a dozen Palace soldiers came running out of a dugout underneath the stronghold's gate, their weapons spewing blue plasma fire. Alpha company took cover, returning green colored plasma fire. Niles and his fireteam flanked the enemy from the right, and cut them down mercilessly. The firefight lasted less than five minutes, but it felt longer.

Colonel Andros and his men rigged the gates with explosives, all the while sounds of battle could be heard coming from within the fortress.

"Explosives primed. Take cover!"

Niles and the rest of Alpha company took shelter behind whatever cover they could find, and after a ten second countdown, the gates blew inward, finally allowing Alpha company to join the fight.

Andros took the lead, opening up on any Palace trooper he saw. A Ranger ran up to him from the left, his unit patch designating him a member of Dog Company.

"Sir, Lieutenant Darr here, we've linked up with Sorin and Kando, and we've managed to push back the Palace into the final defensive ring of the fortress. But we've taken heavy losses."

"Who's the highest ranking officer here?"

Darr wiped the blood off his forehead. "You sir, any other ranking officer is dead."

Alpha company had assembled with the rest of the 45th outside The Black Palace inner fortress. Company medics helped dress wounds, and rangers shared ammunition with one another.

Dog, Sorin and Kando companies had each taken over fifty percent casualties, meaning all three companies had lost half their men fighting to take the outer fortress. All three units had also lost their commanding officers.

Luckily, Alpha had barely taken any losses, so with them reinforcing the attack, it finally allowed the rest of the 45th Regiment to make the final push necessary to complete their objective.

Black Palace flags waved in the air atop the inner wall's battlements; the battle in space could be faintly seen in the sky above.

"This is Andros, any Rangers who can fight, muster with me at the entrance of the tower's stronghold."

Over a thousand Rangers, Niles and his fireteam included, made their way to Andros's position.

Each Ranger was tired, others more than most, but each one had fought bravely. Smoke and blood covered their olive green and gray armor. They could feel it, this was it.

The final push was about to begin. Andros quickly laid down orders.

"This is it, we blow open these gates, we take the tower, and kill anyone we find in there."

He switched the safety off his weapon. "Everyone ready?"

The 45th let out a resounding "Hoorah!"

"Let's begin."

Rangers armed with energy scatterguns took breaching positions, ready to cut down anyone close to the breach once they blew their way in.

"Do it!"

The entrance blew open, and the 45th rushed through. Enemy plasma burned down the first few rangers that pushed in, but their sheer numbers allowed them to overwhelm the first line of Black Palace defenders.

Rangers and Palace soldiers met in close quarters battle. Armored gauntlets struck hardened breastplates, energy swords parried by syro-steele machetes, plasma rifles discharged at point blank range. Blood flowed like water, and the screams of the dying reverberated through the courtyard.

After twenty minutes of brutal, bloody fighting, it was over. Rangers recovered their dead and wounded, and policed the surrendering Palace soldiers.

Andros, flanked by Niles and a dozen other Rangers, entered the tower gun's command center. It was mostly intact, a few plasma burns littered the walls. This was expected, it being a high value target, the Anrachi didn't want to damage it too much.

However, the one thing Andros didn't expect was finding the Black Palace garrison commander dead by suicide. The officer, a General, had shot himself in the head with his own sidearm. On his desk, a final message from The All Father looped behind him.

"Die well General."

The Black Palace were loyal until the very end. Andros shook his head, looking around at his men. He wondered if they were that fanatical in their belief of The Allegiance.

Maybe, maybe not.

He stepped outside and activated his universal com. Before he could speak, he heard the other regimental commanders' voices.

"Tower Alpha, secure."

"Tower Beta, secure."

"Tower Gamma, secure."

"Tower Echo, secure."

"Tower Kilo, secure."

Andros couldn't help but smile. They did it, it was hard fought, but they did it.

"Tower Delta, secure."

Two Months Later

The *Hawkmoon* command bridge

Kyrosi orbit

The Kyros campaign was over. On Anrach, President Lycan heralded Operation Iron Dawn an overwhelming success. The losses they had sustained would say otherwise. Of the three million that had deployed, over half of them had been killed or wounded.

Vallick gazed out the command bridge's central window, Kyros's snow covered landscape filled his field of view. Iron Dawn was hard fought. After the Rangers had taken the planetary defense towers, the rest of the army had landed, putting The Black Palace on the back foot, permanently.

The Palace had attempted to counterattack, but they were met by Anrachi mechanized and armored units in open battle; and were easily crushed.

News of Lord Corrin's victories had made it to Vallick and the Anrachi army. It had motivated them, fueled them.

The war was ramping up, with The Allegiance claiming more and more worlds every day. The sparks of rebellion had flared into a full blown firestorm.

Vallick wondered what Anrach's place was in all this. He wasn't opposed to fully committing Anrach and its resources to The Allegiance; but if it failed, the consequences would be devastating.

But there is no reward without risk. No change without action. And the universe was ready for a big change.

ALLEGIANCE COMMUNICATION

Message from: Zhao-Lan

To: General Gaffen

Location: Arcadia

General! The Aoweiinians have arrived with planetary defenses. Emissary Emoran, although I was skeptical at first, came through with the promises he made. The Elves have returned back to Aoweii to work on new naval ships to aid in your sea battles against The Black Palace. Corrin has provided blue prints for the manufacturing, and expected completion of construction will be provided to you shortly. We are with you General.

Zhao-Lan

SOLDIER BOYS

"You think we could beat Corrin?" Fehir asked. "My brother and uncle both say none of the fleets can stop him."

Corrin had been the only force that could ever oppose The Black Palace. His father, The All Father sought to raise his son to rule. The entirety of the universe has witnessed the potent power of the Spear.

The All Father—wielding the Spear of Space—commanded all worlds to beware his power. His son eventually grew to stand against the primordial creator's brutal reign. One of the two beings who could stand against the commander of the Spear of Space. The All Father commanded Corrin to undergo intense training to hone his innate ability to harness the power of the Spear, the most natural source of universal energy. A wielder can extend their eternal energy to their will to enhance their natural strength tenfold along with a host of abilities, making them unstoppable.

"He's worse than unstoppable," Seb said, "He has the power to destroy entire nations, same as The All Father."

Seben's tone deepened as he ripped the head off a cherri daisy.

"If only I had that power," he said, "no one would be able to boss me around again. I could crush armies with my bare hands, just like The All Father did to the Itarians."

He and his friends often spied on deputies, studying how they talked. Observed how they valued strength and rejected weakness. Seben started to jab his fists through the air in an overconfident attempt to mimic the soldiers whom he and the other yard boys eavesdropped on during their drill courses. He had fierce concentration on his face while he landed the finishing spin kick. Fehir chuckled at Seb's off-balanced landing. He sat with his legs folded while he admired the color of the flowers he picked.

"You think you could do better?" Seb asked while he smacked the petunias out of Fehir's hands. The fog began to roll along with the passing wind. The gust scattered the flowers down the hill. Fehir started to give chase but halted after a few steps. The fog throughout the meadow, coupled with the dark storm clouds above clogged any chance of seeing further down the hill.

Fehir was often mocked for the way he used the crop plow by the yard boys and—even more so—what little fighting ability he had. He avoided the yard boys altogether whenever he saw the chance. As a result, he favored spending his time immersed in the pages of the Galefer Collection by himself in the library.

"I don't even know why I hang out with you," he said, "All you and the others do is mess with me."

"No, I mess with you," Seb said, "The other kids wanna beat you up."

"So, what? You're supposed to be the one who stops them?"

"Duh. You're not that much fun unconscious."

The yard boys were once ordered to chase the invasive swamp dogs off the marsh fields. It wasn't a shock for anyone when Fehir was caught feeding the rodents. They held him down and made him watch as they swung them by their tails until they came off.

"At least I have one," Fehir said, "All those jerks do is drool over the deps and bash each other's brains out."

"Hey, watch it," Seb said as he tugged Fehir toward the other side of the hill, "My brother says it's hard work being a deputy."

With the overbearing darkness, it was impossible to tell that it was morning. The glimpse of their sun poking through the storm clouds grabbed their attention. The patch of land that rested over the hill had spots of the sun's rays burning the turf. They raced each other to the group of warm patches that were sprawled all over the meadow.

Fehir looked over to Seben, a cat stretched in its place.

"Do you really believe it's alright for them to enter our homes whenever they want?" Fehir asked.

His head tilted back as he embraced the ray of sunshine on his face. It was seldom to ever get the chance to see the sun. He was drunk with the warmth of the sun's glow. He often savored the small moments of peace to himself without the drag of having to answer the daily routine inspections. The deputies would've also hated the procedure had it not been for the patriotic ankle biters they accompany to the academy transport train filling their bulky egos.

Seben ignored his question as he continued to relax his hands behind his head, soaking in the rays before they inevitably fell behind the oncoming storm clouds.

"I don't see what the big deal is about them anyway," Fehir said, "just because they can fight doesn't mean they have what it takes to fight armies. What are they gonna do against the Fargulkians?"

"Careful," Seben said.

He had his eyes trained on Fehir like a predator preparing to pounce on its prey.

"You're close to sounding like a traitor."

"How do I sound like a traitor for speaking my mind? Have you seen any of them try to use a Casper piler? I saw one almost blow his fingers off with it."

"Sounding like a traitor is sounding like a traitor."

Fehir was mostly captivated by the universal laws they were taught in school over the political propaganda shoved in their faces at all turns. So much so, that his parents weren't surprised when he was nominated for the district's junior science division. Fehir stood from his spot in the sun as the dark clouds moved in front of the rays. The sky cast a heavy shadow on his face.

"It's up to us," he said.

"What are you on about, now?" Seb asked. He stood with his back facing Fehir while he threw rocks at the trees that led into the forest.

Fehir often allowed his mind to explore the realm of possibility. He stared intently at the clouds. He watched as the lightning returned to coat them. The meadow groaned in the muggy darkness between the flashes which brought out the slew of insects that had buried themselves underground all night. A small glow attached to the end of their abdomens flickered one by one as they began to float and congregate in the middle of the garden.

Their dancing ends that illuminated the area along with the lightning that cracked across the sky reflected deep within Fehir's eyes.

"Sorry, Seb," he said with the humid air clinging to the back of his neck, "I guess I've been thinking more about my final project. It's almost finished, and I've been nominated for the sci-cap."

"You have got to be tougher than that if you're gonna survive the war."

"That's the thing. I could do more to help end the war."

"You mean to win it, right? What could you even do?" Seben asked.

He squeezed the sleeves of the jacket around his waist with a tight grip that was almost threatening.

"You're no fighter."

He was almost the size of an adolescent, even at his young age. His physique allowed the coat to fit better than Fehir's did for him.

"My father tells me there's more to a war than your fists."

"That's because he knows you're too weak to fight."

The flowers in the garden that surrounded them fought against the smog that choked the life out of the bush daisies. Fehir's eyes adjusted to the heavy fog. He sat straight up with a frown.

"I just want to stand against the destruction of our home."

"My father says every war has a price."

"Why do we have to be the ones who pay?"

"Careful not to sound too rebellious around the other yardies."

After a stint of silence, Fehir tackled Seben as he burst into maniacal laughter. Seben surprised himself with how fast he flipped Fehir on his back as he easily pinned him to the ground.

"You're right about one thing at least," Seben said, "you'd make a terrible soldier. All the guys say so. I heard you even failed the Wranglers exam."

Seben's relentless prodding struck a loose chord inside Fehir that lay dormant inside.

Fehir didn't wish to waste time trying to see the point of all the violence among the stars. Why should he be forced to grow up breathing in toxic fumes? Drinking the remnants of hazardous waste dumped into watering pools. Would he watch himself be forced to digest minuscule amounts of plastic the council tells them isn't in their food?

He lay there with a bloodthirsty indoctrinate on top of him, cursing him for not having the stomach to snuff out a man's life with his bare hands. Ridiculing him for wanting more for himself than the cycle of violence that's waiting for him. He struggled to shift his weight and throw Seben off of him. His arms quaked with a terrible tremble as he failed to raise himself off the ground.

Something fragile within him snapped. He felt a burning singe on the inside of his lungs. His hands stung with a bright blue light that flared between his knuckles. Seben looked around them as the fog began to rise over their heads, suspended in a bubble. They inhaled a space of pure air. Seben's hands were struck by an electric sensation that stuck with him as he tried to pull them away. Seben witnessed Fehir's dark brown eyes morph into a white-hot blue flare. His grip began to loosen the longer he held against Fehir's strength. He used his legs to push against the ground, which finally broke his hold.

Fehir sat straight up, silent as he stared in awe at his palms engulfed in a brightness that shattered through the dark.

His hands were aflame, yet he didn't feel any burning sensation. Only the calming bliss of total awareness. He closed his eyes as his retinas began to burn, but another breath of air allowed his vision to blossom as the garden around him did the same. He exhaled a tight-lipped gust of air, and with the push of a thought, the flare was gone. The fog returned to wrap around them like water filling a bowl. The air smelled fresher like each flower in the green was revitalized with a new coat of petals.

Fehir opened his eyes to a baffled Seben, who stood speechless before him, with his guard raised. His un-eased position stirred in Fehir's gut as his mind lapped itself twice over.

"Sorry," Fehir said as he scampered off past the forest border.

He ignored Seben shouting his name through the trees, though his voice continued to ricochet around him.

Fehir's desk and walls were littered with hide sheets with half-finished markings on them, along with torn-out pages scattered about the floor. He paced back and forth over the disheveled notes, crumpling with each barefoot step he trotted in front of his mirror. The amount of energy within each breath shook him to his bones. He jumped at the light thumping on the wood of his bedroom door, but his mother's soft voice on the other end put his heart to rest in a matter of seconds.

"Fehir, honey," she said, "your food is getting cold. Come down and eat."

He stared at the closed door in silence for a moment.

"Okay," he said, "I'll be right down."

He hadn't decided how he'd tell them. Those who trained their entire lives would seldom have any chance at joining the Black Palace's forces, but beings connected to the power of the Spear were almost always abducted by the Palace forces. The thought of being forced to live with strangers just as terrified as he —ordered to eat, sleep, and tear each other apart for the sake of training. He couldn't bear to imagine the pain mother would have to endure if he were to be stripped away from his family and forced to hone an ancient ability he didn't ask for.

Most Spear Energy users were rounded up as children of the crop due to their unusual display of energy. The sound of a whip cracking through the air sent a cold shiver down his spine. He wanted nothing more than to push those thoughts from his mind and forget the entire afternoon, but there was a sinking presence in the pit of his stomach that immobilized him. *What am I gonna do?*

He rolled a slab of Gorgoshu meat around with his fork as he stared intently at the plate.

"What's on your mind, son?" Fehir's father asked.

Even with Fehir's disinterest in joining the ranks, the same as he and Fehir's older brother, father was proud of Fehir's dedication to science.

"If you had the power to end the war," Fehir started, "how would you do it?"

Mother widened her eyes while sharing a glance with father.

"What makes you ask that, honey?" she asked. She'd sooner fist-fight wild mountain foxes than let him anywhere near the battlefield.

He shrugged while he twirled his fork in a pile of steaming noodles. Father grinned as he nodded back to mother with a wink.

"Right now, son, we're at that crucial point where the only answer is a violent one. The only solution The Allegiance would understand. Corrin has lost sight of the perfect order."

"There is still hope," mother said, "that the prodigal son will reunite with his father. He only wants what's best for us. But don't start worrying about the war now, honey."

"I guess I just don't see the point of so much violence."

Father glanced over at mother with a coy expression.

"Your mother is right. Leave the war to the warriors, boy. Although, pinheads do usually plan the battle-winning strategies.

Mother placed her hand over Fehir's— smiling as she brushed over his knuckles with her thumb—she looked him in the eyes.

"Wherever you decide to apply your talents," she said, "we'll be right there."

Their smiles faded after they heard three consecutive pounds at their front door.

"The deputies don't do inspections this late, do they?" Mother asked father as he rose from his seat.

Fehir wished he'd grabbed father by his arm. Tugged him back down to his chair. Told him to ignore it and come back to the table, but father was already speaking with a Black Palace soldier who stood in their doorway.

"Stay here," mother said as she left to join father in the foyer, with Fehir tailing behind her. One of the soldier's heads turned to face Fehir peering from behind the kitchen wall. The boorish man nudged his comrade's shoulder while he flashed jagged teeth at the boy. He turned to step back out of the doorway while another man, tall and pompous, invited himself in.

"Greetings," he said, "My name is—"

"Commander Troi'tn," father said while he placed a balled fist over the left side of his chest. "It's an honor to have—"

"This is no inspection," he said.

He towered over father when he stepped further into the house. Father strengthened his chin while he stared the men down.

"What can I help you with?"

Commander Troi'tn stepped to the side, allowing Seben to lock eyes with the terrified Fehir. All it took was one finger pointed at him for his heart to stop beating.

"That's him," Seben said as he shoved the guard out of his way. "That's the traitor with Spear Energy."

Fehir never experienced the weight of despondence. It was hard to hear anything else besides mother's screams as she tried to push the intruding deputies back. She and father were made to lie on their bellies while the men persisted into their home. Among the orders being shouted throughout the foyer, Fehir's shock didn't come from the collective stun darts fired by the overzealous soldiers. It didn't come from being forced to watch his parents seized during their dinner. It was Seben's cold gaze that built up a fiery rage inside of Fehir as the soldiers began to close in.

A betrayal that was the combustible fluid lit aflame by a spark of passion. The only thing he could do was watch himself scream.

There was a seismic blowback that was packed with an intense field of energy—which devastated the neighboring transport vans. Everything within the epicenter's distance was displaced—shredded to small remnants before the energy dissipated. The electric jolt of the commanders's temp canon brought an abrupt end to the boy's screech.

Commander Troi'tn grinned as he stood to his feet, hovering his head above the aftermath. The commander waltzed over the lifeless bodies of his platoon. He kneeled by the still bodies of father and mother. He shook his head in disappointment as he left their carcasses where they rested.

"Well," he said with a grin as he gazed upon Fehir sleeping soundly on the kitchen floor, buried under his unfinished dinner.

"We have a lot of work to do, boy."

UNTITLED

I am so sorry little cricket.
There is no one here to hear your song.

You see these woods are kept vacant of melody,
Though I understand why that feels very wrong.

Yes the winds feel lovely I admit.
And yes the trees still stand strong.

But the creatures here dare not risk cacophony,
Lest no longer may they carry their lives along.

I think you'll find it hard to find a smiling face,
and peace, I'm afraid, is far from commonplace.

-HORACE VA'ROLIKUN

Letter from Captain Tan'ya

Black Palace Occupying Forces stationed on Catovaz

My love Olan,

I'm writing to you from the infirmary on a Spearcraft Carrier. We were overran by Ice Warriors on Catovaz and lost our outpost in New Var. I am amongst the few that were able to escape before losing the planet completely. This war, this childish rebellion is ridiculous. I don't want our children to see this. I still have favors and friends in The Black Palace. Go there with the kids and relay to Military Command you are my husband. My love, I beg of you, once you receive this letter go immediately to The Black Palace. If these insurgents plan to uproot Black Palace command, every planet will be at war. Tell the children that their mother sends them her love. Moon, I dream of you every night. Your wife,

Tan'ya

THE LAST ENTRY OF THE LEGENDARY ASHER KELLS

I have lost my propensity to see color. I've spent who knows how long down in this simple labyrinth and it appears I cannot see one damn bit of color. My trademark red scarf with yellow tassels has lost its radiant hue and all I can do is sit here and wait for... something to happen. Things have gotten so out of hand that a recording of my experiences of some kind is due.

It's regrettable that a tome such as mine should end here, alone in front of a Void. I've spent close to a decade building my story, crafting my legacy. I've been on the Black Palace's Most Wanted list, uncovered secrets of the universe, fought in wars—and much of what I have done has been made of half-truths and exaggerations.

I guess I should give some context; what is the Void? Why have I lost sensation? And most importantly—who am I? Unlike everything else in this journal, this final chapter will be the truth.

Secret Dealings

I received a message from a drop point on the planet Rashalon informing me to come to the outskirts of the F. Jaeger Nebula. I was to meet Vander Hox—THE Vander Hox of The Hox Pirates—for a business opportunity.

Captain Hox is a man of great power; he holds on to that power by building connections. If you ever get to read this journal, you will get to read a version of some of these tales. I'll try to render him in the most realistic light that I can muster.

I docked in at his Satellite. If you've never seen it before, it's a large and round orb of gold surrounded by a rotating ring of silver. He calls it "The Dragon's Hoard". I exited my ship in the Hoard's hangar, surrounded by a small armada of ships of all sizes. A small group of well-dressed pirates greeted me at the bottom of my ramp.

They took me to the dining room. A great hall with scores of tables for the crew to eat. Elevated in front of them all were the V.I.P. seats where Hox and his Vice-Captains ate. Though I've never seen Hox eat or drink myself. He was always keen on watching through his helm.

The guest list was incredible, if small. The first I recognized was Suny Havok, the weapons smuggler. We worked on a few jobs together over the years. Maybe even shared a few rooms. She looked over at me as she took a drink of something harsh. She winked and gave a slight salute with her pinky. Sat to her right was the go-to getaway pilot for many of us in the Subspace Underworld, Kagra Zed. His stoic demeanor could drag any party down. I took my seat across from Havok.

"Asher Kells," Kagra grunted. I waved back.

"Kagra and Havok," I eyed how close they appeared to be. "How crazy is it that we've never all been together in the same room?"

"Different jobs I suppose," Kagra replied.

"If the Captain needs the three of us it must be something big," Havok said between drinks.

We shot the shit for about an hour. All the while I couldn't help but notice those subtle nudges and smiles they would pass each other. Now I'm not the the jealous type, but Suny was an early supporter, let's say.

Enter Captain Vander Hox.

A small band of pirates followed behind him. The pirates didn't wear uniforms, so it was always odd watching them march like they were a part of the Black Palace Military. Many even wore repainted Black Palace garb over their layman's clothes. The captain was different though. He had a slick red and gold coat adorned with silver and gold trimmings and buttons.

He wore a helmet shaped like a dragon's skull. A ceremonial Itarian artifact. Most of that old empire shit had been melted down into Black Palace weaponry. But the Captain is a man who can get what he wants.

Kagra stood at attention. Havok and I shared a confused glance. Kagra lightly smacked Havok across the arm and motioned her to stand. She rolled her eyes, but not without complying.

"Asher, how did I know you would be the one without any manners?" he said through his teeth.

He took his seat at the end of the table, right next to Havok and I.

"To what do we owe this intimate dining experience?" I said to him.

"Work, obviously. Why would I want to ever hang out with you mother fuckers?"

He sat forward in his seat.

"And I know we are all scum here, but this requires absolute silence."

"Kagra has that covered," Havok remarked.

"Black Palace?" Kagra asked, ignoring Havok's comment.

"Exactly." Vander pointed at Kagra.

"Hence why you got the best pilot this side of the galaxy, the premiere weapons smuggler of the system, and the greatest thief who possibly ever lived. Must be pretty fucking big." My mind was spinning over the possibilities.

Vander motioned to one of his crew members to bring something over to the table. An impish pirate brought over a large briefcase.

"Lady, gentleman, thief. Especially the fucking thief. Take a look."

Vander opened the briefcase.We were all stunned. We are no strangers to large stacks of cash, but this was huge.

"There has to be tens of millions of BPU." Havok could barely speak.

Vander slammed the briefcase shut and said, "We are talking about billions."

I should have known then that this was too good to be true. However, as a thief risk is just part of the business. Want to know a secret about us? NEVER offer us a job that could set us up to retire. ESPECIALLY one as young and good looking as me. Our business is based on trust. Trust that we won't screw each other over. See, if you want to keep working in the underworld you don't fuck anybody over. That's how you get killed.

We agree on a split, we take the fucking split. But when you offer something like this, something where you know you never have to see these people again... that's when greed takes over. And dear reader, greed was taking over.

"Billions?" I asked.

"This was just the deposit. My buyer is prepared to shell out big for this thing."

Vander sat back down.

"Well, what the fuck is it then?" Havok blurted out.

Vander leaned in. We all instinctively moved in.

"On a small moon around the planet Raisa IV, there is a Black Palace Military Base," Vander whispered.

"Why there? There's no tactical or cultural advantage to having a base there," Kagra interrupted.

"That means they probably found something," Havok said.

"Or they needed somewhere to hide something," I chimed in.

"Both," Vander said. "The intel we have suggests that The Black Palace has gotten a hold of rock made of concentrated space Spear Energy."

While people out there have created machines that can harness Spear Energy, and beings such as The All Father can control the energy around them, it's unheard of for the energy to compound in such a way as to form a material substance. Energy like that could fuel a star, could end worlds. That's damn near priceless.

"So," Vander said, expectantly, "Are you all in?

All In

A few moments later and we were on Kagra's ship. It was a small thing, meant to be inconspicuous. It's a sleek black and quite angular. The interior was quite utilitarian; a set of five seats, two-by-two behind the pilot's seat—and a small cargo hold behind that. This was a get-in-and-get-out vehicle.

We flew in silence through The Black Palace space. Oddly enough, the holes were easy to spot, and we were through in no time. The ride towards Raisa IV was uneventful. We expected to catch Black Palace communication signals on our interceptor; but nothing. It was quiet.

"I think we should turn back," Kagra broke the silence.

"Nope," I told him. "I'm not giving up that big ass chunk of money because of your cold feet."

"But—"

"Have to agree with Asher," Havok interrupted. "That kind of money could take us to the edge of the universe. Away from this war, away from our debts, away from this life."

"That kind of money isn't easy to get, Havok," Kagra said, but he kept flying anyway.

A few hours later we spotted the moon by Raisa IV. And it's only barely a moon. Small thing.

"Prepare for entry. This stealth craft doesn't have stabilizers." Kagra flipped several levers and knobs. "We're gonna feel every bump."

He wasn't wrong. I felt my stomach drop as we descended towards the moon. Moon Drops are always so surreal. No clouds, no sky. The moon just… gets closer.

We dove through a chalk-white valley below the jagged mountains. They eventually narrow into a long, tight corridor of rock and dust. Kagra got through no problem. Though, sometimes it felt like parts of the chasm repeated. Eventually, we came to a base embedded within one of this moon's mountains.

"I'm starting to get freaked out here," Havok spoke silently. "This felt like a turret run, but where are all the turrets?"

"We should turn back," Kagra shook his head.

"Why?" I shouldn't have asked, but I did anyway. "Even if there ends up being no treasure, I would like to see what got these fascists all scared."

Havok and Kagra muttered their meek protests, but I was quite persuasive.

We landed in the base's hangar. The few ships that were still there lay derelict. Dust coats their priceless metal exterior. I grabbed a few of my supplies and placed them in my satchel. I looked at Havok and Kagra. They cautiously stared out the window.

"Havok," I tried to get her attention. "Are you coming?"

"Yeah," Havok replied.

"Don't take too much time out there," Kagra pleaded, "I have a feeling the longer we stay here the more we will regret it."

"Well, Vander may be the bigger threat if this goes tits-up," I quipped, "It'll be fine. We'll be back before you know it."

Havok and I wandered through the empty halls of the base for several minutes. The layout was surprisingly simple. An entrance, a hallway, a left turn, another hallway, a door, a hallway, another door. It just kept going.

"What the fuck kind of base was this?" Havok asked. "Why the hell would they abandon an object of pure Spear Energy?"

"Scared?" I prodded.

"You are fucking right I am. The Black Palace values control and power above everything else and they left that rock here?"

"Probably because it was dangerous."

"No shit. But what kind of danger?"

That's when we reached the door. We didn't think anything of it at the time, but who knew we wouldn't be able to come back.

Greed Takes Over

We wandered the halls for what felt like hours. At first, I thought we were just going in circles, but we'd see a new sign or lighting fixture and keep going. Then we would run into the same lighting fixtures and the same signs. Was the base reorganizing itself?

"Did they bury this thing in the middle of the fucking moon or something!" I lost my patience.

"Fuck this," Havok said, "I'm going back."

"Seriously?"

"We've been roaming these halls for hours. If this just leads to a locked door with a space rock behind it, I'm sure you can handle that."

"If you go back, how can I guarantee you wouldn't leave me?"

Suny turned to me with a curled brow. She gave me that look a few times when we were younger, when our fights would get out of hand. That look told me that deep down I was in the wrong, but every time she gave it to me, I was too stubborn to believe it. It would only be after I had time to think about what I said that I would understand what I had done.

"Don't trust me?" Suny said.

"You've done it before," I shouldn't have kept going.

Havok stopped in her tracks and grabbed me by the wrist.

"Touch a nerve?" I shook her off me.

"I never took you for the jealous type, Asher. Just the androgynous play-them thief."

"I'm not jealous. I just know where I stand with you."

"Meaning?" she asked with her tongue in her cheek. She did that when she got angry.

"Meaning," I hesitated, "You will strand me here."

"Then come back with us. We'll explain what happened to Vander."

"There's no way Vander is giving that money back to his buyer. If we don't get this, then we end up dead.

"Get it then. I'm going back."

"No the fuck you are not," I said with my sidearm in hand.

"This is a mistake, Asher."

She was right, but I didn't care.

We had a stare down. And I remember thinking, I shouldn't have drawn my gun.

She reached for her weapon, but I had already drawn mine. I hit her shoulder. It didn't stop her, so I shot again and took a few fingers. She fell, clutching her hand.

"Why?" she asked.

"Because you would just leave me."

"What now?" she could barely get the words out.

"Stay here." I holstered my weapon. "I'll come back for you."

I turned my back on her. A shame. I don't think I'll ever see her again.

Lost

I think I walked close to a day. The same halls, the same signs. Each step I took brought me closer to all those fights Suny and I used to have. As I drifted through this unending maze I also relived every fight we ever had, every time we found ourselves against the wall, every laugh, every passing glance, every time we thought we'd never see each other again.

I kept going. I kept walking towards the end because all of those memories couldn't have been for nothing. All I had to do was find that stupid rock. That dreadful rock. I would come back for Suny, I would collect from Vander, and we could just live in peace as she recovered in my arms.

But that's not how a story like mine ends. That's never how a story like mine would end. I was in the gnashing maw of this universe since the day I was born. I have lived a life of crime and betrayals since I could speak. This end was inevitable.

I came upon one final hallway and one final door. I walked through like the hundreds I did before and that's when I saw it. That's when I saw the rock, but more importantly, that's when I saw the Void.

I reached into my satchel and pulled out a small noisemaker. I tossed it near the rock. It didn't get sucked up, so it wasn't gravitational. I tossed another into the Void itself. It disappeared. That meant I could get close so long as I didn't touch it.

And I did get close. I got low and made my way to the rock. I tossed a third noisemaker at the rock. Nothing happened. I grabbed it, cautiously, and backed up. There it was, just sitting in the palm of my hand. Pure Spear Energy.

I chuckled to myself then walked out the door I came in. I walked down the hall, took that turn and there was the Void again. I stealthily walked by and through another door. But it was the Void again. Then I ran. I probably ran through a dozen of those hallways with the same result. The Void was there.

Just a trick, I thought. I'll probably just need to keep going, for hours, for days if I have to.

And I did just that. I walked and walked and walked before I passed out from exhaustion. I must've been walking for over a day since I've landed here. When I came to, I found that noise began to slip away from me. The low hum of that black hole disappeared. The faint echo of my footsteps through these barren hallways left my ears as well.

I soon learned that this was a cycle. I walked and walked and walked until I passed out and then I would wake with something else missing.

Now

I'm starving, I think. I haven't eaten in weeks, possibly months. I had hunger pangs for a while, but then the pain disappeared. I couldn't feel at all. Writing is difficult because of that fact. I lost my ability to feel, I lost my hearing a while ago, I can't see color now. I'm worried I will lose a lot more before I die. If this place will even let me die.

What scares me most is when I look into that Void. I believe I see something in there. It may be my sanity slipping... but I think I see myself. It was faint at first, but the longer I'm here the more I see it. I'm losing all my senses, but this I see clearly. I get what why no one was here. This rock shouldn't exist, and the universe knows it.

I'm sorry, Suny. I'm. Just. Sorry.

Signed,
Asher Kells

RETURN TO THE VOID

There are only two hours of sunlight on Nyla.

And that's being generous. It's more accurate to say that a day on Nyla lasts two hours on average, because you must remember to consider the length of dawn and dusk, which are a part of the day. Both of which are beautiful, but I don't know many people that would think of those twilight minutes as full sunlight. This is why the people here are mostly nocturnal, because if you want to accomplish anything at all, how could you not be?

That makes seeing the light of day a luxury, albeit, a simple one. One easily attainable if you are okay with foregoing sleep every now and then. I had done it before, many times, and I will admit that the beauty of light is not overstated. I certainly wouldn't mind seeing more of it. However, and this is where my view starts to differ from many on my planet, I also find the darkness quite beautiful. I think it may be a generational matter, but it seems to me that people are becoming more and more discontented with their lives in the dark. It's very understandable. On most other planets, the main characters of stories told to scare children are often creatures of the *night* and dangers hidden in *shadow*. It would be easy to start to see your own world as the odd one out. Maybe you start to yearn to prove you're not a monster hiding in the dark. A villain lurking in the shadows.

An important lesson, often learned too late, is that not all villains hide in the dark.

I sat in my rocking chair on my porch as the last fraction of the sun was swallowed by Warin 3, the largest moon of Nyla and the fifth largest in the universe as I understand it. With the new night up and about, I figured I should get up as well. There were a few chores I had put off from yesterday, and I needed to go to the market at some point. Besides that, all I wanted to do for the rest of my time was read a book, though which one I had not decided yet. I had just finished *Of Kings and Fools* again, so I was thinking I might read something more comical.

I sat up and made a futile attempt at stretching. The soreness in my back was an unkind reminder of my lately sleeping habits, which is to say I was hardly sleeping. When I did manage to sleep it wasn't the restful kind. I had my dreams to thank for that. Do you realize how dark darkness has to be to frighten a Nylan? I had been consistently dreaming of getting lost in the dark, and I couldn't decide if I found that scary or confusing. Or both.

I went inside. My old house consisted of four rooms total, five if you count the attic, and a porch and a backyard. I remember when it was first built I thought it was a grand house, fit for stuffing full of people and material possessions. Then Iinya was born and I worried it might not be big enough. Now, it feels entirely too large.

I cleaned what I left from supper the day before, though one person's amount of food and dishes didn't quite count as a chore. More of a slight inconvenience, but it had to be done all the same.

Satisfied with the kitchen, I went to tidy up the bedroom. Mostly moved things around. Made sure I didn't need to do laundry. I folded the blanket and left it neatly at the end of the bed, even though I thought it a silly thing to do. I would be back in bed later, why the blanket shouldn't be open and waiting for me never made sense. But my wife (her name was Radia) liked things to look well kept. Said it helped declutter her mind. So I always did it for her. That makes it a particularly hard habit to break.

After I took care of the bedroom, which did nothing to the clutter in my own mind, I went to the backyard to tend to the crystal garden. It occurred to me, why on this day I'm not sure, that the amount I've been growing was noticeably less than last year. In a way it makes sense; I had been eating less. I wasn't as active, I wasn't eating as much. I reasoned that I subconsciously reduced the amount of food I was growing to match my lacking appetite. I still had plenty of phosthyst, with a few long stalks ripe for picking. The orange magnerald had some nice clusters coming along. And the potazz I planted a few days ago was finally starting to gain some height in the tank.

After I checked to make sure the temperature of the water was consistent, I returned to the kitchen. I dried the phosthyst and set them aside on the counter. They would do well for supper tonight I thought, but it wasn't enough to stop me from going to the market. I knew I wouldn't be considerably hungry, but I'd still desire a well-balanced meal.

Having changed into my street clothes, I went outside. The street was already awake and active. It's the same scene on many planets. Children played with toys in the streets. Some parents repainted the shingles on their roofs. Peaceful domestic scenes. The only difference was the neighborhood was lit fully electronically, and the sky was filled in with many layers of beautiful gray clouds. The horizon was tinged a lovely shade of gray, and the black sands of people's lawns were decorated with rainbows of non-edible crystals. I could feel the happy thoughts around me, and it made me glad that I had left the house.

I liked how much that side of the city stayed the same even though the city had developed so much over the years. The skyline in the distance spread wide and tall, and there were a few additions to it that weren't there when I was a younger man. I didn't really want to raise a baby in that clutter. Though I suppose the outcome wouldn't have turned out any differently.

The market was busy that day as I remember it. Every store had a constant stream of people coming in and out and there was always a customer standing at any of the stands. I wish I had the strength to revel in that community energy, but I could already feel the soreness creep into my feet from the walk, and my back was protesting having to be upright for so long. I went into a store (my friend Kelv's place) and quickly purchased a gallon of mineral water, a box of Captain Hexagon, and a box of Krystal Krunch. When I was checking out, Kelv came over to me and slipped a bag of chromium chips into my bag before dashing back to business. That's a real friend.

Next I stopped by Tera's mineral stand, mostly just to say hello, but sometimes she has some very tasty stuff that the other stores don't get their hands on. When Tera was younger, she was a gatherer. She knew the local cave systems better than anyone, or at least that's what we told everyone to get her more business. It might as well be true though. Gathering was becoming more and more automated, and drones aren't programmed to brag. She would dive down for days going deeper than even a robot would want to go, and her haul would be worth it. Now she's taken up gardening and her son has taken the mantle of best gatherer in the city.

"Hello Tera," I said to her while pursuing her selection. Her son, Jing was his name, certainly had her nose for the good stuff.

"Benjar, my old friend!" She called with her back still turned to me, hunched over multiple boxes behind the stand. I heard a chorus of clanking and clinking as she rummaged through her stock. She stood up smiling with her arms full of raw geodes and rocks. Her delight almost always made me wish I hadn't retired.

Tera quickly laid out the items giving me a once over out of the corner of her eye. I knew she was going to criticize my diet in a moment. Nylans of course also change appearance based on how much nutrition they put into their bodies. But the differences in our physiology are much more stark. Our skin and hair are naturally translucent, so they take on the color of what we ingest much more quickly and vividly. Our hair is especially susceptible to drastic color changes. Our skin less so, but it does darken when exposed to the minerals in the air and ground. You can tell a lot about one of us just by our appearance. Tera had dark brown skin, so it was easy to guess she spent a large portion of her life underground. She looked like she was gently hugged by the earth and soil, and I'm sure she may have been many times whether it was intentional or not. Her eyes were lightly golden and bright, the eyes of someone who can see in the dark even better than the normal standards of a species that grew up in the nighttime. Her hair was so red it was almost scarlet. That meant she favored red crystals, and I knew her favorite food was ruby soup. It also meant she was neglecting to eat any blupaz. It would be ironic if she were to lecture me about her diet when she wasn't eating blupaz at our age.

"Hey, was last week the last time you stocked up on groceries? You have money trouble or are you not eating enough for a reason?"

"I'm eating plenty thank you." Then in her mind I added. *Jing not finding enough blupaz these days?*

She rolled her eyes and flashed a picture of what she was seeing in my mind. I have to admit, I didn't notice my skin was as clear as it was. I should be outside more I suppose. I've just been so tired. And my home is still so cozy. Still, my hair looked pretty good. A healthy shade of purple, maybe with a few too many streaks of silver, but I refused to stop eating chromium. I wasn't going to let age keep me from my snacks.

"Blupaz is much too hard to chew for something that tastes terrible. I'm not a child, I don't need to finish my vegetables before I can have dessert."

"Well why don't you soak them then?" I asked, nudging her mind with sincerity.

"Making a whole bottle of water taste like blupaz creates more problems than it solves you crazy old man." She pushed back, rebelling against the sincerity in favor of teasing.

"Well I like it, I soak it with some phosthyst and I think it tastes refreshing."

Good for you. She thought. "By the way, how are your magneralds coming?"

"Not too bad," I told her, "They're just so slow."

"Yeah I keep thinking mine aren't going to take to the seed. I love when the rapid growth starts happening, but the waiting until then just kills me."

I felt her send me a feeling of saudade. In the caves, when she found crystals, they were fully bloomed and plentiful. The only patience she needed down there was to wait until she found them. And until then she had a labyrinth to adventure in and map out.

I placed a hunk of raw blupaz, which she had placed on the bottom shelf in case her distaste of it was unclear, on the counter and offered her payment for it. She laughed and gladly accepted the money.

Good get that stuff out of there. She thought at me. Outloud she said, "You remember we're all meeting tomorrow at the diner right?"

"Yes of course."

"But do you remember the time?" She asked

"Yes...do you remember the time?"

Just tell me the time, stingbum.

Rude. Meet at 1800.

Have a good night Benjar.

And with that I started my way home. But I didn't get too far. There were two people in black robes talking calmly to a man that was not talking calmly to them. I recognized the robes, those people must've been Mornur preachers. I didn't mean to stop and watch, but as much as I disliked religion, I disliked random people getting angry at other random people for what they believe.

We're not preachers you know.

I didn't notice a young woman had stepped next to me. She was also wearing black robes. Her hair was bright green, her face was a little tan, and her eyes were very black. She smiled politely at me.

"It's rude to mind-read without introducing yourself first," I said, making my annoyance clear.

"My apologies, but you were thinking very loudly.

She offered me her hand.

"I'm Sibyl."

I shook her hand.

"I'm not interested."

She laughed.

"But what's your name?"

I wanted to just leave, but I felt bad about my own rudeness.

"Benjar."

"Nice to meet you. So I take it you already know all about Mornur?"

She sensed I did not. People her age are so annoying sometimes. "He's your god of death." I said pointedly.

"Not quite. He's often called the 'The One who Accepts Death'. So that might be what you're thinking of."

"Yes perhaps. Yet, that distinction would hardly make me more interested." "What is it that makes you so disinterested?"

I slowly started to step away. "I have little patience for the real gods and the religions built around them. I have less for the religions built around fake gods."

"I don't want to waste your time with something you don't care about, but I would be remiss if I didn't tell you that Mornur is not a fake god. And in fact, he is the only god that truly cares about the people of this universe, and he is from our planet."

That made me remember a book I read when I was a teenager. "Wait I remember that part, your god is the same one from that book series. *Behind the Dream Veil.*"

"As much as I like those books, they are not very accurate representations. Mornur has been called *The One* Behind the Dream Veil, but those books don't deal very much with the facts from his or this planet's history."

"And your cult does."

I sensed the frustration flare up in her head. To her credit, she didn't show it as much as others her age would.

"There hasn't been a cult in Nyla for many hundreds of years."

We both turned to watch the man walk away from her two friends, who seemed annoyingly unbothered by his insults. Sibyl went over to check on them. I took advantage of the opportunity to continue on my way without the need of additional conversation.

When I arrived home, I put away my groceries and had a bowl of cereal for supper. I wasn't in the mood to crush the phosthyst. I didn't put water in the cereal. Some cereals like Captain Hexagon need to be dissolved a little for me to enjoy them. But I like Krystal Krunch dry and, well, crunchy.

After cleaning up my low effort meal, I ended up choosing *Strap Bakagen* to read. A collection of short stories about the misadventures of a snarky gatherer.

Another difference between Nyla and the rest of the universe; every other people of every other planet have gardens too, but theirs are full of organic material. They grow beautiful living things. But we are the only living things on this planet, and as such, we are the only species that learned to sustain ourselves on inorganic matter. Apparently that makes us hardier and more adaptable to many cuisines. We can eat a lot of other people's foods, and they can either only handle ours in very small quantities or not digest it at all. I'm not too big a fan of a lot of alien food. So much of it has very strong smells, and it's also very inconvenient. A lot of cutting is involved, and heat. There's like ten different ways to apply heat to the ingredients, fire being one of them and a popular one at that which is crazy to me. All I need is a small induction stove to heat water and I can cook anything.

All of that to say, there's one alien dish that I think is absolutely brilliant. Bread. Eating at restaurants became so much more fun when bread came to Nyla.

There were five of us at dinner: Kelv, Tera, Druan, Maki, and me. Kelv and I went to school together before he went into the grocery business and I into tailoring. Tera and I met because Iinya and Jing were friends in school. Druan was a welder and used to live in the house next to mine, but he sold it after his husband passed (a decision he always regretted). And I met Maki because she was childhood friends with my wife; they both got into intergalactic commerce, mostly salt. We all had more friends at one point, but as the years passed they either left, died, or simply grew apart. One time, Kelv tried to lighten the mood and said we were down to the best ones, which is a very nice sentiment when you remember he's mostly referring to the friends that left on bad terms, but the three of us who had had spouses couldn't take as much comfort in the idea.

We were all on our second round of breadsticks. Nice thing about telepathy, you don't need to stop eating to talk. Potentially bad thing about it, if you have a group of friends prone to making funny remarks, you may choke a few times. So we were all thinking at each other and enjoying our food and drink. Thoughts were better in this group too because Druan's hearing was starting to go, so we tended to save the verbalities for loud outbursts.

Tera had finished updating us all on Jing's exploits. She was so proud of him. She also made sure to question everyone else's diets, not just mine. This earned her some playful jeering in return. A few spit takes were made. Then Kelv tried to get everyone to agree with him on the best brand of mineral water. I pointed out that his nostalgia was getting in the way of good taste.

You're insane. Kelv thought. *Crystal Ale is the definition of good taste.*

No. It's much too sweet.

Maki interjected. *I like Raindrop.*

Do they still make QB? Druan thought with a far away look in his eye. *I feel like I never see it anymore.*

If you're thirsty, you drink Cave Nectar. I thought with pretend authority. *If you want dessert, you drink Jetsi Purple. No contest.*

I don't know what's more upsetting. Kelv thought. *The fact that Cave Nectar is such a boring choice, or the fact that you brought up Jetsi Purple.*

I didn't think they sold Jetsi Purple here anymore. Druan thought.

They don't! Maki replied. *It was discontinued so many years ago.*

I said what I said. I said.

I like the store brand stuff. Tera thought peacefully.

Kelv put his head on the table in defeat. There was no recovering the conversation from that, we all were laughing too much.

After a fifth round of breadsticks, the group started to lose energy. Druan had an early doctor's appointment he had to get to tomorrow and Maki was driving him, which was the whole reason we were meeting a day earlier than we usually do. I didn't quite feel like going home yet, and it was my turn to pick up the check. So after we all said our goodbyes, I stayed at the table and ordered a stronger drink. I was trying once again to declutter my thoughts.

That morning I had a strange dream. I was wrapped in a thick cloud of dark smoke and I couldn't move. I cried out but no sounds came. I reached out in my mind, but it felt empty. It was awful, to be perfectly aware of the dream I was having in my head but for my mind to be so completely uninhabited at the same time. It felt like choking after getting hit so hard all of the air gets knocked out of your body. The only reason I knew it was a dream, was because my head is never so quiet. There's always something in it.

What kind of things are in your head?

I shook myself away from my thoughts and looked up. It was the woman from yesternight.

I answered out loud. "*Personal* things."

Sibyl was at the table across from me, giving me an inquisitive look. She was alone.

"I'm sorry. I intruded again. But you were thinking very hard about your dream." Her eyes turned away from me. "And it looked familiar."

I frowned. "Familiar how?"

"There are many different interpretations of the Void." She said simply. I could tell that she wanted to say more but was stopping herself. I recognized the look of annoyance on her face to be directed at herself, not me.

"You said your name is Sibyl?" I asked gently.

She nodded, confused.

"Sibly, I'm sorry for what I said when we met." I wanted to explain, and I didn't want her to feel bad. "I meant it when I said I have no patience. I'm impatient about everything now, and gods are things that particularly annoy me. But I hurt your feelings and I'm sorry."

She looked surprised, but some of the annoyance was gone. That was good enough for me. I wanted to right my wrong. I didn't want to leave someone worse off having interacted with me.

Sibly smiled, then she stood up and walked over placing her hand on the back of the chair Druan had sat in. "This seat taken?"

"No," I said matter of factly, "But I'm not staying long," I said more matter of factly.

She sat down. "You didn't have to apologize to me. Why did you?"

I took a deep breath. "I don't like leaving people worse off than how I found them."

"Well that's a very noble way of looking at it."

"It's not a question of being noble," I protested. Then I had a small coughing fit which I'm sure made me sound even more convincing.

She looked at me, concerned, as I took a shaky drink from my glass. "Are you feeling alright?"

"I feel old." Eager to change the subject, I decided to humor her. "What is the void?"

She hesitated. "I'm not looking to force you to talk about something you don't like."

"It's fine. Void sounds familiar but I don't remember what it's from."

The waiter brought her meal and set it down in front of her. Amethyst soup with side of bread.

She tore off a piece of bread and threw it into her mouth. "You may recognize the Void from school, when they told us how The All Father created the universe."

She paused when she saw my clear disgust at the mention of the universal tyrant, but I motioned for her to continue.

"The All Father tells us that he populated the Void with space and planets, essentially destroying the empty state of the universe before life was made. But we have ancient tomes that tell of a different start of the universe. Tomes left to us from the time that *Behind the Dream Veil* was supposed to take place."

"Tomes written by the...people who thought they could raise Mornur to conquer the universe?"

"The cult, yes. They were a cult. And they were wrong. The universe had three planes of existence in the beginning. Space, Time, and Void. The All Father ruled Space, and made plans to create all of life to be in service to him. Zaman, ruling the Time domain, only cared about maintaining the proper flow of time. A vital job to be sure, but it blinded him to what was going on between his two brothers. Mornur was the Lord of the Void, and the Void is a special kind of energy that balances the energy of space. Mornur wanted to live in peace with The All Father, and create his own race of beings that would live in harmony with the beings of Space. The All Father was furious when he found out. He saw this as his younger brother questioning his right for total dominance of the universe. So he fought him, and he thought he killed him."

She raised her glass and gulped down her beverage. Then she continued.

"But The All Father was wrong. Mornur was alive, but he and his Void were cast out of the universe, so to speak. Remember I said the Void compliments Space, that continues to be true even today. It's a law of nature even The All Father can't change. In a way, the Void has become the space in-between Space. Mornur's domain now works in harmony with The All Father's in a much more intimate way than what The All Father originally tried to prevent. Beings that are particularly in-tune to Spear Energy can sense it, though they can't tap into it."

"Except in their dreams?" I asked.

"And in death. And some think it's where you end up if you travel into a black hole. Though I think that's just a specific example of death."

"Death?"

"The All Father doesn't care about us when we're alive—"

"You don't say?" I asked sarcastically.

"—even less so when we are dead. But Mornur does. He's made it his job to look after the souls that leave this universe. And we can see the Void sometimes in our dreams. The divide between universes is much thinner when we dream, and even thinner for those with telepathic abilities."

The idea of souls being taken care of after life, I admit, softened my facade for a moment. But reason (or skepticism, I didn't care) won me over again quickly. "And even thinner for a telepathic race that lives in the dark? You're starting to quote the book again."

She shrugged. "Sometimes there's good points in fictional stories."

"But doesn't everything you just said seem a bit...I'm not sure the word. Fantastical?"

"Well how do you explain your dream?"

"Well yes I suppose a member of a telepathic race that grew up in the dark who also happens to be dying would practically have nothing dividing him from the planes of life and death."

Now Sibyl looked guilty. "I-I'm sorry. I didn't mean to suggest you were—"

"You didn't," I said waving my hand, "I'm the one suggesting it."

Silence.

"Are you sick?"

I sighed and shook my head. "Everyone is dying my young friend, some of us are just ahead of the rest of you."

More silence.

"Thank you for the company," she said.

I nodded. I waited for her to finish her meal before leaving. I didn't like to see people eating alone. I did feel very tired though, and I had a feeling I didn't have restful dreams awaiting me at home.

Nothing happened in the dream. However, it still felt like it lasted entirely too long. I saw someone's silhouette floating in nothingness. But I don't think it was a silhouette. Everything around me was already so dark, the sight in front of me looked more like an impression in the darkness. Like how the other side of a curtain would look if you pressed your body against it and tried to reach through. Then, completely shattering my metaphor, eyes opened where the silhouette's face would have been. This sent an unexplainable uneasiness throughout my body.

I woke up to knocking on the door. I slept in way too late. I was meant to meet Kelv today. I hoped I wasn't so late that he left the store to come looking for me.

I scurried into some clothes and went to the door. Coughing all the way. I opened it and Sibyl was standing in front of me.

She looked as shocked to see me as I felt to see her, though I'm fairly confident there was some annoyance mixed in with my emotions. I just wanted to right my wrong, I wasn't looking to make this person a regular in what's left of my life.

"Benjar. Hi." She was holding a pamphlet.

A pamphlet. Oh good grief.

Sorry. She thought.

Before I had a chance to complain, she started talking.

"I'm sorry. I didn't know you lived here." She motioned to the two other people in black robes at the door of Druan's old house.

"Good evening, Sibyl. I don't mean to be rude but I'm late for lunch with a friend," I said, stepping past my door and locking it behind me. "Why are you always by yourself in these situations?"

She shrugged. "I'm a little more understanding of people's skepticism. I don't push as much, and some people in my group don't like that approach."

"I think that's the scariest thing you've told me yet." I started down the street.

She laughed, and started following me. Of course.

I'd hate to see what more pushing looks like.

She laughed in her head in response. Which I admit made me smile.

"I'm glad I ran into you again," she said, "The way you were talking at the diner worried me. I was hoping I'd be able to make sure you were alright?"

"What do you mean the way I was talking?"

"What you said about...your health."

"You have an impressive way around words, I'll grant you that," I said, stifling a cough as I did not want to validate her concerns. "I'm fine. It's nothing I haven't thought of before."

"I wondered, if what I said comforted you at all?"
"Which part?"

"The part about Mornur looking after us. Your face almost looked...eager, or hopeful when I mentioned it."

I didn't stop walking toward town, but I slowed my pace. "I don't care what happens to me after. Didn't ever spend too much time thinking about it. Thought it was a waste of time. Even when my wife died. Sad as I was that she was gone, she had left on the best terms. In her own bed, at home with me, in a room surrounded by the people that loved her."

I could feel Sibyl's apprehension.

"My daughter...did not. After we mourned her mother's passing, she told me she wanted to leave Nyla to join The Allegiance. She wanted to help."

I swallowed, trying to keep my voice steady. "And I spent her last few days here trying desperately to convince her not to go. I didn't care about the universal family feud The All Father and his son decided to start. But she did and she tried to tell me it was important. I've always respected the things that were important to her, but I was supposed to take care of her. I'm the one who's supposed to look after her. Was I meant to assume someone who used to to call themselves the Shepherd of Fire would? And I'm not only afraid that she died in a horrifying battle, lightyears from the people who cared about her, I'm also *terrified* that she died thinking I stopped respecting her or loving her when she left."

I started to walk faster again, breathing heavily. I think Sibyl put her hand on my shoulder and asked if I was okay.

When I was walking normally again, I said one last thing. "So maybe, maybe the idea of someone taking care of her after all of that, maybe someone knowing that I'm still loving her and being able to tell her that I was proud of her even though it wasn't the last thing I told her..."

I didn't know how to finish that sentence.

Sibyl held onto my shoulder once again. I didn't look at her, but I heard her thought.

I think a parent trying to keep their child out of danger is one of the clearest ways of telling them how much they care for them. How much they love them. You wouldn't need Mornur to tell Iinya that.

I felt the waters rise in my eyes.

Kelv started lunch without me on the bench outside of his store. I realized in my rush to get here I neglected to bring anything to eat. It was either due to my haste, or to the fact that I felt no hunger.

He smiled at me. "I was getting worried, old friend. But I hope you're late because you're finally sleeping better. You look great!"

I returned his kind look and comment, though I did not feel great, my mind felt more at ease. I suppose he was referring more to my mental state than to my physical one. Perhaps my last talk with Sibyl did more to declutter my mind than I thought it would.

I joined him on the bench. "How's work?" I ask.

He shakes his head. "Everyone keeps telling me I need to get something called freezers so that we can start carrying more off-world food."

"Not a fan?"

"Well I don't mean to be against progress, but why does progress have to be such a pain in the ass?"

"I think that's how you know you're progressing."

"Well my ass is tired. I'd hate for Tera to beat me in this whole retirement standoff we find ourselves in, but I mean it. I'm tired."

"I understand my old friend. I'm tired too." I thought to myself for a moment. "Kelv, do you dream?"

"Do I dream? Yeah sometimes. Why?"

"Just curious. What do you dream about?"

"Well lots of things. Sometimes it's just part of a memory. Other times it's something bizarre like playing cards with a talking loaf of bread. Every now and then I just see shadows and nothing interesting."

"Shadows?" I asked, trying to mask my astonishment that he might have similar dreams to mine.

"Yeah it's a weird dream I've had every now and then. I'm in something like a dimly lit space and there's just these weird blobs of, well, nothing. I can see them but they're too far away for me to make anything of them."

At the mention of the shadows being far away from him, I felt myself relax a little. "Well at least you don't dream of that all the time."

"Yeah It kinda makes me uneasy if you can believe it. A Nylan letting dark creep him out."

"I think I can believe it."

"What do you dream about?"

I paused. "Things I don't really understand."

"Well it can't be less understandable than trying to talk politics over a card game with a sapient piece of off-world foodstuff."

We both chuckled at the idea.

We watched the hustle and bustle in the street. Mothers and fathers dragged their kids to do errands with them. Teenagers on the cusp of adulthood ran to and fro, excited at the power their part-time wages earned them. Young adults roamed almost aimlessly and enjoyed the energy of it all, as if they had nowhere else to be.

"We're lucky to live on Nyla aren't we?" I asked more to myself than to Kelv. "What do you mean?"

"Well, looking at us all here, now, you wouldn't know there was a war going on. In a way, being ignored for so long, by the Itarians or the gods, actually turned out to be a good thing."

Kelv looked at me. I could feel his worry. "Been thinking of Iinya?"

"Always."

He sighed and patted me on the back affectionately. "She was really fantastic. Almost made me want a kid."

"Almost." I chuckled.

"Well there was that time she tried to steal half my carts because she wanted to organize a 'kids only parade' or whatever she called it."

My laugh burst out fast and loud, more like a snort. It actually kind of hurt my chest.

We spent the rest of the day sitting on that bench. We reminisced about lots of things, and talked about unimportant topics. Kelv grew more and more certain that he wanted to retire with each passing hour. I told him he earned it.

We ended up talking until sunrise, and decided that we would simply go home and sleep in after watching it. Kelv said we earned it.

"You know, Iinya once told me, when she was a child, that she learned in school that Nyla sunsets are the most unique and beautiful in all of the cosmos. It's because we're the only habitable planet orbiting a blue sun, so it's the only place you can see the unique colors a blue sun gives off when setting. And our dark atmosphere and all the moons affect the light so it stays blue somehow or something like that. When she was that young, her dream was to travel the universe and see all of the sunsets. I hope she got to see some of them, while she was out there saving the universe."

"You know Benjar, I would bet money that she managed to see most of them."

That was a really good day.

For the next week, my dreams were much less scary. I still saw the Void, if that's what it was, but I didn't feel as trapped as I did before. Though there was still something unsettling about being there. And on the same day the next week, I was walking back to that bench, eager to be the first to hear that Kelv was hanging up his smock. Our friends supper was on the usual night again, which meant I would be ahead of everyone else in the gossip chain.

However, as I got closer to the town, the more I walked toward Kelv's store, the worse I started to feel. My breathing was more labored than it had ever been. I even started to feel dizzy. By the time I got to that bench, I basically collapsed on it. My vision was blurry, and I knew I wasn't hearing things right. Everything sounded far away. Almost like in my dreams.

I didn't focus on anything again until I saw Kelv's face right in front of mine. He was stooping down to support me. I didn't realize I couldn't sit up straight; I kept leaning to the left. I vaguely managed to understand that he was going to take me to the hospital. I'm also, fairly certain, he was not wearing his smock.

I woke up a few times, in a hospital bed. The feeling of a tube in my arm and the sound of faint blips on a monitor were enough to rouse me, just not for long. But I know for sure, I woke up six times. The first time Kelv was asleep next to me, hunched over and clearly uncomfortable. I woke him, relieved to see relief flood his face. We didn't talk long, but I made sure I thanked him for being a good friend to me for all our years. He told me to shut up, but I didn't need to be a telepath to hear that he was thinking the same thing about me.

The second time Tera was with Kelv. She had been crying, and I hated that I was the cause. I was sure I was dying now. I could feel the weakness in my body pulling me back into sleep. I wasn't sick, I was just tired, and my body was telling me to rest. I was stubborn enough to resist the urge long enough to tell Tera how important she was to me too. I drifted back to sleep in the hug she gently wrapped around me.

The third time I woke up alone. I was pleased to think my friends were getting some rest themselves. I didn't want them killing themselves over my death. Besides, I had a window, and I woke up to a sunset; the night was just starting and I could see the light vanishing over the skyline. I entertained the idea of staying awake long enough to talk to my friends when they arrived, but I did not have the strength. Still, I was grateful to see one last sunset. It reminded me of watching them with Radia and Iinya.

The fourth time I managed to catch the doctor. Not that she had anything new to tell me. I already knew what was happening. I just wanted to thank her for keeping me comfortable, and to not hesitate to send any of my friends in.

The fifth time everyone was there: Kelv, Tera, Druan, and Maki. I knew that I had been asleep for longer this time since Kelv's hair had turned gray, no doubt from only eating hospital food. I felt bad about that. I told Druan and Maki that I loved them. I said it again to Kelv and Tera for good measure, while also mentioning that they should get some real food because I didn't want them starving themselves just to watch me sleep. I also reminded Maki how much she meant to my wife and for that I was always grateful that she was in our lives. And I told Druan that if he wanted it, I left him my house in my will because I knew how much he hated his small apartment. This made even him tear up, and Druan was notoriously not a cryer. Maki reciprocated my feelings and went to hug me, but I fell asleep too quickly.

The sixth time I managed to stay awake for a while actually. It made everyone hopeful, even though I still didn't feel like I was getting better. They all stayed with me in the hospital, talking to me, playing cards, and telling me how much they cared about me. All of these emotional declarations were things we had told each other before, but when you love each other as purely as only best friends can, you can never confess your emotions too much. Especially in times like these.

The last thing I saw before I drifted off to sleep for the final time, was Sibyl. She was outside the window, preaching in the street. I don't know what kept bringing her near me, but this time I was glad. Talking to her made me get over some things that I had trapped in my mind that were doing me no favors. Spilling everything out to a new person would've done it I suppose, but that's not important because she was the one who pushed me to interact with it. It may not have been the help she was offering, but it was helpful nonetheless. And I actually think it made me ready for the next part. But maybe that was just a coincidence of cosmic timing.

I hoped her telepathic aptitude for nosiness worked at this distance. There was one more thing I wanted to say to her.

Thank you.

Sibyl spun around, looking excited. Then she saw me in the window. When she realized where I was and what I was doing, she still looked happy. She was still smiling at me. But I could feel the pang of sadness she was trying to hide, as she waved goodbye to me.

I went.

My dreams did not do the darkness justice. Thick wasn't the word. Drowning didn't explain the sensation. It was so dark, I was actually giving off my own light... which seemed wrong. Was this glow the Spear Energy inside me? It hardly mattered, all the light did was let me know where my own body was. Without it, I'm not sure I would've known where my limbs began and ended. When I closed my eyes to try to wake up, the darkness was absolute. I could feel myself extending throughout the emptiness. I was somehow a part of this infinite abyss.

I knew it wasn't a dream when I saw him flying towards me. He wasn't the silhouette that had made me uneasy. Or if he was, I saw him completely differently now. Size was hard to judge, but he was much taller than me, though nowhere near as large as a Fargulkian. His skin was somehow blacker than the darkness that surrounded him. I only saw him by the outline of his body, which was bathed in a faint gray glow. He wore no clothes, unless what looked like dark smoke engulfing him was actually one long flowing garment. Faint little white lights, like distant stars, glimmered in the middle of his eyes. I could tell he smiled once he approached me because his teeth shone a dim silver color.

Welcome back to the Void, Benjar.

"THE NEW JOURNEY"

I saw him clear as day
though his form was dark as night.

Too solid to be called a shadow.
Too brazen to be called polite.

He told me it was my time now,
that I must leave with him at once.

I confessed to him my dread,
and this was his response:

"I am no more frightening than Life,
and I'm just as, if not more, fair."

And so I went with him,
on that journey we all someday share.

-MAKISIA BULAREM

GROCK AND SANDS

Grock stared at the bottom of his empty glass as he waved over the bartender for another round. He looked down at his newspaper; nothing but Black Palace propaganda. Ever since The All Father woke up, Grock spent most of his time drinking. He had been a commander in the military, but when The Black Palace army showed up he ran. He'd rather leave his position than fight for the tyrant.

Now he just drank and pretended the war wasn't happening. For the most part it worked. He crumpled up the newspaper and threw it over his shoulder. As he went to down the new drink the bartender had handed him, he felt a tap on his shoulder.

"You dropped this," a voice said behind him.

Grock spun around and nearly fell off his stool when he saw the man who had tapped him. He was dressed from head to toe in Black Palace garments; full military armor with a pistol at his hip and a rifle slung over his back. He extended an arm with the crumpled up newspaper in hand.

Grock spit at the soldier's boots.

"Don't need that garbage. And we certainly don't need your kind in here."

He spun back around and gulped down his drink, once again waving down the barkeep.

The soldier sat in the stool next to his, "Look man, I'm not here to cause trouble. I just want a drink."

Grock looked at the bartender wondering if he would serve The All Father bootlicker.

The bartender just shrugged and poured them both a drink.

"Long as he's paying."

"Whatever," Grock said, grabbing his drink and getting up to leave. He didn't want to stick around to find out why The Black Palace was in town.

"I'm not here for you, didn't mean to ruin your night. Sit down, next round is on me. What's your name?"

He eyed the soldier up and down. The tag on his breast read 'Sands'. Above it was a mark showing his rank: commander.

"Name's Grock."

Reluctantly he sat back down.

"So if you're not here for me," Grock said, grabbing his glass, "why are you here then, *commander*?"

The soldier raised an eyebrow at the way Grock said 'commander'.

"Official Black Palace business."

He gulped down half of his drink.

"You military?"

"Ex." He wondered if he should be telling this guy anything but the drinks were starting to hit him. "Left when they wanted me to serve your *leader*."

He said 'leader' with the same distaste as 'commander'.

Sands looked down at his drink as if that's who he was talking to.

"Yeah, The All Father's not exactly what they make him out to be."

He closed his eyes and thought for a few seconds before sighing and turning to face Grock.

"Truth be told, I'm not here on Black Palace business."

"Oh?"

"I was sent to slaughter innocent people, all to prove a point. I was on the rock the night The All Father fought with Corrin."

He was shaking his head by this point.

"I had to get out before things got worse. I took a ship and left."

He sounded so disappointed in himself.

"You did the right thing, commander," Grock said, putting respect on his rank this time.

Sands ripped off the rank marker on his armor.

"I don't deserve this," he said looking down at it before letting it fall to the floor.

Grock looked down at his own drink, feeling remorse for leaving his post. For leaving his troops. He started to wonder if he had ever deserved commander in the first place.

The bartender tapped on the bar to get their attention. He was staring out the window near the door. Grock and Sands both turned to see what he was looking at. Outside the bar stood seven Black Palace soldiers, full suits of armor like what Sands was wearing.

"They must've tracked the ship," Sands said, scrambling to get up.

"Come on Grock you gotta go out the back. I'll distract them," he said, grabbing his pistol.

"I'm not leaving," Grock said appalled that he would even suggest that.

"They have you outnumbered, give me a gun."

With no hesitation, Sands threw him the pistol and grabbed the rifle off his back. By this point the other patrons had caught on to what was happening and they began clearing out. All except the bartender who was now sporting his own gun.

"Come on, get behind the bar."

Grock and Sands obliged and hopped over the counter. The three of them were crouched behind the bar when the door swung open and the soldiers made their way inside.

"Commander Sands, we know you're here. Surrender your weapons and come with us."

Sands racked his rifle.

"If I turn myself in, I'll be executed for desertion!"

Grock could hear the soldiers walking towards the bar. He knew there was no turning back now. He peeked over the counter and took a shot, hitting the soldier closest to them in the neck. He was aiming for the head but after more than a few drinks he was glad to have hit him at all.

The soldier crumpled to the floor causing the other six to topple tables and take cover behind anything they could find. The bartender rested his rifle on the bar and began taking shots.

Sands whispered something that was either a prayer or a curse then he started taking shots at his former allies. Shots were fired from both sides for a few minutes. Glasses shattered and napkins flew through the air. Half the furniture was full of holes and there was blood all over the floor. Finally shots stopped hitting the bar and Sands was the first to get up.

He signaled 'all clear' and Grock and the bartender both got up. Grock counted; five, six, seven. All seven soldiers were dead. They all sighed and wiped the sweat off their brow.

Sands dragged a few stools over.

"Three beers please."

Grock chimed in.

"Put them on my tab."

The bartender chuckled and said, "No worries boys, they're on the house.

ALLEGIANCE COMMUNICATION

A letter to Corrin

To whoever is reading this, I am most likely long gone by now. Please give this letter to Corrin, who I thought was our leader.

I joined this cause. I wanted liberation for my family, for my world. But I didn't expect to see brother turn on brother, sister turn on sister. I didn't expect to see mothers kill their sons for having a different political opinion. Is this what you started this war for?

I left Braroclyn a man, but now I'm barely a person with a soul. What we were commanded to do on Scav was…horrendous! Killing anyone, even children, who side with The Black Palace…Are these your orders?

Others voiced their concerns. Some were shushed away, but others were killed by our own! You were said to be different, but is that even true, or are you just another version of your father?

Unknown

BLACK PALACE CORRESPONDENCE

Hey dad, got your last letter. Sorry for the late response. The Allegiance tried to take Veer but The Black Palace defeated them. I think after witnessing some Black Palace soldiers in action, it made mom be more at ease. I don't think she's mad at you anymore for enlisting. It's either that, or she's happy the BPUs you sent us finally arrived.

How are you? Based on what people are saying, this war shouldn't last long. Seems like you'll be able to come home soon. I got your gift from Fargulk too. Were the giants there really that big? This bone is almost as big as my bed!

I'm helping mom more around the house too. After training at The Black Palace Youth Center, she makes me do the stuff you usually do. At first it seemed hard, but I think I'm getting stronger. I'm probably almost as strong as you now.

Have you met The All Father yet? All the kids are saying his Spear is extremely powerful. If you do meet him, can you ask him if he can really speak into space. Some of the older boys said their parents heard him in the clouds before most of us were born, but I don't really believe that.

Anyways, I'm running out of space and mom needs me to help her with dinner. Talk soon dad, can't wait to read your next letter.

SERVE THE BLACK PALACE

"Serve The Black Palace."

I grew up surrounded by that phrase. The Itarians had ruled over us for a full Cycle, purging our great land, enslaving our intellect, and perverting our technology. We had never known war, the concept in and of itself was frightening enough and it led to our easy enslavement. When The All Father returned and his decree rang throughout the cosmos, the people of Myero had become joyous once again. Myero joined his empire and became a valuable asset, allowing his influence to spread and grow.

My name is Kai-Lung. My Father told me stories of how The All Father returned and it led to the liberation of our people. He told me of the Itarians and their brutality, and it lit a fire inside me. Ever since I was young my dream was to serve The Black Palace and bring peace to the universe. My father ignored my dreams and eventually stopped telling me stories of our planet's past. He said we traded one tyrant for another, yet I believed he was wrong.

My only outlet became my longest friend, Takeshi. He alone was the only other person who understood my call to The Black Palace. Now, as The All Father wages a new war with The Allegiance, my time has come to join his ranks. Peace will be maintained throughout the universe, and we will be a part of it.

The Black Palace instantly felt more like a home than Myero ever did. I became a part of something larger than myself, fighting for justice across the universe.

Takeshi and I both enlisted in the Infantry. We were top of the class and excited to finally become real soldiers. Finally, we were assigned our first mission. We were to be sent to a small moon on the outskirts of the universe which has become more and more unsettling.

Although not a part of The Black Palace due to its far away location, the time has come for it to join The All Father.

"The day has finally come," Takeshi said.

"Indeed it has, brother," I replied.

Takeshi and I were lined up right next to each other as we waited to leave our carrier ship.

"There he is," Takeshi whispered.

Our company leader, Markovitch, parted the sea of troops to make his way to the front of the infantry line.

A blue aura formed around him as he rose six feet into the air in front of the line of troops.

Markovitch's voice pierced through the chatter of the soldiers.

"O.S.G. Kartov wants this to be a clear and clean mission. I'm expecting the best out of all of you. I understand this is the first mission for many of you so let me make one thing clear, my word is law, you are to do what you are told as my orders come directly from the top. That being said, let us go over the mission one more time before we deploy. We alone, our company, is being sent to the small moon of Thrax. The inhabitants of this moon, Thraxians, are a small culture of beings with technology far less developed than our own. This puny civilization is to finally be brought into The All Father's empire. This is a diplomatic envoy mission, however, if they refuse they are to be terminated. Is this clear?"

"Yes, Company Leader Markovitch! For the Spear. For the Father. For the universe," the room shouted back.

"Good."

An eerie smile formed along Makrovitch's face before he continued.

"We just entered the atmosphere, prepare yourselves."

Markovitch once again parted the sea of us soldiers, this time passing directly in front of me and Takeshi. As he walked by I heard him mumble something to himself, yet was unable to clearly hear what he was saying.

"Did you hear that?" I asked Takeshi.

"The company leader? No," he responded.

"Do you think the Thraxians will join?" I asked him.

"Beats me, but I don't expect much from what we are about to see. I overheard Markovitch talking to Kartov yesterday and it seems like this moon is more primitive than Myero, more primitive than any other culture I've read of."

Just then, the bay doors opened and the bright light of Thrax's sun rushed in. We quickly hurried out onto the moon's surface and headed toward the capital city.

As we lined up outside the city's gates, Markovitch once again gave us our orders.

"The moment the gate falls, sweep in and round up all civilians into the capital square."

"Sir yes sir," everyone shouted out.

I leaned over to Tekashi.

"The capital square, why? Isn't this a diplomatic mission fir-," before I could finish my question, Markovitch blew up the gate and a sea of soldiers pushed in, splitting me up from Takeshi.

As I too began to run through the city streets, I quickly started sweeping buildings and handing off civilians to other soldiers to be taken to the capital square.

An hour passed and the streets were dead. Every citizen had been rounded up and was waiting in the capital square surrounded by Black Palace forces.

Markovitch's voice boomed out toward the crowd.

"Attention citizens of Thrax, this is your final warning. Join The Black Palace and The All Father's rule, or face war with his empire."

"We yield," an old Thraxian responded. His voice was frail and filled with fear.

"Forgive us, for we are ready and willing to join The All Father. We want no trouble," the old Thraxian continued, terror in his voice.

"Excellent," Markovitch replied.

The same eerie smile from before formed along his face.

"Do you have any inhabitants akin to Spear Energy?"

Markovitch began to form Spear Energy in the palm of his hand. I had never seen power like this before. Although I knew of its existence, I had never witnessed it firsthand until today when he blew up the gate. His strength at this low in the military, is far above what I can do as a soldier. I could only imagine the power The All Father possesses.

"No, we do not," the old Thraxian answered.

"Unfortunate," Markovitch said as he hovered a few feet into the air.

"Sadly, The Black Palace has no room for weakness."

Markovitch unloaded his Spear Energy from his hand into a powerful blast directly into the old Thraxian. His body fell to the floor.

The other civilians began to cry out as Markovitch's voice reigned over their screams.

"Exterminate them," he yelled with a cold emotionless demeanor.

"I want this sad excuse of a civilization wiped off the map!"

Before I could react to the atrocity I witnessed, blaster fire began to ring out all around me. A million thoughts instantly swarmed my mind. Was this why we came here? They were willing to join The All Father, why are we murdering them in broad daylight? Was this the plan all along? Was this why I joined the Black Palace Military? Is this war? Was I so eager to join a group of people willing to blindly follow these orders? Then only one thought echoed through my mind. All I did was watch. I watched as an entire population of men, women, and children were gunned down in front of me. I watched as a culture was eradicated and did nothing about it. I didn't move, I didn't say anything. I neither partook nor attempted to stop this execution. All I did was watch.

The screams of a thousand lives were quickly snuffed out and for a moment all was quiet. I stared at the onslaught of bodies in front of me before I snapped back to reality. I turned around to see Markovitch staring directly at me.

"All right, head back to the carrier ship, we're going to rain hell on this sad excuse of a society. There is no place for primitives in this empire."

Just like that the entire company began to walk back to the carrier ship. Markovitch locked eyes with me before he turned around and headed to the ship as well.

I slowly made my way back, unable to turn around and face the crimes I witnessed. As the ship's bay doors closed I quickly went to my quarters. I tried to sleep as the sound of the ship's artillery began to open fire on the moon and officially destroy what remained of the Thraxian society.

I awoke the next day, drained and in a daze. Sleeping was hard. Every time I closed my eyes, all I could hear were the screams of a thousand souls. I looked outside my room's window to find that we were still in the orbit of Thrax. As I wandered the halls of the carrier ship, I tried to remember why I had joined the Black Palace Military. Was I not bringing peace to the universe? Were we not meant to be liberators and soldiers of justice? Does The All Father not value his creations and is he not the benevolent ruler of all space? Why would he condone the extermination of Thrax? Is this what I wanted as a boy, is this the justice I had wanted to serve? Then I remembered Tekashi. Did he partake in the genocide? He has been the only person I could confide in for all my life. He will listen, and he will know what to do.

I waited outside his room until he finally arrived

"Hey Kai, how are you?" he asked.

"I need to talk to you," I responded.

"What's up?"

"Are you not affected by what we just did. How do you feel?"

"Feel about what"

"Us exterminating the Thrax race, wiping their society off the map."

"What do you mean?"

"You don't feel anything? We just killed thousands of people. Is this why we joined the Black Palace Military? This isn't what I signed up for. Aren't we supposed to be bringers of justice? We're no better than the Itarians-"

"Don't," Tekashi interjected. "Do not compare us to the Itarians. We are bringers of peace, The Black Palace had no room for the Thraxians and their weakness. After all, they were a primitive race and would not benefit the empire. Remember why we do this. For the Spear. For the Father. For the Universe."

"I don't need to hear that right now. How is this for the universe? How could you say that about them? There were children, innocent lives-"

"Quiet, do not question The All Father again."

"I... I just don't think I can do this anymore."

Tekashi stared at me, a deep stare that I felt could pierce my soul. Something had changed, this is not the boy I grew up with. How could he say such horrible things? He walked away after staring at me for what felt like an eternity, not uttering another word.

As I walked too, back towards my room, a horrible feeling washed over me. Not long into my walk, other soldiers began to look at me. They stared at me as I passed them in the corridors. Two even pointed at me, then a few began to follow. Something was wrong. I had to get out of here.

I began to pick up my pace and was eventually sprinting in the halls toward the escape pods. As I turned the corner, a figure awaited me in the darkness at the end of the hall. A blue light began to form as Markovitch emerged from the shadows.

"Is this him?" he asked.

Before I had time to react, a familiar voice answered.

"It is."

I turn around to see Tekashi standing behind me.
The sound of a blast rang into the air, and I
immediately fell to the floor, overwhelmed by pain.

I opened my eyes to find my left leg had been
incinerated from the knee down. My blood spilled out
and I realize Markovitch must've hit me with his Spear
Energy. I began to scream out in agony as Tekashi
walked over and stomped on my face, making me lose
consciousness.

I faded in and out of consciousness as I was being
dragged between the halls of the ship. I could feel my
body being thrown down but was unable to do a thing
about it. I opened my eyes to see Tekashi and
Markovitch standing on the other side of a large glass
door.

The airlock, it hit me, this was the end.

I was going to get sent out into the vacuum of space
to die. I couldn't do anything about it. I couldn't speak,
I couldn't move, in the end, I was never able to do
anything about anything, all I ever did was watch. My
father was right, one tyrant for another.

I could hear the muffled voices through the glass as
Tekashi and Markovitch exchanged words. Then I
heard the last thing I would ever hear.

"Do it," Markovitch commanded.

"There is no place in The Black Palace for weakness," Tekashi said as he pressed the airlock button.

"REMEMBER BEFORE"

There was before a simple time that all knew,
Everyone fulfilled in their own value,
With days of laughter and nights of amity.
The universe reveled in its own melody.

The meadows sang to the sky,
The forests without fear stretched high,
The rivers rushed freely without any ploy,
All relaxed in this oblivious joy.

These memories we hold so dear,
Remind us of a time sincere.
That simple life was all we knew.
May our hearts keep the feeling true.

-THE RAT

MY WAR TOO

I saw Corrin once. I was pregnant with my first child when he arrived on Catovaz. How long has it been now? Maybe twenty years? Yea, something like that. Handsome he was. On the shorter side but still striking to see. I applauded when I heard he rose up against his father. But screamed when The Black Palace retaliated against my village.

Six months this war has been going on. Many of the men left to fight alongside The Allegiance. Some women joined up as well, leaving the rest of us to look after the children. How annoying. Leaving to fight a war while the rest of us are defenseless against Black Palace occupying forces.

Everything seemed fine at first. The presence of The Black Palace was always felt, and of course it was felt more after the war started. I expected more patrols. I expected harsher rules and laws to be implemented. But I didn't expect to be plunged into a battle of life or death.

My village sat on the ridge of Mount Ita'r Rus. We had mountains to our back, perfect for The Black Palace to close us in. Which they did.

Our village was designated to be shrunken in size. Easier to control I guess. Night raids began to happen. It was a few drunken deputies at first, coming in and talking to the women. The visits then became more frequent. Eventually it became an everyday thing, with violence being a common prerequisite.

I was helping my youngest lay flowers on the grave of his father, my late husband, when I heard the first shot. My eldest came running over, blood splattered on the hide covering his chest. He was holding a blaster. The girl he was seeing had tears running down her face. My eldest muttered out what he had done. He shot a Black Palace deputy who was trying to harass his girlfriend.

I reacted quickly. I took the blaster from him and tried to calm his nerves. Many of the other mothers were already rushing children and the elderly into the mountains. More shots rang into the air. I grabbed my sons and motioned for them to follow the others. My eldest protested but I shut that down quick.

As I watched my sons and the girlfriend disappear into safety, I quickly ran back into the village. Some bodies were sprawled across the snow as drunken Black Palace occupying deputies stumbled about.

I held the blaster in my hands. I remembered some of the men had left weapons for us just in case we needed them. I felt stupid for showing my eldest where they were hidden.

There were five deputies. They were kicking the dead body of Mrs. Hollan. She was my neighbor. As I was about to do something, more deputies appeared. They seemed right in their mind, not loose off of a few drinks. I glanced back towards the mountains. My sons were out of sight. The number of deputes grew from five to fifteen.

I couldn't hear what they were saying but one pointed toward the mountains. I made my way to where the weapons were hidden. A bunch of blasters were bundled together. My husband and I would go shooting together sometimes when the snow wasn't too thick. I remembered him always telling me to breathe before pulling the trigger.

I grabbed a blaster I was familiar with. The neck was long and had a scope on it. I peered back at the mountains. I either hold these Black Palace bastards here, or allow them to attack my people.

This was my war now too. Not for The Allegiance. Not for Corrin. But for my family. No one was going to harm my sons and I'll die, taking as many as I can with me, before allowing anything to happen to them.

I laid on the snow and took a deep breath, my finger on the trigger.

SHAKEDOWN

Central command bridge, the *Sylvana's Kiss*

Jotuun Orbit

Captain Aphriss Reya sat in the command chair of her cruiser, the *Sylvana's Kiss*. A *Constance-Class* Cruiser, the *Kiss* was a state-of-the-art Anrachi ship of the line. Being her first command, she couldn't have asked for a better ship. Bristling with railguns, plasma casters, fusion missile pods and a robust barrier point defense system, she was ready for anything The Black Palace decided to throw at her.

Aside from the *Kiss*, Reya's command included two other starships, the destroyers *Vyruuck* and *Corvath*. Her small flotilla was in charge of patrolling the northern sector of the Jotuun Defense Perimeter.

A year ago, the Anrachi government had declared independence from The All Father and The Black Palace, after Corrin's brazen attack on his father's fleet. Alongside their declaration of independence, the Anrachi set to work rebuilding their once proud Military.

The Anrachi Defense Fleet was reorganized into the Anrachi Navy, being brought up from 400 outdated ships to over 2,000 modern warships. The *Sylvana's Kiss*, *Vyruuck*, and the *Corvath* were amongst the newly modernized Anrachi armada.

As these new ships were being built, the Anrachi got to work training the crew necessary to man them. Reya and her crew were a part of that training program. For six grueling months, Anrach's new cadets were given a crash course in naval combat, ship maintenance, maritime navigation; and for their new starfighter pilots, dogfighting.

Earning top marks in her class, Reya went through another four months worth of training to become a Captain. Once the Captain program ended, she took command of the Sylvana's Kiss.

The Black Palace had sent small battle groups to test the newly independent Anrachi. In response, the Navy had created the Jotuun Defense Perimeter, using the moon Jotuun as a forward operating base for their fleet.

A few small skirmishes flared up here and there, with the fleet only sustaining light losses against the enemy. But High Command didn't want to take any chances, so here Reya was, commanding her own small battle group, keeping watch for any enemy movement out in space.

She leaned back in her command chair, and hit a comlink button on her left hand side.

"Wolf-1, this is Reya, anything?"

Wolf-1 was the squad leader of one of the *Kiss's* Skyclaw fighter squadrons, Wolf Squad. Wolf Squad was currently out on patrol, looking for any signs of the Black Palace.

"Nothing yet ma'm."

He took a look at his fighter's fuel levels, he was currently at 75% fuel. Not bad, not great either.

"Do another sweep Wolf-1, then get back on the *Kiss* for some R and R."

"Aye, aye Cap. Wolf-1 out."

Reya got out of her chair and paced around the command bridge, her arms clasped around her back. Her bridge crew worked in silence around her.

"We got anything on the sensors?"

Ensign Romeo turned around in his chair. "Nothing ma'm. All clear."

She sat back down in her chair. The last Palace incursion was over a month ago, on the western side of the perimeter. It had been quiet ever since.

Alarms began to emit from the computers all across the bridge.

"Ma'm, we've got something coming out of spacefold!"

A massive Black Palace Spearcraft Carrier thundered into real space, it's sleek angular form menacingly hanging in space.

Lieutenant Darrius, who headed the *Kiss's* weapons systems, spoke up.

"Why aren't they launching any fighters?"

Black Palace Naval combat doctrine called for the immediate launching of their F-Class Starfighters. But oddly enough, this carrier wasn't doing so.

"Ma'am, we're receiving a hail on the com."

"Ensign Rudy, send it to my chair."

A light chirp notified her that it was transferred to her command chair. Reya tapped on the display, and a text screen popped on. It was a short message from the enemy ship:

This is the S.C.C Darkstar, surrender your ships and prepare to be boarded.

Reya immediately tapped back a response:

Fuck off.

Reya inhaled, stood up, put some bass in her voice, and yelled "Battle Stations!"

Alarm klaxons wailed, and a soft red light settled within the command bridge. Her crew quickly brought the *Kiss's* weapons online, and their four other Skyclaw fighter squadrons quickly deployed. On the command screen in front of Reya, the commanders of the *Vyruuck* and *Corvath,* Commanders Orkick and Lyle, came on screen.

Orkick sat with his left leg crossed over his right.

"Reya, what's the plan? The bastard's already drawing up firing solutions on us."

Without hesitation, Reya relayed orders to her fellow commanders.

"Orkick, Lyle, split your ships up, try and get him in a crossfire. We can't let him focus fire on any of us. I'll take the *Kiss* directly at him, give him something to think about."

Both commanders nodded in agreement. Lyle raised his hand in saute. "Aye Captain, we'll be seeing you on the other side."

"Romeo, get a message out to command, we've engaged the enemy."

The Anrachi had set up Rapid Reaction Forces at different points within the perimeter. Incase the Palace decided to show up, they'd be called on to reinforce whatever part of the perimeter that was under attack. But it would take some time, which meant that Reya and her ships would have to hold out for a few minutes until they arrived.

And in a naval engagement, a few minutes can feel like a lifetime. At flank speed, the *Kiss* rocketed at the *Darkstar.* The enemy ship had launched it's own fighters, who were already engaged with Wolf Squadron and the other Skyclaws.

The *Vyruuck* and The *Corvath* had begun their maneuvers, breaking left and right respectively.

The *Darkstar* let loose a salvo of plasma at the *Kiss*. It impacted her shields; a deep shudder vibrated throughout the ship.

"Shields at 85% Captain," reported Commander Roxy from her console.

"Thank you Roxy, Darrius, return fire."

The *Kiss* fired back with a salvo from all eight of her railguns. Her plasma casters let a stream of superheated plasma fly at the *Darkstar*, mixed with over a hundred fusion missiles. The munitions made contact with the Spearcraft Carrier, red glows of light across her hull indicating from her shields where they had impacted.

The *Darkstar* fired off another round of plasma, and broke right at full speed.

Reya raised her eyebrow in confusion.

"What is he doing?"

At navigation, Commander Roxy turned in her chair back to Reya. "Ma'am, their course will take them on direct impact wi-"

She was interrupted as the *Darkstar's* massive hull collided with the *Vyruuck*, shearing it clean in half.

The command bridge stood silent. They could see the bodies of the crew of the *Vyruuck* floating lifelessly in space.

One beat.

Then two.

After the third heartbeat, Reya's training took over

"We need to get in close, engage them at point blank range. Romeo, get me the *Corvath.*"

A pair of enemy Spearcraft fighters tried attacking the Kiss's command bridge before they were promptly shot down by the ship's point defense systems. Commander Lyle popped up once again on the bridge's command screen.

"Ma'am."

"Lyle, I'm going to engage the *Darkstar* at close range. Keep the *Corvath* mobile, and overload its shields. Once their shields are down, go for the engines."

The *Sylvana's Kiss* shuddered from another plasma impact.

"Shields at 50% ma'm."

Lyle saluted Reya and disconnected from the com. Another salvo of plasma from the *Darkstar* narrowly missed the *Kiss's* hull. The *Corvath* unloaded on the enemy ship with its weapons, not allowing the *Darkstar* to focus all of its firepower on it. The plasma weapons used by the Spearcraft carriers could easily overpower the destroyer's shielding if all their shots hit home.

The *Kiss* and the *Darkstar* were now up close, and both ships held nothing back. At point blank range, neither ships' weapons could miss. Blue and green plasma energy collided in space, rail gun rounds impacted at super sonic speeds, and fusion missiles were destroyed by enemy flak cannons.

With each impact, the *Kiss's* shields began to overload. But so were the enemies.

The *Corvath* continued its hit and run attacks on the *Darkstar*, its harassment helping to keep the enemy from bringing its full compliment of weapons against the *Sylvana's Kiss*.

Enemy soldiers attempted twice to board the *Kiss*, but both boarding parties were destroyed mid flight.

"Those boarding parties are getting a little too close for comfort, Darrius."

Darrius nodded and tapped away at his console, his eyes fully focused on the screen in front of him.

"Yes Ma'am."

"Any word from the RRF?"

Ensign Romeo shook his head, "Nothing yet Ma'am."

They were already down one destroyer, and the Kiss's shields were almost spent. The enemy was holding its own despite being outnumbered. If this was what it was like against one Spearcraft Carrier, she couldn't imagine fighting a full fleet of them.

Those reinforcements needed to get here, and get here fast. The *Corvath* came in for another attack run when the *Darkstar* turned to face it.

Already committed, the *Corvath* had no room to maneuver when the *Darkstar* fired all its weapons at it.

The plasma overloaded its shields and burned through its hull, gutting it completely.

Escape pods were launched from the *Corvath*. As they left their mothership, the *Darkstar* fired homing missiles at each one, destroying them.

Reya stood up from her chair in shock and anger, her fists clenched in barely contained rage.

"I want every weapon system we have firing on that ship now!"

Without saying a word, her crew executed her orders with no hesitation. Everyone on board the *Sylvana's Kiss* were in shock at the brutality displayed by their enemy. But each crew member, from the maintenance techs to the senior bridge crew were well trained. While they were in anguish and dismay at the loss of their fellow ships and crew, they pressed on, doing their duty.

Wolf Squadron was the last Skyclaw squadron from all three ships still left flying. Each member had became an ace pilot after destroying six Palace starfighters after the start of this skirmish. They had watched the *Vyruuck* and *Corvath* be mercilessly destroyed by the Darkstar.

"We need to get down there, the *Kiss* is standing alone."

Wolf-1 agreed. Most of the Palace Spearcraft fighters were destroyed, any that were left had docked back in the *Darkstar*.

Before he could form a plan and relay any orders, Captain Reya came over his squad com.

"Wolf-1, their shields are down, go for the engines!"

"Yes ma'am!"

All twelve Skyclaw fighters dove down at the *Darkstar*. The *Darkstar's* anti-aircraft cannons were laying down a thick wall of flak, barely allowing the wolves from seeing clearly through their cockpits.

The *Darkstar's* captain had to have picked up on Wolf Squadron's intended target, given that its already intense wall of anti-air had begun to further intensify. Five wolves were shot out of space, with another fighter's wings disabled on their descent down, crippling it.

"Keep going!"

Wolf-1 yelled through his squad com.

"This is Wolf-8, I can't see, I have to pull up!"

Wolf-8 broke formation, and almost made it, but was nicked by an anti-aircraft round.

She spiraled out of control, and finally exploded against a fragment of the *Corvath's* destroyed hull.

"Stay together!"

More and more starfighters were destroyed until Wolf-1 was all that was left.

Wolf-1 expertly maneuvered his way through the enemy fire, and centered his sights on the *Darkstar's* engines. Smiling, he loaded the last of his fusion missiles into its launch tube.

"Got you asshole."

The fusion missile launched, its contrail leaving a white streak in space. It hit the *Darkstar's* central engine, destroying it in a fabulous purple and orange explosion.

"Direct hit Captain. Your turn Ma'am."

The *Sylvana's Kiss* triumphantly brought every single weapon she had to bear on the *Darkstar*. Fusion missiles peppered it's hull, streams of plasma burned their way through it's decks, and rail gun rounds tore through the carrier.

Reya's comlink chirped. It was a message from the *Darkstar*.

Well played.

Reya smugly responded to the communique.

We'll be accepting your surrender now.

Before the Darkstar's captain could respond, the bridge's nav station began to chirp an alarm.

"Captain, we have more Palace signatures!"

A dozen Spearcraft carriers space folded behind the *Darkstar*. Reya felt a cold spike of adrenaline course through her body. She sat back in her chair, looking at her crew. Thousands of enemy fighters were already on their way to the *Kiss*.

"This is it ladies and gentlemen, let's make them work for it."

But then, before they were overrun by the Palace fleet, the Rapid Reaction Force finally arrived. First ten, then twenty, and then finally seventy five Anrachi ships space folded next to the Sylvana's Kiss.

Frigates, destroyers, cruisers and five battleships cruised their way to meet the enemy fleet, led by the *HawkMoon*, the flagship of the Anrachi Supreme Commander Roan Vallick.

The bridge crew watched in awe as both fleets collided in space. On the command screen, Vallick himself came on screen.

"Reya you did good. Get back to the Jotuun dockyards, we'll take it from here."

Reya nodded in acknowledgment. "Yes sir."

Vallick nodded back and ended the communication. Reya sighed and sat back in her chair. Her crew looked back at her, awaiting her orders.

"You heard the man, set course for Jotuun."

Victorious, the *Sylvana's Kiss* limped its way to the Jotuun docks for repair, it's crew settling for some much deserved rest and relaxation.

The fifth Battle of Jotuun would end in Anrachi victory, with all thirteen Spearcraft Carriers destroyed. However, the Anrachi would lose forty eight of the seventy five ships they set out with. Recognizing the need for a change in tactics, Anrachi High Command would revamp the Naval Academy's training program. For her valor in battle, Captain Reya would be promoted to Admiral, and put in charge of the Battle Fleet that would be sent to help retake Kyros IV.

BLACK PALACE CORRESPONDENCE

Approved by OSG Kartov

Sent by Commander Byeron to Allegiance Forces on Vaxlier:

This is Byeron, commander of the 1st Infantry Division stationed on Vaxlier. This letter is directed to the leader of insurgents currently trespassing on Black Palace territory. Your forces are surrounded and your equipment is inadequate to ours. You have twenty four hours to surrender and dissolve all positions.

If these demands are not met, we will begin to lay siege. Current prisoners will be executed upon direct orders of Overseeing General Kartov, and any insurgent still on Black Palace territory will meet the same fate.

You have twenty four hours. Be thankful The All Father has granted you this mercy!

Commander Byeron
1st Infantry - Vaxlier

SOLDIER BOYS PT 2

The Network was the dark stain stitched to the tail-end of the Black Site—tucked away on the forbidden moon, Foryo—a frigid wasteland left to the sands of time. A multifarious assortment of skulls was the first to greet the misfortunate modicum collection of young, despondent subjects with their eyes glued to the chains that wrapped around the ankles of the child in front of them.

Fehir watched from his cell in the Grand Tower while the latest batch of subjects lined themselves to enter Ge Hinnom, abode of the damned. He scribbled on the leather pages of a journal that had the skin of an animal as its cover. The sheets had been crudely sewn along the book's edge.

It's been six months since I've been brought to this place, and this is the tenth cyber-tram I've seen crammed with kids older than myself. I don't know how much I can take living like this. I don't know how I'm surviving. Every time I think I've pushed my body, my powers, to their limits, the Butcher sets a brand-new bar that seems impossible to reach until it is once again my turn to step into the black. I buried Rory last night. He was the closest person I could call 'friend' in this place before the house went silent. Even with the no talking rule, his kindness was louder than any words that could be shared. Jessipe is still locked in the black room for her noise. None of the guards have even checked to see if she's still alive. I wake up every day, and I don't know if I should be grateful or not. All I have to do is get through the next one.

Fehir hurriedly slammed the journal closed upon hearing the distinct sound of the knock against his thick wooden door. Twice with a pause, then a final one followed by footsteps that continued down the cemented corridor. Fehir fought against his legs that kept dragging him closer to the exit. The fresh taste of iron in the air settled on his tongue after stepping in the hallway.

The dark building blocks of the damp dungeon's corridor stretched until they converged behind General Troi'tn, the Black Butcher. His unorthodox method of igniting one's natural latent power of Spear Energy led him down a path of innumerable wild experiments and bizarre theories.

Fehir slowly made his way in line behind other subjects—zombified in their movements—inch-by-inch. They marched after one another while they each found themselves in the clutches of his talons. He held their mouths open, inspecting them for any contraband. Troi'tn shoved them along into a large room with a reinforced glass ceiling that peered out into the stars. The room had padded white walls that were only soft in appearance.

A young pink-haired girl spun her head over her
shoulder to face Fehir before she grinned to herself with
shy eyes, avoiding his gaze. He recalled her name to be
Lyd'da from the overseer's roll call.

When it was Lyd'da's turn to approach the Butcher,
she snatched her head away from his hands with a sour
expression. It could have been a myriad of excuses; his
hands were often cold to the touch; it was evident that
he didn't cleanse the dried blood from his fingers after
an experiment. Either case, Fehir didn't have time to
ponder the reason as he winced at the sound of a loud
slap that slid across her face.

The violent note bounced sharply off the narrow
walls. Without a word uttered, the Butcher grabbed
Lyd'da by her teary chin while he dug his bare fingers
between her teeth and under her tongue. Troi'tn
smacked her again after he was finished before pushing
her into the yard with the others.

She moved in cadence with the subjects who circled
aimlessly through the enclosure. There were dark glass
windows above their heads that overlooked the center.
Fehir followed the line that lapped the perimeter.
Troi'tn took to the middle of the herd. He held his fist
in the air and it ignited a powerful light that drew the
attention of the room.

The light reached the top of the glass ceiling and by
then, the subjects circled around Troi'tn, sheep to a
herder, as his voice stretched across the room. The

surrounding subjects anchored themselves in place while they focused their sights on Troi'tn, who's burning fist began to release a stream of vapor as it cooled above their heads.

"Spear Energy. You have all recognized its power, but none of you have mastered its potential," Troi'tn said.

"In order to hone your innate abilities, your body and mind must endure rigorous stress to tap into the power. Today, you will learn how to release the stored energy from the various exit points of the body."

Troi'tn sharply waved his hand while looking at the closest subject, a frail boy with fair skin matching his light hair. He straightened his back while Troi'tn made space for him in the center. All the other subjects, including Fehir, watched disquietly while subject and master circled one another, the ouroboros trapped in an abusive and endless dance.

Fehir felt the craven abyss that plagued the young subject's heart as he faced the Butcher. A fierce wave of uncertainty surrounded the boy in a brittle aura that shaped him. The taste of the boy's fear settled on Fehir's tongue. His eyes locked onto Troi'tn's footing while the others were glued to the Butcher's fluorescent glow. He pointed his open palm toward the subject in front of him.

The air reeked of black iron and burning ire. A flash of light bathed the subjects in the yard in a dim flare of blue, before an immense boom erupted their eardrums. Fehir's bones trembled while he tried to maintain his balance. Once his eyes refocused to the mayhem, it was clear that Troi'tn had assaulted his subject with a beam of pure Spear Energy.

Fehir shuddered after seeing the steam radiate off the boy's flesh. He threw his head in disgust, signaling a pair of guards to remove the boy's body.

Fehir wondered what went through the kid's mind while facing down the Butcher. What would he himself think? To stare down the proprietor of their daily torment while he's ready to strike anyone of them down in the name of science. A twisted perversion of groundbreaking discovery with a bastardized methodology as his primary instrument.

Fehir longed to use his scientific aspirations and talents to end the war, but in the hands of Commander Troi'tn, the Black guard Butcher, he'd be molded to meet The All Father's abnormal standards. An army crafted out of Spear Energy and hewn into soldiers.

The Butcher faced the crowed of subjects.

"That," he said, "is how you harness Spear Energy. Who else would like to demonstrate theirs?"

He scanned their surprisingly dull and expressionless faces after his display. He succumbed to mild confusion as if they had not been impressed. He then focused on each of them individually before recognizing the jaded lifelessness buried within their eyes.

His delight grew while he jumped from one pair of dead eyes to the next. Most, nearly gray with thin and faint blue veins pulsing against the skin on their necks. He locked eyes with Fehir, surprised at how healthy he looked amongst the heard. He had arrived with most of this batch and didn't look like he aged even a day.

How could that have been possible? Troi'tn withdrew a sword—pointing it into the crowd where Fehir stood.

Fehir had to use his tongue to suppress the bile that seeped between his teeth. The compound hardly fed them, so imagining having to summon energy struck along the shriveled chords of his empty stomach. His brain started to cramp when he remembered the last trial he had against the Butcher. He hadn't wondered why Commander Troi'tn's blood thirst ran on a violent loop, only that whatever was in his path would beg for the sweet release of death.

Fehir felt a tug on his arm and he was pulled back by Lyd'da who stepped in front of him. The Butcher's eyebrow bounced up upon seeing the girl's rosy flesh. She stared him down with a lowered head. Her dark eyes refracted a glimmer of light from the wall behind the Butcher. A slight flash of red shimmered in the girl's eyes, catching Troi'tn's full attention. A coy grin formed across his lips before quickly fading behind the madness in his eyes.

"Lyd'da," he said, "would you like to demonstrate your talents for the new batch?"

He asked with a sadistic tone as the foundation for his proposal.

"Wouldn't you like to show the rest of the subjects what you can do?"

She glanced over her shoulder before turning toward Troi'tn who was shocked at the devilish curl on her lip.

"Okay," she said, "they'll love this."

Lyd'da was one of the few subjects Fehir had seen and not heard from much since he'd arrived. He hadn't remembered if she was there before him or if they arrived at the same time. If she was already there, how had she retained her pinkish skin? As a native from the planet Wan-Ri, Lyd'da had been saturated in the planet's radiant atmosphere while living on its energetically rich surface. She stood a few dozen feet away from the Butcher who assumed his attack formation.

There was a still silence that filled the space between them. Not a dust particle could be seen circulating with the current of the yard's artificial air draft. The crowd had livened up their attention to focus on the two of them as they occupied the center stage.

The subject's sparring lessons for the past few months have been modeled after a tormentor toying with his latest play thing. The unnerved Lyd'da kept her legs from shaking and her eyes bolted to her target.

Fehir shuddered in unison with the deep inhale of her breath. The enclosure around them was painted with the black stillness of the two being's growing and conflicting auras. Both their energies pulsed from their centers, burning through their flesh and spilling out around them in the exhibit.

That powerful smell in the air returned at the sign of Fehir's flaring nostrils, only, the blinding cauliflower light had been replaced by an off-hue magenta, with a stream of sweet lava forming beneath the subject's bare feet.

The room itself began to shake as a pulsing thump of a rapid heartbeats slammed against the walls with an odd rhythm. For a moment, stood a tall and handsome beast built from Lyd'da's energetic material. The pink monster flaunted its fluorescent glow around the room as it pranced around the enchanted subjects. It was somehow weightless, yet carried the mass of a herd with each glorious stomp of its hooves. Its many horns stacked on top of each other in an irregular pattern, resembling the sehck-rams of the Ood-li jungles of her home planet.

Troi'tn looked upon the beast with the same admiration that could be found in a prideful pet owner.

He witnessed his trained subject harness its latent ability into a work of art. He almost didn't mind when it was sent crashing into him—throwing him into the white padded walls.

Lyd'da fell to her knees, a singer out of breath, overwhelmed by the incredible rush that befell her. She only just began to regain her balance before the Butcher was only a breath away from her in the blink of an eye. All of her energy had been used in her attack. She'd later crucify herself for not using enough of her hate for him to fill the construct's power and kill him. She'd question whether or not it'd be worth it. Each time she harnessed her energy thus far, a sizable piece of her mental fortitude could be felt peeling off with each construct and blast.

With each aura she summoned at the request of the Butcher, she watched herself mutilate her soul and disgrace her flesh only to leave it in the gutters of the wind.

The Butcher studied her closely for months. He'd recognized her potential, yet was only thinking of the limited possibilities for her development.

"You've been holding out on me, Miss Lyd'da," Troi'tn said with a revolting gargle in his lungs.

He coughed into his glove—his greasy hair obscured his vision—he lightly chuckled to Lyd'da's confusion. He glanced behind her, waving his hand forward to signal the on-duty guards to approach.

"Not to worry," he said, "we'll start from square one."

"You can't—" Fehir said, spectacularly failing to stop himself from speaking out before the Butcher used his telepathic ability to choke the boy by his throat with a violent jerk.

"Subject Fourteen," Troi'tn said with grit in his teeth, "you have broken the ninth rule of the batch."

He wrapped Fehir tight in his clutches and brought him uncomfortably close for either of them.

"You will not speak in this house."

The punishments for breaking the house rules were as wicked as they were diverse. Fehir sat strapped to a chair with wires running along the legs and lumbar piece. A metal helmet was placed over his head, shielding his eyes and nose—drowning him in complete darkness. Each round of electric volts that ran through the wires were glaives that had been rammed through his chest. His hairs were uncontrollable coils that spiked upward, with each wave running through his nervous system. His screams were shrouded and smothered by the masonry walls. Through the cracks between the foundation, Lyd'da peered through to bear witness to Fehir's torment.

The next morning, she sat with her eyes closed and hands folded in her lap—humming to herself on her cot. There was a lit torch that hung innocently on the damp wall directly in front of her. It flickered violently, the light pushing against her closed eye lids.

The light's movements danced on the parapets of her eyes while she cautiously hummed in the quiet darkness that she surrounded herself in. She kept her ears fine-tuned to hear each rat scurry across the floor.

Her pattern of breathing remained consistent until a large blushing bubble began to spill out into reality with her as the epicenter. The aura began to overtake the torch light that drooped above her as the dancing shadows morphed into a rampaging herd.

She flinched, twitched, and trembled while she accumulated a small puddle of sweat around her crossed ankles. She opened her eyes to see a magnificent beast before her, made out of the very essence of her being. She opened her eyes and gasped at the sight of the construct. Lyd'da had only ever created mere images; however, there was something noticeably different she figured out as she inspected the creature.

"How are you so still?" she asked to herself, but loud enough for the creature to tilt its head in reaction. It looked at Lyd'da with dumbfounded eyes.

"Because you are," it said with a mocking tone.

Lyd'da was only surprised that it took a conversing construct completely made from her energy to break her hold on reality.

"Isn't that something?"

Fehir laid across his cot, each breath was a dagger in his throat followed by an intense wheezing wince. The very composition of his being suffered the unrelenting sting of his inflicted punishment. He gently picked his body up to turn it over when the side he was lying on grew to be too painful.

The Butcher kept him in the black room for over twelve hours, longer than any precedented holding. He silently pushed out frustrated tears while he ripped the fabric of his cot—fiercely and valiantly combating against the scream he'd wish he could shriek. He'd been stuck in an unending nightmare and was angry with himself for being incapable of waking up.

A bright flash of magenta peppered against his face behind his closed eyes while he sniffled in the darkness. He lightly lifted his head to get a clearer view of the phenomena before him. His cell was overrun by the dominating ominous field of energy that had him surrounded.

He could barely peel his torso off the cot without the excruciating burn of movement tailing close after him. A boisterous thump struck the cold brick that made the floor. He inched his arm over his cot's edge as it only hovered a few crawls above the surface, while he blindly searched the frigid ground.

After a moment of sightlessly tapping the area under him, his palm came across the smooth skin of a round object. Without looking, he grazed his fingers along the curves and grooves of the item, following them until his fingers wrapped around it completely while the sensitive skin under his nails had begun to peel off.

A ball?

His sense of environment had been utterly distorted as he laid bathing in the confusion that followed the questions that plagued his mind. He brought the strange object to his face, the tears in his eyes obstructing his field of vision. Coupled with the vain fire from the wall torch, it provided little defense against the cell's abundant darkness. Yet, he was able to make out the object to be a perfectly preserved green apple.

He stared holes in the fruit for what seemed like hours, but that was only due to time having all but altered into a futile commodity to him. As he held it in his open palm, he thought back to his first few weeks in the batch. Everything had been extremely different from a simple academy where parents would send their ruffian offspring. This was where dogs were sent to be trained, grossly contorted into weapons of mass destruction. If their strength ran dry prematurely, or tested their luck in running away, they'd be caught, rounded up, and put down accordingly.

One morning in the dining hall, Fehir had passed by the table where Lyd'da occupied. He took notice of the untouched red apple among the remains of the sloppily prepared meal. His eyes fell onto her, only to find that she had been hungrily stalking the freshly plump green apple that rested on his tray. He chuckled to himself before he placed the apple on the corner of the table to her bewilderment. He himself didn't hate red apples, but could tell that she did.

"I like red apples," he said.

Their only direct interaction happened before the Butcher implemented the silent rule, yet Lyd'da didn't say a word or phrase in response to him. She merely watched him walk to one of the far tables near the back of the cafeteria and eat quietly to himself.

Another wave of tears befell his face before he sank his teeth into the apple's sweet and sour juices.

I'd been silent for so long I've forgotten the simple pleasures like uttering a single sentence. The sweet vibrations in my vocal cords. The Black Guard has ears everywhere. Writing down my thoughts feels empty as I start to forget what my voice sounds like. Lyd'da sends me small constructs of animals with messages. I can hear her voice in my head. Her gift acts as the line that connects us. Through this, it feels like we've spent a lifetime together in a matter of days. Our conversations put me back in high spirits. The Butcher spent an allotted amount of time tearing my flesh from my bones while putting me back together again with little empathy. He brought up my parents, how I was responsible for their murder. He's right. I didn't know what came over me. He says the cause was my emotions. He didn't mention that I was to use my power to elevate myself from the pain until late in the process. I was barely conscious at that point. He views his actions as making me stronger. I'd be lying if I said I didn't notice it. The amount of power within me burning to be released. My anger and hatred. All for him. All for this place. It's knocking on the doors of my mind and I do not have any strength left to ward against it. Whatever the Butcher is doing, he is snipping away the final pieces of myself that I recognize. I fear—

His ears twitched, and his head snapped behind him at the sound of the knock against his door. A bright blue aura engulfed his fist and with a flex of a muscle, the book was tucked under the rough cot. He levitated his body inches from the ground. The sharp pain from the peeled skin of his feet scraping against the infested floors grew too severely.

The door opened with a pair of Black Guard squad drones standing over the frame. Fehir nodded at them and in turn was guided to the black room on the far side of the compound.

He stood behind his escort while they performed a familiar rhythmic knock against the off paneled door.

The Network was fashioned as one would do a rat maze.

Fehir grew to understand the rule of code during his time in the camp. The subjects who were worth a damn were studied and observed by the Butcher himself. The others who lacked behind were shuffled between the work sites and testing labs on the west wing.

Scientists have developed limited technology over the years since the compound's inception. Although most of the mechanical designs have functioned exceptionally for the Black Guard thus far, the glow in Fehir's eyes allowed him to gaze upon the inner-workings within the walls. The pulling operators, attached to tied wires, that traversed a vertical line—opening the door.

The performance was outlined for him with a strangely clear view, admiring the way the gears grind together in a seductive symphony. The door fully lifted with a cool draft against their faces. The guards stepped aside— turning with dead pupils as they stared blankly ahead—allowing Fehir to float into the room.

The Black Guard, genetically bred, had been Troi'tn's saving grace to secure his position as commander. He was given Spearhead after Corrin left to start a family on Arcadia. His first actions were to recover the forgotten moon, and reform the compound; following unusual practices and forbidden methods in the name of science.

The Butcher slaved for countless hours over his research, pouring his energy into discovering new ways to break down the body to its barest roots, and reassemble it back into a weapon.

"Fehir," Commander Troi'tn said.

He stood with his back against his floating subject. He inspected the cleanliness of the tools on his workbench.

"Did you find the escort alright?"

"Why the hell do you give a damn about the escort?"

The commander's sadistic grimace on his face was his trick to dull the boy's spirit. It was something he'd let slip to Fehir during his reconditioning.

"Is that anyway to talk to your master?"

His eyes beamed with a cold glare that chilled the room. Fehir had hidden his fear behind a muted face, but the Butcher still tested the façade.

"I watch over you now, Fehir," he said, "I can bring out your innermost latent abilities, for the good of The Black Palace. But I can also stop your experiment whenever I please."

His fist raised with a sudden jerk, and to his bewilderment, Fehir refused to flinch at his master's hand. With a haughty glance, the Butcher tugged his arm forward, summoning a chair in the center of the room.

After some time, Fehir sat defeated surrounded by a pool of his own sick. The Butcher's dirty tools rested scattered across one another on the disheveled cart standing next to him. The Butcher finished wiping blood off his fingers before he turned to approach his subject.

"And how are we feeling, Subject Nine?" Troi'tn asked.

The boy's silence drove a pestering wedge through the commander's thin patience. He snatched a clump of hair on the front of Fehir's head to deter its uncoordinated and incessant bobbing as he slipped in and out of consciousness.

"Subject Nine," he said, "Answer the question."

An incoherent gather of words and phrases left Fehir's lips with a slurred pattern and noticeable gaps in processing. The Butcher knowingly nodded while Fehir continued his senseless babble. Troi'tn clicked his fingers together twice at a working lab assistant—directing him to bring forward a journal. After snatching the book out of the assistant's hands, he wrote furiously with small characters in the empty spaces around the cluttered page.

"This is immaculate," he said, "The subject's access to his internal Spear Energy appears to be unfazed, despite his total lack of awareness and limited brain functionality. As if his supply has reduced itself to solely keeping him alive. Subject Nine has been the only one, of all the batches, to do so. This warrants further study."

"No," Lyd'da said while she held a sharp instrument against the lab technician's neck, "You are going to unfasten Fehir's restraints, and then you are going to stand aside."

Commander Troi'tn tried to hide his ever-growing smirk through tightly tucked lips, regardless of the deranged girl who stood no taller than his workbench and commanded his respect in his own lab.

There was an uncomfortable silence in the room, except for the slight ramblings that came from Fehir in the center of the chamber. Lyd'da slowly walked behind the frantic lab assistant, avoiding everything else in the room but the Butcher.

"And hello to you, Subject One," he said, "Is there something you'd like to discuss?"

"How about safe passage off-world once you've done as I said, and release my friend."

"He isn't your friend, girl. He is on his path to becoming one of Black Palace's finest assets."

"Because of what you've done to him, tried to do to all of us, but now you will listen to me. Untie Fehir."

"As you wish."

I can't remember what happened after my restraints came undone, but I keep replaying the sound Lyd's voice over and over again in my head. A gut tearing unease settles inside of me each time I hear her cry. In the empty black behind my eyes, I see the outline of the Butcher's sharp face. His warm breath slides off the back of my shoulder. Then I remember tearing in two.

Fehir stared motionless at the dark spots throughout the rakish laboratory. Lyd'da's hands gripped his shoulders, sinking her nails into his skin as she screamed in his face.

"What have you done to him?" She asked Troi'tn who sat quietly at his workbench, reviewing his notes.

"Exactly what I've been striving for since the beginning," he said, "What that fool Corrin didn't have the stomach for. I've just started a new era, one where beings like us, connected to the Spear, can rule. I've saved us."

"You're sick. You've taken our freedom, our bodies, even our lives. In what era could one see you as their savior? What about those who can't harness the energy? You expect to rule over them all?"

"I do! Do you not understand what the power means? How unique you are? Your unique color has kept you here thus far. Your 'pets' are no more than puppetry nonsense, and only serve to leech the energy from your brain. But I'm afraid you've surpassed your usefulness, dear girl."

I remember her cry.

A sharp sting coursed through the air. *I remember the smell of sulfur.* A scythe, with a color of death smeared on the blade, corrupted the skin of her aura. The only time Fehir had smiled since he'd arrived at the compound was seeing the magenta animals prance around his room. He loved nothing more than the sound of her sweet voice running through his mind. She was as innocent and pure as the meadow Fehir scampered with Seben.

Fehir's time spent with her reminded him of the pureness in life and the innocence of soul. The only memory of his old life.

I remember her body lying at my feet. Then I remember crying.

End

THE HEART OF OLD SKY-VIEW
BY SYD JAY

He never took off his apron. That's why it took me a second to recognize the old Sky-View baker. It wasn't the grey hair, nor the fact that he was standing at the register ringing me up. It wasn't even the lack of warmth in his smile as he was bagging my generic Myeran coffee cakes—much to his chagrin, I suppose. No, it wasn't any of that. Kei Yu-Lung never took off his apron.

That's what I remember most about the Sky-View Bakery, located in the shopping district of B-4, Mid-Level Province. The Sky-View shopping district was a bastion for kids who didn't want to—or couldn't—go home after the bell rang. The arcade by the electric fountain was our hangout. The old scientists outside the diner would place bets on us. Couples sit on the soft metal construct under the eponymous Sky-View, a window to the sky through the miles of steel above us. At days end, you would see everyone at the Sky-View Bakery.

I came back a few days later to pick up my mother's medication. I took a turn down an aisle when I saw him again. He was programming the stockbot with a list of cough meds to manufacture. I reintroduced myself to him—it had been close to a decade since he had seen me. It took him a moment to take in what I had said. He stood with his arms crossed, eyes pointed to the ceiling.

"Coffee cake. Extra sugar with a light touch of frosting." He remembered my order perfectly.

We sat under the Sky-View after he clocked out from the Tinako Mart. We were able to find a bench near the center of the Sky-View. A consequence of Kei Yu's late hours. I used to spend my childhood staring up from this bench, trying to imagine what life was like up above.

It's funny. It's hard to make my way down here now. Even with my credentials, securing access to an express elevator is difficult, and I dread the several days long trip with the public elevators. I've only gone back four times since I moved up to Sector A-3 in the High-Tier. And every time I come home, there's another piece of my childhood gone.

"Kids used to play out here. Do you remember that?" he asked as he stared at what used to be the local Gadget and Gizmo, but is now a fast food walkthrough.

"We grew up," I told him.

"But there were kids before you that did the same thing." He crossed his arms and leaned back on the bench.

"I used to play at Granny Notches card shop before it became the Gadget and Gizmo. You and our kids played at the arcade across from my shop. After that…"

We both sat with that thought for a while. At some point when I was growing up, children faded out of my life. I thought that was normal as you grow into adulthood—only seeing them occasionally when out grocery shopping; there certainly wouldn't be a whole group of them laughing and playing. Why didn't I ever think that was strange?

Kei Yu must have known what was going through my head. All those years serving as the heart of the Sky-View shopping district seems to have sharpened his sense of empathy.

"Getting older, I was sad about all the things our children couldn't do that we got to do. I didn't expect to still have that feeling when you guys grew up."

His eyes went misty. There was a lot his son Kai-Lung would miss out on.

Several months ago, Kai-Lung joined The Black Palace. I remember the arguments he and his father had at the old bakery. His son believed, like so many young men believe, that The Black Palace would purify the galaxy. Kei Yu-Lung told him that's what the Itarians wanted too. As a young adult, watching this teen's mind fall so thoroughly to propaganda was disconcerting.

Once he turned eighteen, he left to join The Black Palace with his friend Takeshi. A few months later, he was labeled a traitor. The Black Palace killed him.

"After Jen died, I knew I had to hold on to Kai," Kei Yu said with a light grunt as he readjusted himself in his seat. He leaned forward so I couldn't see his face, though that's an assumption. "I was just so tired, and I let him go. I shouldn't have given up on him. I should have—"

Kei Yu was a man at the end of his rope. His wife Jen died a several years ago from an accident. The funeral costs ate into the funds from the bakery. It lasted longer than most of the other shops here. He held out as long as he can. But less and less people came here to hang out. The community was gone and replaced by brands. His bakery suffered because of it.

The Black Palace offers a hefty settlement when a soldier dies in battle. It's macabre, but when reality hits as hard as it does, it's hard to turn that luck down. Unfortunately, The Black Palace considered Kai-Lung a traitor, so they would not pay out. Kei Yu even had to pay out-of-pocket to get his son's body back. At the time of writing this article, The Black Palace did not deliver Kai-Lung's body despite Kei Yu having paid to ship his son's body back home.

The bakery was finished.

We left the Sky-View that night missing a piece of ourselves; left behind on that bench in the center of that vertical corridor to the only natural light there is down here. There's nothing for us here anymore. I had no opportunity, so I left, but Kei Yu stayed.

That's a benefit of my youth. I could leave everything I have behind, secure in the knowledge that I can make a life for myself anyway. I don't know if that's true for Kei Yu. He grew up here. He had a family here. Many of his kin died here. He's as part of the Sky-View as our ancient skyscrapers are a part of the mountains of Myero.

THE SURFACE CHRONICLER
[REDACTED]
[REDACTED]
[REDACTED]

Mr. Syd Jay

[REDACTED]
[REDACTED]

Dear Mr. Jay:

Thank you for submitting your article for review. Unfortunately, due to the controversial nature of your article we have decided not to move forward with it.

Given your recent track record with our publication and other controversies that have surrounded you, we believe it best for both you and our publication that we end our professional relationship. While this piece is one of your least radical works, we do not think it best to write something so tastefully against The Black Palace in times of war.

We hope you take our advice, and we wish you luck in the future.

Best,
Tai-Elle Anhil

ALLEGIANCE COMMUNICATION

You were right, I am dying for this cause. But I couldn't be happier. It's Graida, your little sister. I'm in a medical tent on Itarus. We got here about two weeks ago. Fighting started immediately but oh man Grodun, it was amazing. We took out so many Black Palace soldiers in the first few hours. They had no idea what hit them. The days after is where things got more intense. An influx of infantry soldiers arrived and our numbers quickly meant nothing. A few friends I met along the way died, others abandoned their posts. But I stayed!

And I'm happy I stayed. I pushed with my comrades up the lines, inch by inch, day by day, until the Black Palace infantry that came to kill us off, shrunk. They thought they broke us, but they were wrong. We took Itarus, and liberated it from The All Father. I was apart of that Grodun, me, your little sister.

But I'm writing to you now from a medical tent. Yea, I should be angry or sad, but I'm not. After we liberated Itarus, some Black Palace loyalists infiltrated camp and set off some explosives. I took the initial force of the blast, rupturing every bone in my back. By doing so, I saved more lives than lost.

Don't cry for me my brother, I am an Allegiance fighter. And soon, I'll get to see Mom and Dad.

-Graida

THE BATTLE OF DARK & LIGHT

A beautiful woman quickly rushed down a hall. She was dressed in lavish gray robes with golden jewelry all over her body. She took a deep breath before entering a small room where two boys, one dressed in black, and one in white, were waiting.

"The viceroy has done it. Rasho boys will not be conscripted into The Black Palace," the woman said.

The two boys beamed with joy and began to glow blue as they slowly rose into the air with excitement.

"Kurai! Stop!" The woman yelled.

The boys both descended back to the ground and ran to their mother. The three embraced in a long hug.

"Raito, Kurai, your powers are a gift, but one that must be kept secret."

Raito, the boy in white responds, "Yes Mother, we're sorry."

A new figure appeared in the doorway. A tall man dressed in black stayed in the shadows of the hall and began to speak in a low voice.

"Siphra, I need to talk to you."

The woman quickly turned around and faced the man.

"One second Dagon," she responded.

She looked back toward her children before going into the hall with Dagon. The door shut behind them. Raito ran off to the window but Kurai snuck over to the door. He leaned up close against the wall and remained silent. He could hear Siphra and Dagon's conversation. It was muffled and quiet but he listened in.

"I need the funding now, Siphra."

"It's coming I promise. It takes time, The Black Palace can't know about these transactions. I may be wealthy but my money is not infinite and it is still tracked and monitored."

"If I don't get the funds soon, I won't be able to pay the arms dealers and help free Rashalon. Our rebellion will fail without weapons. You want a better life for those boys do you not?"

"I do...Raito has something inside him, I know he can do great things. Just, just give me another day and you'll get the money."

"Good, I'll be back tomorrow then."

The next day, Raito and Kurai waited in the same room with Siphra. She paced back and forth before finally rushing out into the hall. She screamed and the two boys sprinted out to see Dagon laying at the end of the hall with a hole straight through his chest and a massive pool of his blood slowly growing.

Raito comforted his mother, crying over Dagon's body, as Kurai watched behind them standing in the shadows.

After that incident, Siphra fell into a deep state of depression as Drexa, a city on the planet Rashalon, began to fall. The rebellion was quickly crushed without Siphra's funding. Drexa turned from one of the wealthiest Rashalon cities, to a small community built in the remains of a once-populous town.

Many months went by and Raito and Kurai now lived in a small hut on the edge of town near the ocean, where they took care of their now-ill mother, a shell of the woman she once was.

Raito and Kurai sat beside their mother. Her breath was faint. Kurai clenched his fist and stood up. He began to walk to the front door.

"Where are you going?" Raito asked.

"Away," Kurai responded.

"What do you mean, why? What about mother?"

"I can't be here anymore Raito. Leave her, leave here, with me," Kurai said as he mounted his Vasari.

Raito stepped outside their small hut as Kurai extended his hand out toward him.

"Come on. We are destined for greatness. We can become something. Let's leave this life of poverty behind and make something of ourselves."

"I...I don't know," Raito said back.

A shriveled voice called out, interrupting them.

"Boys."

Raito looked back toward their mother and then at Kurai. Kurai sighed and bowed his head.

"We'll meet again brother, I promise," Kurai said.

Raito stared back at him.

"Don't look at me like that, you look just like her. I'm sorry," Kurai angrily said before riding off into the night.

Raito watched from the doorway as Kurai disappeared into the abyss of darkness.

It has been eleven years since Kurai left Raito that night. Only a year after his departure, their mother died. Since then Raito, has been living alone in that same hut trying to get by.

As he wanders through the town market a voice calls out to him.

"Hey, Raito over here!"

Raito looks down an alley to see a young girl gesturing him over. He quickly sneaks over into the alley.

"Tama what do you want?" Raito asks.

"You can use Spear Energy right?" Tama asks. "I need your help with something I'm planning today."

"Shhhh, not so loud Tama," Raito sternly exclaims. "What are you planning?"

"Word is a new commander is arriving today to take over the occupation of Drexa and I want to give him a little surprise."

"This sounds like a bad idea."

"Well, he won't expect an uprising on his first day. It's time to take our city back."

"Tama, I don't think you should do this and I want no part in it. Drexa has suffered enough, don't make things worse."

Tama frowns and Raito leaves her in the alley and continues on his way. He arrives back at his hut and passes through to the backyard where he stares at a small stone slab in the ground. Carved into the stone it reads: *Here Lies Siphra A Loving Mother. The goddess who birthed the moon and sun.*

As Raito ponders on the words of his mother's grave, a huge shadow comes sprawling over him and he looks up to see a Black Palace carrier ship. He looks once more at the stone slab before heading out again.

Raito arrives at the Drexa docking port to a crowd of people. He watches as the ship's doors open and a fleet of Black Palace soldiers flood out. They form two lines and the town goes quiet as everyone watches in

awe as the new commander makes his way out of the
ship.

"I wish to tour Drexa alone," he says, his voice
booming over the commotion of the crowd. "You are to
wait here until I am finished then you may return to
your lives as normal."

Black Palace soldiers form a perimeter around the
crowd as the commander and two soldiers head into the
town. Raito watches them leave when he notices Tama
slip out of the crowd and begin to follow the
commander.

"Don't do it Tama," he mumbles to himself, before
he glances at the soldiers around him. He sees a blind
spot in their perimeter and sneaks out quietly, running
after Tama.

The commander walks through the city and arrives
at Raito's hut. He stops outside of it and clenches his fist
when two shots suddenly ring out. The soldiers
accompanying the commander fall and he turns around
to see Tama standing a few feet behind him holding a
pistol.

"Drexa wasn't always this way," Tama says.

The commander stares at her, his face is covered by
his helmet.

"It's time we take back our land from you."

The commander begins to laugh as Raito watches
from behind a building.

"I know Drexa wasn't always this way. I was here when it first fell. Take this land back, huh? Foolish girl, it is I who has come back to my home."

The commander begins to amass Spear Energy into his right hand. Tama aims her pistol toward him and lets out a shot. The commander dodges it and sends a blast toward Tama. Raito quickly covers his body with Spear Energy and pushes Tama out of the way. The blast hits Raito and he gets knocked to the ground. The commander hesitates before beginning to amass more energy into his hand.

"Another Spear Energy user. No matter, this one will kill you," the commander states.

Before the commander could send his attack, Raito launched his own weaker blast toward him, hitting him in the head and knocking him down.

"I knew you could use Spear Energy," Tama says.

"Is it over?" Raito asks.

The commander begins to laugh as he starts to get up. His helmet falls from his head, shattered from Raito's attack.

"TAMA RUN!" Raito yells.

Tama escapes as Raito stares down the commander still unable to clearly see his face.

The commander begins to speak.

"It's been a long time huh, eleven years to be exact."

Raito's heart sinks and his face drops into horror.

"Kurai?"

Kurai and Raito look at each other in silence for a few moments. Each one sizing the other up and seeing how their brother had grown and changed after all this time.

"Why?" Raito asks.

"Why what?" Kurai responds.

"Why did you join The Black Palace?"

"Isn't it obvious? Look at me. I have reattained wealth, status, and power. Everything we were destined to have, I have achieved. What about you? Why are you still here living in poverty in Drexa? I hoped from the bottom of my heart I wouldn't find you here."

"You mean, you came back for me?"

"Of course I did, everything I have ever done has been for you."

Three Black Palace soldiers came running up to Kurai. Two of them pointed their rifles at Raito while the third threw Tama down in front of Kurai.

"Sir, we heard gunfire and found this girl running through the city."

The soldier points his rifle at Tama as she kneels on the ground crying. Raito looks at Kurai, his face in horror.

"Does this girl mean something to you? Do you care for her?" Kurai asks.

"Yes. Please don't kill her, she's just a child." Raito says, his eyes beginning to tear up.

"Then she will be spared."

Kurai turns back to the soldier aiming his rifle at Tama.

"Take her back to the docking port. Treat her with care."

The soldier nods and reaches for Tama, but she suddenly grabs at the soldier's rifle. She pulls it from his hands and fires three shots into the soldier. She then points the rifle at Kurai.

"TAMA STOP!" Raito screams out.

But it's too late, Raito watches in terror as in merely a few seconds Kurai once again dodges Tama's gunfire. He coats his arm in Spear Energy and plunges it through her body.

Tama's body slumps to the ground in front of Kurai, the massive hole in her chest leaking blood.

Raito looks down to see his white robes stained with Tama's blood splatter. He slowly raises his head and stares with piercing eyes at Kurai.

"Please...please don't look at me like that. You look just like her. Those hateful eyes. I had no choice, brother. I had to defend myself. Please understand."

Kurai's voice is filled with contempt and sorrow.

Kurai reaches his hand out toward Raito once again, as he did when they were children.

"Please join me. Together our power can grow to heights the universe has never seen. Our abilities are a gift, not something to be hidden. We have power, so let's use it for good. That's what Mother never understood, that's why she had to go."

Raito's eyes shift back and forth between his brother and Tama's corpse. His eyes turn to daggers.
"What do you mean she had to go?" Raito looks once more at Tama's body, he remembers the day they found Dagon dead with the same hole through his chest.

"Listen Raito. I have done horrible things, but listen-"

"You! You killed Dagon, didn't you? What...what did you do to Mother!?" Raito screams.

"I did kill Dagon, Raito. He had to go and so did she. Listen to me, please. Everything I have ever done has been for you. I killed Dagon thinking it would change Mother, that she wouldn't fund his rebellion and she would focus on us, on you. That man was a horrible influence and the rebellion he funded through mother is part of the reason Drexa fell. The Black Palace does not stand for insurgencies. It doesn't matter anyway, I was wrong, she was too weak to continue after his death and didn't change. She hardened her heart and I realized she needed to go to. I poisoned her, made her weak and sick, you never knew, you thought she was just letting herself go from depression but even then you wouldn't come with me. I waited months for you to come around and realize we needed to leave her... but you didn't. So I left on my own, unable to remain in this place...but I'm back now. I've gained power, and status to show you what we could be."

Kurai kept his hand extended out to Raito.

"Please, join me this time."

Raito's eyes formed daggers once more. He began to coat himself in Spear Energy. Kurai's smile faded and he shut his eyes, coating himself with Spear Energy as well.

Raito explodes with rage, flying through the two Black Palace soldiers, and throws a punch at Kurai.

Kurai blocks it. Raito throws punch after punch at his brother, each one being dodged or blocked. Kurai dances around Raito's attacks.

"Raito stop, you can't beat me. I have been training for years. You have been hiding your powers," Kurai states as he grabs and throws Raito away from him.

"It doesn't matter, you killed Mother," Raito mutters. His voice had never had so much anger.

Raito charges Spear Energy into his fist. He throws another punch at Kurai. Kurai grabs it, not knowing Raito has charged his fist with energy. It explodes in a blast sending Kurai flying back into a ruined building. The building crumbles on top of him, trapping his arm under debris and pinning him down.

Raito breathes heavily as he and Kurai face off in opposite positions of power now.

Black Palace soldiers suddenly come rushing in from around every corner. Tens of soldiers begin to surround

Raito, pointing their rifles at him. Raito increases his aura and charges Spear Energy into his fists. He starts to float a few inches off the ground.

"WAIT RAITO! DON'T, PLEASE!" Kurai screams.

He begins struggling to try and lift the debris off his arm. The soldiers follow Raito as he floats, with their rifles pointed at him. A sergeant raises his hand into the air.

"STOP! He's my brother!," Kurai screams as he reaches his free hand toward Raito before he charges Spear Energy into his hand.

"Fire," the sergeant orders as he pulls his arm down.

The soldiers all begin to fire at Raito. Kurai blasts the debris with his energy and quickly shoots up into the sky. In an instant, he points his hands down at the Black Palace soldiers and rains beams of Spear Energy upon them.

Kurai descends back to the ground. He wanders through the cloud of dust, stepping over Black Palace corpses and body parts before finally finding Raito laying on the ground.

He flips Raito onto his back and sees that he has been shot. Kurai was too late. Raito's body is rapidly losing blood and he is barely conscious.

Kurai picks Raito up and carries him to the shore. He sets Raito down and sits beside him watching as

Rashalon's sun begin to set. Kurai listens to Raito's wheezing gasps for air and starts to cry.

"Why? Why wouldn't you just join me? We're supposed to be brothers. A bond stronger than anything else. Why wouldn't you come with me?" Kurai says, tears streaming down his face.

Raito looks over toward Kurai and he smiles before looking back at the sunset. His body then falls into the sand.

A month has passed, and Kurai stands with a lone tear running down his face. He is standing in the backyard of Raito's hut. He looks down at the two stone slabs next to each other. One for his mother and one for his brother. Raito's grave reads: *Here Lies Raito. The Brightest Sun Of Them All.*

A Black Palace soldier runs up behind him.

"Sir, are you ready?" The soldier asks.

Kurai puts on his new helmet before responding.

"Yes. The future of Drexa begins now," Kurai says as he turns and walks back toward the city.

BLACK PALACE CORRESPONDENCE

To OSG Kartov from Commander Smin

OSG Kartov, this is Commander Smin once again writing to you on an urgent matter. Another battalion under my command has taken leave to the planet Qibbi.

I ask you to put a permanent travel ban on all Black Palace personnel from going to that forsaken world. Upon returning, my men are in a delirious state of mind. They cannot perform their duties, and their ability to be soldiers is inhibited. And sir, those are the ones that come back.

Many of my men do not return from Qibbi. I have not sent a scouting party in fear of losing more men than I have already lost.

I hope this message finds you quickly and we put an end to this unnecessary distraction!

Commander Smin
4th Infantry
Mehdias JX7 System

ALLEGIANCE COMMUNICATION

Message from: Kreeden Kray

To: All Allegiance forces across Telamor

To my brothers and sisters in arms, I salute you. I hope this message finds you well and the weather and terrain here on Telamor isn't kicking your asses.

I'm sending this message out due to some issues we have experienced in Ga-Gadan. There seems to be some sort of creature, or native species here, that is disrupting our operations. The locals call it a "MagiDa". One of our translators says it means "Deliverer".

We're not sure what the hell THAT means, but the MagiDa hasn't harmed any of us yet. One of the men got a glimpse of it the other night. He described it as a four legged beast, with scales, yellow eyes, a long tail and snout, and a tongue that hisses.

I don't know if this is an isolated issue, but I recommend all Allegiance forces across the planet keep an eye out. I spoke to Allegiance Command and the consensus is not to harm the creature, as it might offend the locals. Stay safe out there, and lets kick some Black Palace ass.

- Kreeden Kray

THE WEAPONS MAKER'S DAUGHTER

An early morning was nothing new to Rylan as Lumina's best weapon maker. He dressed himself in his work clothes, packed himself a lunch and left breakfast for his daughter. Before heading out he cracked open his daughter Elara's door and watched as she slept peacefully. He walked over and kissed her head. On his way out he looked back to see her sleeping face. She looked just like her mother, if only she was here to see the beautiful girl she was becoming. Rylan closed the door and headed to work.

At his shop Rylan greeted his employees and headed to his office. He began to sift through the pile of order requests he had received overnight, with so many orders to fulfill he had to pick and choose which got priority. With the war going on he had lost most of his workers. The Black Palace military was paying a lot more than he ever could so he didn't blame them. A few small orders from locals and a slightly larger order from Fargulk might be worth it.

He reached the bottom of the pile and saw the largest order he had ever received. The bottom of the page had a number that could change his and Elara's lives. Only one issue, the order was from The Allegiance. Rylan had his men start working on the small local orders while he contemplated if The Allegiance's order was worth the trouble. Most of Vaxlier supported The All Father and the people of Lumina had made it evident who they sided with and what they thought of the rebels.

As far as Rylan was concerned all The Black Palace was doing was taking his men and making it harder to put food on the table for his little girl.

Rylan spent the rest of his day manning the forges and thinking about his predicament. Even with only a few men they managed to get the local orders done and even start the Fargulkian order.

He sent his men home and went back to his office, he stared down at The Allegiance's order. He went to toss it away when he saw his picture of Elara on the wall. Her smile reminded him of his priorities and he wrote up an approval for the request. On his way home, Rylan stopped by the mailing office and sent in the approval.

When he reached the house, he was greeted by a bear hug from his daughter. She asked her usual questions about his work, always so interested in what her father was up to. They talked and joked while Rylan made dinner with the little food they had left. He looked at the small portions and then at Elara, he knew he had made the right choice taking The Allegiance's order.

The next morning Rylan went through his daily routine and headed to the shop. He showed his men the order and told them who the order came from. Luckily these men hadn't left with the rest to join The Black Palace for a reason, so they were okay with helping the rebels of the universe.

They went down the list of weapons needed by The Allegiance and got to work. After about an hour a loud bang was heard at the front door. Rylan said he'd check it out and told his men to keep working. When he opened the door he was greeted by a group of four men with Black Palace insignia on their clothing. They obviously weren't military but Rylan had a bad feeling about this. He recognized one of the men from the mailing office.

"Hello Mr…," the man at the front of the group said looking down at his name tag, "Rylan."

He had a big belly being held by some old leather suspenders and was clearly their leader.

"We were just wondering if you had received a…large order this past week."

So that's what this is about, Rylan thought. Rylan looked the big man up and down and replied "That's none of your business."

"You hear that boys?" Said the leader, raising an eyebrow. "It's none of our business."

His lackey on the left tried stepping through the doorway but Rylan didn't budge.

"If that's all," Rylan said, getting annoyed, "I've got lots of work to do."

"I'm sure you do," the leader said, peeking over Rylan's shoulder.

By now the working had stopped and everyone was staring at the door wondering what the problem was.

"Let's go," he said, turning around.

Rylan rolled his eyes and shut the door. He walked back to his station and continued working. His workers just looked at each other and shrugged then went back to work.

He spent the rest of the day in silence wondering what those Black Palace loyalists were up to and how they knew about the order. After a long day Rylan sent his workers home but he stayed working until sundown. He finally called it a day and closed up the shop, eager to see his daughter after the strange day he had.

When Rylan arrived at his house he noticed the front door was ajar. He grabbed his knife off his belt and slowly pushed the door open.

"Elara?" he called out.

No response.

He walked inside and made his way towards the bedrooms down the hall. He heard a loud creak in the

floor behind him. He spun around expecting to see
Elara but instead he was met with a fist.

When he finally came to, he was tied up to a chair,
his knife was gone, and he was surrounded by the men
from earlier. The fat man was facing him holding up the
approval request with Rylan's name signed at the
bottom.

"Mind explaining this?" he said, throwing it at his
feet.

"Where's my daughter?" Rylan demanded.

One of the men behind him grabbed him by the
hair and said, "Hey traitor, he asked you a question."

Rylan looked up at him and spat in his face. The
man responded by punching him in the stomach. He
doubled over in pain and asked for his daughter again.

"Bring her," the fat man said.

One of the lackeys, a tall, bald man walked over to
the room and brought out Elara. She was kicking and
screaming, calling out for her dad.

"Please," he begged, still out of breath from the gut
punch he just endured "let her go, do whatever you
want to me but please let her go."

The men laughed and the main guy spoke up again.

"No, I think this is a lesson you need to learn. The
All Father is our ruler and the puny 'Shepherd of Fire'
is not going to change that."

The man who had Elara threw her on the ground and pulled out a knife. Another man grabbed Rylan's head and held his eyes open, forcing him to watch as they murdered his little girl in front of him.

He let out a wail as he watched his daughter's lifeless body hit the ground. The men just looked at him and laughed. They all took turns beating him as he sat there, numb, unable to process what he just witnessed.

They punched and kicked him, knocking over the chair leaving Rylan on the floor facing Elara's body. When the loyalists got bored with him they left, and Rylan just laid there and wept.

Rylan awoke, hoping everything he remembered was nothing but a terrible nightmare. His hopes were quickly crushed as he realized he was still laying on the floor, tied to a chair and staring at his little daughter's corpse.

He managed to free himself from his restraints and he crawled over to Elara and held her as he cried, cursing The All Father and all those who followed him. He spent the morning burying the only person he cared about.

After he was all cried out he was consumed by anger. Anger towards The Black Palace, anger towards The All Father, but most of all, anger towards the men that did this.

Rylan made his way to the warehouse of his shop and spent the day prepping and gearing up with the weapons he made for The Allegiance. He went back to the mailing office in hopes of finding the man from yesterday.

The mailing office was all but empty with only a receptionist at the front desk, her eyes widened as she saw Rylan's bloodied face and all the weapons he was carrying. He demanded the name and address of the man who killed his daughter.

The receptionist said he hung out at a bar on the other side of town. As the sun was setting he reached the bar and found three of the men sitting at the bar drinking and laughing. The only one missing was the fat leader. Rylan, consumed with rage, walked up to the bar and stabbed the guy from the mailing office in the back.

The patrons of the bar began screaming and the other two men got up in shock and tried to run out. Rylan managed to grab one of them by the shirt and turned him around so he could look him in the eyes while he slit his throat.

By now the last man had regained his composure and broke a glass in half and thrust it into Rylan's side then ran out the door. Rylan screamed out in pain but he managed to follow the man outside and tackled him to the ground. The man began begging for his life.

"I'll let you go if you tell me where to find your boss." Rylan said, spitting out some blood.

"M-my boss?" the man stammered "O-oh you mean Lykard? He lives down the street, atop the hill. He was here, h-he left early. Please I'm so sorry he made me do it!"

The man begged.

Rylan looked at the house sitting atop the hill and stabbed a knife repeatedly into the man's gut.

Battered, bruised, and bleeding, Rylan practically dragged himself up the hill and banged on the man's door. The man came out in a robe asking who was bothering him at this hour.

When he saw the blood dripping from Rylan's clothes he turned pale and tried to shut the door. Rylan put his foot in the doorway and pushed his way inside.

He tackled the man to the ground and they fought.

Rylan cursed at the man, "SHE WAS JUST A GIRL, WHY DID SHE NEED TO DIE?" tears flowing down his face as he asked.

The man punched Rylan in the face and responded, "FOR THE ALL FATHER!"

Those were the last words he ever spoke.

Rylan's knife plunged deep into the man's chest and the house filled with silence. The buzzing of insects outside were all Rylan could hear. He crawled his way out of the house, nearly losing consciousness from the loss of blood.

He made it outside and laid back against the house.

He sat atop the hill watching the sun peek over the horizon. Rylan looked up to the stars, his vision fading.

"Elara my love, I'm coming."

"HOUSE AND FAMILY IN SHAMBLES"

I seem to notice more and more, home has changed
since I was young. At first I heard dulcet sounds ring
throughout each and every room,
But our delights were silenced by His harsh tongue.
Obeyed of course, lest we join our brother in his doom,
Less sure I am, to grant Him the power to judge our
living improper. Curse you, Father.

Our house was wonderful, our house was grand.
Our house is broken, most rooms unprecedented
disrepair, Save those callous and those blind, that accept
the palace brand. The pain I feel for my small siblings is
much too much to bear. Their best failed, to quietly
leave or to stand and holler. Curse you, Father.

You said you were here to secure our house and give us
guidance, That we your supposed children would be
safe in your gaze. You mistake peace and harmony for
subjugation and silence, Yet you claim to be baffled why
some would turn to violence. What manner of creature
would condemn their kin to slaughter?
Curse you! Alleged Father.

-Q.B. YORING

THE ENERGY WITHIN

Spear Energy. A shorthand term to refer to the power that radiates throughout the universe, originating from the Spear of Space and the Spear of Time. Everything that ever was and ever will be is comprised of Spear Energy. Therefore, everything also emits Spear Energy.

This was the first of the few readable passages left in an old book that Amali found in the rubble of the Academic District. Covered in grime, slightly scorched, and on the verge of falling apart. These descriptions applied to the book, the girl, and the district.

Amali was an orphan from the colony of Braroclyn. She was just about fifteen years old by standard time keeping. Being an average native Jargun-Ba, she had dusty, red hair and alert mauve eyes. Her nose was a bit longer than most, nothing that would incite comments from a sensible person, but perhaps it would earn her some jeers on the school yard, if she were to ever go to school. Her skin was brown, besides the parts that were blue and greenish with bruises she hadn't quite slept off yet. She wore a ragged white shirt and tan pants, which she rolled at the ankles to make them her size. Her shoes were made of old leather wraps and new holes. The one article of clothing she gladly claimed

ownership of was a duffle coat she found while looting
an old laundromat. At one time it probably would have
been considered green, now it just looked dirty, but she
loved it because it had deep pockets hidden everywhere.

As for her home, Braroclyn, it is made up entirely of
asteroid settlements the Jargun-Ba's had created after
their moon crashed into their planet. The colony
consisted of domed habitable zones called districts, with
public ships meant to ferry people to and from them at
no cost. That was the law that no one upheld. No one
cared anymore, as they've almost all figured out a way
to bypass the illegal fees. If no one follows the law, it's
difficult for any form of authority to enforce it. Unless
of course, you find a group of people no one cares
about and force them to follow the rules no one else
will.

Amali stuffed the leftover book in her coat and fled
the scene. No one ever cleaned the debris, but if a
marshal caught you scrounging they'd still throw you in
jail for thieving. She ran across the fallen buildings
toward the station. Sometimes, when the orbits of the
star and the planets and the moons are just right, parts
of asteroids will be torn from their stable state and
crash into other asteroids. In the worst cases, whole
asteroids will just be thrown down to the planet Jargun-
Ba, with the people still on them. Trapped. What's left
of the people who still call Jargun-Ba home will ransack
the asteroids, savagery being their only means of

survival. And if the people on such asteroids survive the fall to the planet's surface... they do not survive on the surface.

Every child in Braroclyn has nightmares about their cannibalistic cousins living on the nearest neighboring planet.

Every child shares the nightmare, but not everyone shares the ancestry. Thanks to the Itarian Empire, plenty of people not from Jargun-Ba live in Braroclyn. Or are trapped there, depending on your point of view.

The people who don't consider themselves trapped come from the richer districts, and either work directly for The Black Palace or are pawns in the larger network. The lawmen make a particularly nice living, and make others' living situations particularly not nice. Maybe if any of the people who actually grew up in Braroclyn were allowed to "protect the people" then the people might actually feel safe. But somehow none of them ever made the cut. Depending on The All Father's mood, Braroclyn was a place to send his successful soldiers to reward them with an easy assignment, or the place to send disappointing soldiers that deserved only drudge work.

Amali snuck onto the ferry to the Residential District, all she had to do was pretend to swipe a card and walk fast enough for the sensor to miss her so that it didn't sound an alarm. (The Academic District was poorly maintained.) The ride only lasted a few minutes, so she sat in a dimly lit corner and kept her head down until they docked. Amali didn't get many chances to have fun, especially in the traditional ways kids tend to do, but she did love to skirt official security measures. There is no more enjoyable mischief than being where you're not allowed to be and going where you're not supposed to go.

It was dangerous to hide out on the more populated asteroids, and this one particularly. It was mostly filled with honest people, trying to live their lives to the best of their ability. The pros of hiding in a place full of mostly good people is that they don't care if a group of orphans are running around, so long as they're staying out of trouble in their district. So you didn't need to worry about getting reported if a family spotted you rooting through dumpsters or scrap heaps. You might even take up begging; most of these people barely had enough to get by themselves, but they at least wouldn't call a marshal on you if you asked. The cons were that the marshals knew all the pros, so they prowled here frequently. And they weren't above leaning on the people whose only crime was not wanting to send homeless children to jail. The thing about those people, as kind as they were, they weren't going to risk the safety of their own kids. Amali had seen marshals exploit that fact many times.

All of the domed habitats looked mostly similar, with the same short modular buildings, the same narrow streets, and the same bright white light coming in from the constant sun. The asteroid doesn't rotate, so daytime is perpetual. The nicer domes, like this one, had polarizing glass that could shift the tint level to mimic night and day cycles. The Residential District's dome was still mostly functional, though every now and again there were some patches that would go a few months without maintenance.

In an attempt to give some uniqueness to the districts, artists would be commissioned to paint the buildings and even the streets. Or at least the nicer domes could afford to pay artists for that. You could always tell because the shops and houses would be color-coordinated by function and great big murals would adorn the walls and floors as landmarks. Other districts, such as the Residential, took a different approach. They encouraged graffiti, and if public officials tell you it's okay then it's not technically graffiti. Essentially the people in charge of those domes legalized all public acts of art. As a result, street artists of all ages could leave their marks anywhere they pleased. The more calculating of these artists got together to organize which tags they would leave for specific places, making navigating the city easier. True selfless acts of public service.

For a little less than a year, Amali and her friends had been hiding out in an abandoned mall, affectionately called "the Green Rabbit" in reference to the giant spray-painted bunny on the side of the building. It's easy to find your way back to it because of the green footprints subtly painted along the streets leading to the front doors. The prints went for a while in multiple directions, and were mostly ignored by people since the mall was closed. This made it easy for Amali and her friends to quickly find a way back to their hideout without using the same route every time. No one ever noticed the trail.

Malls are ideal hideouts. Since they're original purpose is to house various storefronts, every room in a mall is designed to be customizable and multifaceted. And if the city forgets to shut off the water lines to the building, an abandoned food court is just a portable generator away from being a fully functional kitchen, not to mention the biggest dining hall of any home in the district.

Living in a mall also allowed each of them to have their own rooms, which is why Fia had the idea in the first place. Amali found her and her other two friends in the designated common area, which was what appeared to be once a furniture store. Fia was chatting while occasionally holding something in an attempt to help Gem, who was tinkering away on some device she had apparently plugged into the wall. Chase was painting on said wall, not in an attempt to be helpful.

Fia, a native Jargun-Ban as well, was from the same rundown orphanage as Amali. The best thing that ever

happened in that orphanage was making them best
friends, or at least they thought so. Once that happened
though, they both decided their best course of action
was to leave.

Fia had a natural talent of talking her way out of
situations, which paired nicely with Amali's natural
talent of punching her way out of situations. They
looked and acted like sisters. Fia's eyes were identical to
Amali's, and her complexion was a little bit lighter. The
main difference in their appearance was Fia's hair; her
hair was as black as the depths of space that knew no
stars, a rare trait among Jargun-Ba's.

Fia moved into the shop next to the one where
Amali made her room. Amali used a wrecked jewelry
store not only as her personal room but also as a
storeroom to stash any loot or money they scrounged
for safekeeping. Excited to find there were still two or
three books on the shelves, Fia turned what used to be
an old bookshop into her room. So excited in fact, she
decided to sleep on one of the larger shelves; she
claimed it was very comfortable.

Her sole outfit, which she did her best to keep well
maintained, consisted of a faded blue long-sleeve t-shirt
and black pants with a belt so ragged that trying to
maintain its status as a belt was a strenuous effort. The
pants fit her perfectly, but the shirt was much too long,
with the sleeves going well past her hand and the hem
falling almost to her knees. Most of the time, she kept

the bottom of the shirt hiked up and secured with the belt, a style more suited for running away. She wore sandals which were not ideal for running but (literal) beggars can't be choosers. She made the most of it, saying that she liked that her toes were free. She also wore a half of a broken handcuff on her left wrist like a bracelet, a fun and audacious reminder of the first time she got away from the marshals.

Gem was a Myeran runaway who had a knack for electronics, power tools, and blind concentration. She had pale teal skin and shiny gray hair. Her eyes were wide and sparkled golden. She wore a black headband that had a fuchsia-colored geometric pattern on it, a white short-sleeved shirt accidentally decorated with grease marks, brown shorts, and socks with work boots. She never took the headband or the boots off, even to sleep. That's how Amali and Fia met her, asleep in an alleyway, not too long after they had run away themselves. Gem couldn't recall why she was on Braroclyn, or even how. All she knew is she didn't like the Black Palace marshals that were charged with her "care," so she left them.

Myerans are native to the planet Myero, an ecumenopolis of technological marvels. Myerans are famous for their natural intelligence and peaceful dispositions. They chose to use their gifts to further their civilization's welfare, rather than advance warfare between their separate peoples. Their ingenuity allowed them to flourish in agricultural, technological, and medical advancements, but they neglected their military for longer than they should have. They had successfully united their planet and developed it to be the most interconnected and self-sufficient city in the universe, which made it all too easy for the Itarians to conquer them. Under the Itarian rule, the Myerans had very little control over their own planet. Most of the population were forced to innovate new weapons, armor, torture devices, and other evil things that horrified the Myerans. When the Itarian Empire fell and The All Father took control of the universe, nothing changed for the Myerans, save for what color they were told to make the armor.

Amali was pretty sure that Gem was here because her parents were at one point forced to work here, and then they were either killed. It was possible that they were sent elsewhere, but just lost the privilege to take their daughter with them. Given Gem's natural talent with electronics and machines, Amali guessed that someone official on Braroclyn meant to keep her here to groom her into being their personal armorer. It's also the only explanation Amali could come up with that explained how Gem got her hands on a Myeran Multitool.

A Myeran Multitool is a self-powered gadget with several functions, with the nicer models having over a hundred implements and settings. Gem's was certainly

the cheapest model, in fact it looked like it was the
cheapest model ten years ago, but that didn't make it
much less valuable. The Black Palace severely regulates
their distribution, so either Gem managed to pull an
impossible heist when she was a toddler, or it was the
last thing her parents gave her before she was separated
from them. She never let it out of her sight.

And they were lucky she always had it with her,
Chase especially felt that way. He was the last to join
their group, though entirely by accident. The three girls
in the early days of their careers would steal from
various vehicles in the Commercial District, if you
currently own your own mode of transportation and
can still afford to shop for trivialities, you can afford to
get robbed. One day Gem pops open a trunk with the
aforementioned multitool and what do they find?
Chase, tied up and squirming to get out.

Chase was an Itarian, an obvious fact gleaned at the
sight of his royal blue skin and dark red eyes. He wore a
sleeveless black shirt, baggy pants, and a multicolored
bandana. His hair was a bright yellow not natural to
Itarians. They recognized that he was the same age as
them and probably in a similar living situation as they
were, so Amali decided to help him even though they
had no idea what kind of trouble he was in.

As it turned out, he had done nothing wrong, that
time. Or at least, not to the people that tied him up.
What landed him in the trunk was the singular fact that

he was an Itarian. People still hated the Itarians. The
reasons for the burning hatred are two-fold. One, the
Itarian Empire lasted a very long time and made many
people miserable. Two, the people were so miserable
that when The All Father came along many of them
actually felt relief. Of course The All Father was not
really any better than the Itarians, so many started
thinking that if it weren't for the cruelty of the Itarians,
maybe most people would have not been so eager to
accept The All Father's rule.

Also, if the Itarians hadn't decimated every other
planet's army, maybe it wouldn't have taken so long for
there to be some resistance to The All Father's
demanded sovereignty. That being said, Chase was only
ten years old (when they met). Even the people who
locked him in the trunk knew that he had nothing to do
with the Itarian Empire. More than that, his parents
and grandparents wouldn't even had been able to have
anything to do with it. But they didn't care; some people
don't care who is punished for a transgression, they only
care that someone is punished.

Amali did care, and none of them had anything
against Chase. Not even Gem, who arguably had the
most reason to hate Itarians because of what they did to
her people. But she was so bothered by the prejudice
and violence currently being afflicted on her fellow
orphan that the possibility of Chase's ancestors doing
something awful to her ancestors didn't even cross her

mind. And so Chase became a part of the group and quickly matched the best friend energy the three of them had cultivated. Once on a dare from Fia, he had once jumped outside of the habitat dome while a ship was leaving and floated to the next district all on his own. It was the two closest districts in the colony, only being about ninety meters apart, but it was still an insane thing to do.

Chase was an amateur street artist and extremely sneaky. By the time he realized how much he loved spray paint, a lot of the street art infrastructures were mostly done in the districts that encouraged it. So he decided to practice his craft not just in the districts that didn't allow it, but in the districts that were *actively* against it. So he had to become just as stealthy as he was artsy in order to get anything done. As a matter of fact, one of Chase's first acts of self-imposed community service was expanding the network of Green Rabbit prints. Each addition was hidden in plain sight more cleverly than the last, and got them out of a tight spot on more than one occasion.

"Ooo this is a nice purple," Chase said as he took his bandana off of his neck. He laid the bandana on the table next to him and sprayed a small patch of the color onto it. He nodded, satisfied, and left it to dry as he turned back to painting the wall.

Amali could tell everyone was much more comfortable than they had been the first time they hid

in this place. They were truly cheerful, and having fun.
When Amali focused on people, she could sometimes
see them glow, and she could tell how they felt
depending on how they glowed. Everyone looked
different, but her friends she could recognize perfectly.
Gem had a brilliant pink around her, Chase was slightly
gold, and Fia shone orange.

They were all happy.

"Everyone having fun on this beautiful day?" Amali
asked sarcastically as she emptied her pockets.

"Morning Sis!" Fia waved at her cheerfully, nearly
dropping the multiple items Gem had handed her.

Chase took a break from painting and went over to
check out what Amali was able to find. He noticed a
half empty bottle of paint and grabbed it immediately.
Looking at Amali for approval, she nodded at him, to
which he responded with an appreciative high five.
Then he went back to his wall.

Amali stood over Gem as she continued to work on
the inner workings of some kind of computer thing that
Amali was pretty sure wasn't designed to be hooked up
to a moldy cafeteria wall. Gem looked up, as if noticing
her for the first time, and smiled.

"Good morning," Gem said, her hands still working.

"Morning, can you use these for anything?"

She handed Gem three power cells.

"Oh these are great! They're drained but they look mostly intact. Definitely will come in handy. Thank you!"

A tinge of satisfaction warmed Amali's mind. Sometimes they don't find very good stuff, or things that would be useful if they weren't so broken. Gem always had a way of reassuring the other three that their efforts were worthwhile. They all tried to encourage one another, but Gem was usually the one that actually made the junk they found into something useful, so they tended to take her feedback a little more seriously.

Gem had managed to make the four of them short-range communicators to wear on their wrists so that they could always be in contact even if separated. She had the idea after the scare of losing Amali for days when she broke her ankle. She had led the marshals away from their previous hideout to protect the others and ended up having to jump from a high building to throw them off her trail. She had to hide until the pain was manageable, and even when it was she was in agony trying to slowly make her way back to them. Gem hated that they hadn't been able to help her until she got back and collapsed.

She also made Fia a digital skeleton key. Fia was extremely good at talking her way out of things, but she wasn't as fast as Amali and she did not have Chase's gift for stealth. There have been a few times when Fia had been detained behind locked doors before she had the opportunity to lie her way out. Gem wanted to make sure to avoid that circumstance again, especially since last time Fia was captured by the worst excuse for a keeper-of-the-peace ever to latch onto Braroclyn. Captain Nequois.

Tilditch Nequois was an unusually tall Gorkonian with a long, shiny mustache and malicious, violet eyes. He had been the appointed deputy director of the security force in Braroclyn for the past four years. He was also captain of his own ship, making him more of a nuisance than previous directors. With a private ship and crew, he had a unique grip on the asteroid colony. Deputy directors of the past had been people of military backgrounds, either recruited by The Black Palace or veterans of it, as such their vessels were property of The Black Palace and heavily monitored. The Black Palace kept a strict watch on how their property is used. But since he had owned his ship, The Star Hook, he could do as he pleased without consequence.

Braroclyn needed a healthy population size to continue being taken advantage of, Captain Nequois knew this and used his ship to stop and search other departing vessels so that he could ensure there wasn't any mass-emigrating going on under his leadership. It was hard to get proper documentation to move from

Braroclyn, done purposely so that really the only people that could leave without being branded as criminals were the elite class citizens who would actually want to come back.

If that wasn't bad enough, Captain Nequois intercepted the trade ships that came to Braroclyn and took the best supplies for himself. And he wondered why people were dissatisfied with him, why they would want to leave their homes. He didn't really wonder; he wasn't delusional, he just didn't particularly care.

No one was surprised by this behavior, as Captain Nequois was already infamous before he laid claim to Braroclyn. There was a reason he went by the title of captain rather than adopting the "Deputy Director" moniker. For the fifteen years before he killed Braroclyn's previous overseer, Captain Nequois roved the universe with his crew, marauding ships and raiding colonies that were unfortunate enough to enter his line of sight. He wanted people to remember he was a pirate first, and a servant of The All Father second.

A sentiment that would surely get him killed if The All Father ever heard him talk that way, but Captain Nequois was a daring man. Though, not so daring that he didn't regularly send The Black Palace the tax money Braroclyn owed. Paid in full. A day early.

The captain chose to stay on his ship rather than adopt the small office in the building the marshals worked in. Most of his crew remained at their old posts, only being deputized when Captain Nequois found the methods of the Braroclyn's bureaucrats unsatisfactory. One of those unsatisfactory bureaucrats was talking to him now. Talking about some kind of administrative nonsense.

"Sir I know you think the administrative process is nonsense but it's an important part of the day-to-day," he said, free to let some more annoyance creep into his voice since he was safe behind his monitor.

He would not be so bold if he was having this conversation in person.

"What is the point of you, Drexy," Captain Nequois said from the big chair in his quarters, "If you don't handle the day-to-day drudgery for me?"

The undervalued public servant named Matzin Drexy took an exasperated sigh and rubbed his forehead. He was exhausted. It was bad enough his home was at the mercy of a band of thugs, the fact that he was often powerless to make any good of the situation only made him feel worse.

"As my commanding officer...sir...there is only so much I can do without your direct approval."

He breathed in through a menacing grin. The kind of grin that shows your teeth as a threat. "Continue," he said.

Drexy continued. "And we are, once again, being asked to increase-"

Captain Nequois pounded the table again.

"WHAT?"

"Sir-"

"How much more could those blasted buffoons possibly need to keep their precious palace all nice and shiny."

Captain Nequois felt the words echo in his throat as soon as they left. Words that could potentially not bode well for him in the future. He'd need to make it clear later that he meant the foolish attendants The All Father was surrounded by couldn't run the place efficiently, and that he had a great love for shiny palaces.

"The All Father, needs support to counteract the activities of the growing number of insurgents," he said this matter of factly. "And it is a privilege to support him as much as we are able," he said this robotically. He rehearsed the right things to say in his mind regularly to prevent slip ups; there was no love of The Black Palace behind any of it. He may have despised the captain for what he was doing to his home, but he put as much of the blame on The All Father for allowing it to happen.

"Make it so that the next payment to The Black Palace matches the requested increase. And make it so to increase the taxes during the next quarter, but don't announce it just yet. Savvy?"

Drexy bit his lip at the thought of further increasing the tax for people, especially since it wasn't necessary. The pirates lived more than comfortably.

"Yes Captain."

"I think that will be all for today Drexy. I'm in desperate need of a break." Drexy, to his credit, did not roll his eyes.

"Unless of course, you have any leads regarding the fugitives?" Captain Nequois said it more as a threat than a question.

Drexy paused, and then spoke slowly. "Are you referring to the young runaways again, sir?"

Captain Nequois slammed his favorite smashing fist on his desk. Drexy hid his apprehension poorly.

"The 'young runaways' have been a blasted pain in my side for almost a year now. You say they'll be no problem with time." His eyes narrowed. "Yet, they run more rampant with time, somehow continuing to elude you."

Not that Drexy wanted to bring those poor children to the feet of the creature he worked for, but the insult to him and his team was frustrating. Afterall, Nequois's crew were no more capable of finding them. That being said, Drexy did find some amusement in this pirate captain being drawn into a fury by a few teenage vagabonds. Honestly they weren't even causing that much trouble. It was strange to think a man in such a position of power could be so bothered by some indirect humiliation. Drexy believed the nickname that their ring-leader gave him was the main source of his hatred. She had commented on how his first name almost could sound like the common name for the

Scuulian mud leech, if you just ignored a few letters that is. Before you knew it, most of the colonists referred to the captain as "Titch" or some variation thereof.

There was nothing more Captain Nequois could say to Drexy about them, so he decided his time would be best spent hanging up on him in a rude fashion, and then proceeding to curse at random inanimate objects around his room.

Though this turned out to be very unproductive, it did improve his mood. However, the news that was about to walk through his door would raise his spirits much higher. Almost as high as they were at the peak of his piracy.

"We could be pirates," Gem eagerly pointed out in an almost wistful tone.

Amali took a deep breath and rubbed her forehead like a parent tired of telling their child they can't have ice cream for dinner. "You shouldn't want to be a pirate."

"I don't mean a pirate like ol' Titchy, not with all the killing and setting things on fire. One of the good pirates. The ones that have their own flag and go around the universe saving people and looking for treasure on abandoned planets. Like in Fia's stories."

"That's not really being a pirate though, Gem," Chase explained with more interest in the conversation than Amali presently had, "That's just being a spacer. The pirates are really only called pirates in those books because kids think 'pirate' is a cooler word. You gotta do a lot of illegal stuff to be considered a pirate. It's not as romanticized."

Amali was using both hands now to rub her eyes. "Those aren't bad points Chase, but in her defense stealing a ship would be more than enough to label us as pirates. They'd come after us. The main thing is that we're trying to keep a low profile. Pirates of any kind don't have low profiles."

"But I could modify the ship!" Gem actually turned away from what she was tinkering. "It would be entirely new, basically. Wholly our own. A real home."

Amali stopped her anxious face massage and looked at Gem. Her orange glow was dimming. She wanted to give her a look of understanding or say something comforting. But Gem had already turned back to her work and started talking again. As she worked, her light shone more, and Amali decided to leave it for now.

"Besides, I don't see how stealing *one* ship is worse than robbing a bank," Gem said pointedly in Chase's direction.

"It's a victimless crime!" Chase said defensively.

"Oy roak, for the last time Chase, it really isn't. Regular people keep their money in banks. Or at least

the banks we would be able to get into." Amali wasn't
fidgeting, but it did look like her right hand was looking
for something to throw at him.

"If the bank gets robbed," Chase not backing down,
"The government needs to reimburse—" "A
government run by a ruthless *pirate* doesn't *need* to do
anything."

"And if we only take the *physical* BPU tokens, then
everyone's digital stuff is still safe. Most people don't use
the tokens anyway."

Amali started physically backing herself away from
the conversation. "Exactly Chase, they don't. Banks
aren't just stocked up with lots of tokens anymore. You
can't just run in wearing a mask and run out with one
of those giant sacks with the money symbol on it."

She left Gem and Chase to debate whether it would
be easier to rob banks with or without a ship.

They kinda do sound like pirates. She thought.

Amali sat on the table Fia was using to read. "Any
luck?" Amali asked her as she was still leafing through
the wrinkled pages of the book from the Academic
District.

Fia did not hear her as she was still entranced with
the book. This did not give Amali any hint as to
whether or not it would be valuable or useful, since Fia
loved all books unconditionally.

She waved her hand between Fia's eyes and the open book, severing the spiritual link Fia had supposedly built with it.

Fia reeled her head up. "This is a Spear Energy tome. Or at least I think it's a tome, it looks a little small to be one though. But it's also really damaged so maybe there's more pages missing than I think. The front cover is gone and I can't read any page numbers so who knows how big it once was. But it's definitely from Wan-Ri; warrior priests there train with Spear Energy."

"What the heck is a tome?"

"It's like a large book."

"...So this is a small tome?"

"Potentially," Fia said distantly, getting distracted again.

"...So it's a book?"

Fia snapped herself out of her literary link this time. She shook her head. "Sorry, tomes aren't just about their number of pages. A tome is different from a book also because it's usually about something important. Like a large volume of history or science or something. Something scholarly."

"So it's useless to us then?"

Fia excitedly flipped through the pages. "My dear friend, prepare to have your mind blown."

"Okay, can it be a short preparation?"

Fia landed on a page, leaned back like someone satisfied with themselves, and pointed with the flair of someone who just revealed something more impressive than a torn page in a burned book that was still somehow a little damp.

Curious all the same, Amali leaned over to read the half smudged text.

Know it or not, consciously or unconsciously, everyone emits Spear Energy. It is a fact of biology. We are all connected to the Spears of the Universe, that is why they are sometimes referred to as the Spears of Life and Death. Spear Energy is life energy. Every living thing gives off their energy as they exist. This is commonly known as aura, and can be perceived by those proficient in the use of Spear arts. Aura is as unique to a being as an ear is to a boar-rabbit.

Amali stood up, confused. "Sorry dear friend, my mind isn't blown."

Fia was practically jumping up and down in her chair.

"Don't you see? This is you! You can use Spear Energy."

Amali was still confused, but those words successfully blew her mind.

"Fia I don't see how—"

"You can still see people glow can't you?"

Amali nodded, now understanding where she was going with this and prepared to disagree.

"That's aura you're seeing!"

"Fia, that's a really cool idea, and it might be true, but I don't think I can use Spear Energy."

"Not now, but with this, you might be able to learn!"

Amali wanted to protest more, but Gem stuck her head over Fia's shoulder to examine the book. Her hands were still working with something even as she spoke.

"You can use Spear Energy? I always thought you were just one of those people that can see music and taste numbers."

Amali didn't want everyone to take this too far.

"And I still very well could be. There's no reason for us—"

Chase put his head on Fia's other shoulder.

"Ames this is fantastic! You can learn how to do those powerful blast attacks and fry up Titch like the space-cod he is."

"That is the opposite of keeping a low profile!"

Fia grabbed the book and sprang out of her chair, not caring for the disorientation she caused her friends' heads in the process.

"Well let's get started! Come on let's go to the roof."

"The roof???"

Amali felt like the only sane person in the room again.

"Yeah of course, if you manage to do a big blast attack right away, you might not have good aim the first time. So we need to go somewhere where you won't blow any holes in the walls. Or my room."

"That does make sense," Gem said as she returned to her own work. Chase nodded in enthusiastic agreement.

Amali sighed. It was taken too far.

"Are you making sure that you 'Visualize the energy in you becoming a part of the energy outside of you'? I think it means you're basically transferring your energy. Do you feel transferable?"

They had been at it for almost three hours. Fia's enthusiasm had not wavered an iota, and Amali felt silly.

"Do I feel *transferable*???"

"And don't forget to breathe. This goes hand in hand with the meditation technique from earlier."

"Believe me, breath is the only thing getting transferred right now."

"Oh that's a great way to think about it!"

Amali hung her head in exasperation, or perhaps it was embarrassment of the failure. She hated letting Fia down.

"Fia can we stop for a second?"

"Anything you need champ," she said with an accent that Amali didn't recognize but was sure was a specific reference to something, "You feeling good? Feeling strong?"

"Fia to be honest I don't feel...very transferable."

Fia acknowledged Amali's serious voice, but laughed at her attempt to keep things light.

"What's wrong?" She said, sitting down on the ledge of the roof.

Amali joined her.

"Nothing's wrong, I just don't think I can do it. And to be honest with you, I'm not sure staying up here for hours trying is the best use of our time."

Fia nodded. She was trying her best not to look disappointed, but Amali saw her orange glow dim slightly. She was a little let down.

"I'm really sorry. I know how cool this would've been. And you were doing a great job with the researching and helping me through the exercises and meditations—though to be *perfectly* honest, I could've done without you sitting on me while I did the pushups."

"We needed to get your muscles past their usual limits! It opens everything up to help the Spear Energy flow through you."

"My spine was bent past my usual limit, does that help?"

"Ames—"

"I also just think maybe we're not, you know, knowledgeable enough to do all of this. I mean you just read that book today, we don't even know if that's a starter book by the way; for all we know that's volume two."

Fia nodded some more.

"Yeah yeah. That's true."

She turned the book over in her hands like it had already been a treasured possession for years. Amali thought it was nice that she could latch onto things like that, to give value to things beyond what they really are. Fia had a great ability to treasure the ordinary. That's how she turned into the heart of their little group. To hear her talk, they weren't ordinary kids on the lam, they were heroes on an adventure.

Amali decided to be the one to remind them that, while they keep collecting the perfect colors or getting lost in books or dreaming of their own ship, being kids, they also needed to survive.

Amali put her hand on Fia's shoulder, thinking of something encouraging to say before she suggested returning downstairs, before she heard

Boots. Not Gem's.

She jumped up quickly and spun around to see five of Captain Nequois's crew on the roof. They had been trying to sneak and were clearly dumbfounded by being spotted so easily. They froze, before coming to their senses and lurching quickly towards the two girls.

Amali grabbed Fia, yanked her up, and made a break for it.

Amali opened her communicator.

"Gem Chase Titch's guys found us grab what food you can and get out NOW!"

The roof was big, but there was nowhere to hide. The little cover the vents provided wouldn't do any good since they were in sight of all five of them. Going down the stairs wasn't an option, she needed to keep them away from Gem and Chase for as long as she could. They're only option was to run for the opposite side of the roof, the side with the smallest gap to another building, and jump.

They dashed as best they could, but Fia wasn't as fast or as agile as Amali. Amali was almost dragging her across the roof, terrified of her falling behind and getting snatched. There were plenty of closer ways for her to escape, but Fia wouldn't be able to follow if she needed to resort to urban acrobatics. Halfway to their point of salvation, Amali's fear was realized.

What she would later describe as the worst feeling she's ever experienced, Amali felt Fia's hand ripped from hers. The five crew members stopped, knowing that Amali wasn't going to run now that they had her friend. Amali's mind raced. There was nothing in her immediate vicinity except for the large vent a few steps to her left. She had nothing even resembling a weapon, just the book that remained in place where Fia's hand should have still been. She couldn't fight off five people twice her size. Fia was making an effort to remove herself from the woman's grip to no avail.

Fine Fia, I'll admit the ability to use Spear Energy would be immeasurably valuable right now.

Amali was worried. The pirates weren't moving, and the roof was just big enough for—

A skiff descended from the sky with the side door open. Captain Nequois hung out of it precariously, holding his hat to keep it from flying off, laughing a stereotypical pirate laugh.

Just big enough for a dramatic entrance. I hope he falls out. Save me a lot of trouble.

"Amali! We meet again! What a pleasure!" Captain Nequois stepped off the skiff with a noticeable bounce in his step.

Amali looked back and met Fia's stare. She sighed and stashed the book inside of her coat before turning to face the pirate.

"I'm terribly sorry, do I know you?"

That made Fia smile. Amali couldn't make an art of talking in circles like she could, but she was snarky and she knew how to exasperate adults.

She saw Captain Nequois's smile waver and his eye twitch.

"Wait, I think I do remember you. Twitch right?"

Some other pirates on the skiff snickered at that.

One of the pirates behind her called, "Actually the nickname you gave him was Titch."

It sounded like he was genuinely trying to be helpful.

Amali made a show of rubbing her cheek and squinted her eyes.

"Titch. Titch Titch Titch."

Titch was losing it more and more each time she repeated it. You could see it on his face.

"I'm not sure I remember that being anyone's name. It kinda sounds stupid. At any rate I don't think I can let you park here. This is private property."

More laughter. Then Captain Nequois drew a laser pistol from his belt and shot the would be helpful pirate's hand clean off. No laughter after that. But a fair amount of screaming. Captain Nequois was beaming again.

"Well," he said returning the pistol to his belt, "Doesn't someone want to help their LOYAL 'mate back to the ship? Maybe retrieve the hand so our fine doctor could try getting it back on. I hope he remembers how," he turned to Amali.

"It's really been a while since he's had anyone to practice on."

Amali stopped. Everyone's demeanor dramatically changed in an instant. Her face turned serious, a face with a dependable strength you usually wouldn't learn until you were older. Two of the pirates behind her helped the whimpering one back to the skiff, one to take care of him and one to hold his hand. Some of the pirates who weren't laughing earlier looked more at ease. Not as though they were happy with the turn of events, it was more that this was the situation they were used to dealing with.

She tried her best to pour confidence into her words.

"Why can't you just leave us alone? We don't do anything illegal and we have no money to give you. Are you so bored that you have to resort to hunting just kids?"

Not a terrible effort, but not the right one. It came off more as demanding with a sprinkle of righteous indignation. An approach that often doesn't work even with people of good moral character. Realizing this, Fia cleared her throat. The situation was dire, but Fia still had a gift for making people do what she wanted while still leaving them convinced it was their idea and to their own benefit.

However, the pirate holding her was clearly informed of her silver tongue. The minute she felt Fia gearing up for a monologue, she gagged her mouth with a rag. Fia looked more horrified at the dirty thing than the fact that her and her best friends were going to be caught and killed.

Captain Nequois sneered at Fia, then at Amali

"Don't do anything illegal? That one over there just gets herself arrested on a regular basis for doing nothing?"

Fia nodded profusely. Amali said "I mean I've never seen her convicted of anything."

"Fleeing custody is a crime too."

"Well that seems intentionally convenient for the marshals."

"The blue boy has trespassed into enough high profile premises to lock him away for life."

Amali crossed her arms and raised a finger

"Allegedly trespassed. Incredibly all those accusations have absolutely nothing in common to confirm it was him."

"He painted a gold celestial fox at each place."

Damn it Chase.

"I seriously doubt he knows how to paint."

"And am I supposed to believe all those little bits and bobs you sell to any low-life merchant that tolerates you are licit transactions?"

"You are supposed to believe that, yes."

"How do you obtain them?"

"I can get them wholesale."

"The Myeran is a blasted war criminal!"

"Says the corsair."

That was a good last line, but Amali and Fia had to admit, the war criminal comment came as a shock. And was concerning. And not true? They'd have to worry about that later.

Captain Nequois drew both of his pistols. "I'm thinking the others will be much easier to track down once they can't rely on your astute guidance, says I."

Amali flinched for only a moment. She didn't want to leave Fia, and she hated that she knew the muffled

scream was her best friend shouting at her to run. She
dove into the vent, the leftmost bolt grazing her right
shoulder. Her last sight was of Fia's aura: shining
bright, but pulsing rhythmically like a frightened
heartbeat. She tumbled downward in searing pain,
hearing the echoes of Titch's infuriated shouts and
curses follow her.

There was always a possibility they would be found
out at the Green Rabbit. That's why Amali insisted they
maintain a secondary location. A hideout that was
more, well, hidden. Albeit, it was far less comfortable.

One luxury that's taken for granted on planets is the
ability to dig. Whether it be underground transportation
or storage, civilizations like to utilize holes in the
ground. A reason the Residential District was so cheap
to live in was its lack of an underground sewage system.
The richer districts were built on the more stable
asteroids, so they could afford underground systems of
all kinds both financially and structurally.

The Residential District found out the hard way
that their asteroid was not suitable for tunneling. There
were natural tunnels spread out and unmapped
throughout the hunk of rock the universe left them
with, and during the early development of the colony,
an unfortunate placement of what would have been
their sewage system broke into one of the natural

chasms. Said chasm, connected to the open universe.
Dubbed the Great Leak, the artificial atmosphere of the
present day Residential District was almost lost to space.
The dome sustained major damage that is still being
repaired to this day, and the tunnel that caused the
breach was sealed and completely filled up. But the
other tunnels, the initial smaller ones, were never filled.
Not enough in the budget. They were only sealed, and
not well.

Chase had happened upon a tunnel with a busted
seal while he was laying out the Green Rabbit tracks.
Later, it would be where the kids agreed to make their
safe room. The embodiment of a last resort.

They didn't have much down there. As time went
on in the Green Rabbit, as they became more and more
comfortable with their living situation, they neglected to
maintain their provisions in the safe room. Amali was
kicking herself for that now. She was also kicking the
few provisions they did have.

"I JUST LEFT HER THERE," she cried as she
repeatedly kicked a defenseless box of canned "bread".

Chase was holding his hands up and out to her, like
someone who considered going for a comforting hug
but ended up looking like they were surrendering

"Listen to us: you *didn't* do anything wrong."

"Ames, he fired at you," Fia said in an even voice,
"You're lucky you got out of the way only slightly

scathed. And getting out of there was your only choice."

"And out of there means you're not dead," Chase continued, "You would be if you had lingered for just a moment. As it is, Fia *and* you are alive so—"

"Really??" Amali took a break from the box and spun to face him. "Are you sure she is???"

She saw them both, with their fearful pulsing auras. What she had never seen before, was her own aura reaching out to meet theirs. It was still its opaque white color, but looked like it was burning. Like it was *made* of fire. She didn't want it to touch them.

There was something else she didn't recognize. The looks on their faces. Shame? No, guilt. Amali realized they must partially feel responsible too. It was unspoken, but they all figured out that the only reason they were found out was because Amali and Fia had spent so much time on the roof. It may not have been technically considered drawing attention to themselves since most people kept to ground level. But they were easily spottable from any ship that happened to fly overhead. That's specifically not keeping a low profile..

She took some deep breaths, and willed herself to calm down. It wasn't working at all, but it was still a good mindset to have.

"Listen, I'm sorry. We-we just need to get her back. As fast as we can."

Chase nodded solemnly.

"I think she'll be alright. She's gotten out before, and I think..." He paused to consider the best phrasing. "... he mainly is focused on you so I don't think he'll hurt her. I think she's bait."

He was right, except on one account.

"He came in his own skiff. He didn't take her back to a local marshal's outpost."

Gem's aura blinked.

"She's on the Star Hook. Even if she escaped her cell, or the brig I guess, she'd have no way off the ship."

Gem's aura flared up and stayed bright (anticipation), but she didn't say anything else. Amali looked knowingly at Chase, who looked back at her unknowingly.

He pointed sheepishly at himself.

"Me? I dunno what to do. You're saying it's bad? I'm confused. I don't know why you're looking at me like that."

She rolled his eyes at his panicked confusion, and the thought of how Gem would react to what she said next actually brought a smile to her face.

"My friends, we need to steal a ship."

Gem was shaking.

"Oh my gosh thank you! Wow guys, listen okay, so, okay. Gosh I know it's way too soon but I'm gonna say it anyway okay. This is DEFINITELY my favorite time that Fia got arrested."

"Oh please," Fia said defiantly, while tapping the electrified bars of her cell, "This arrest doesn't even make my top five."

Braroclynites have no natural resistance to electricity. Fia was no different, but she did occasionally enjoy making people uncomfortable.

The pirate posted to guard her rubbed his hands anxiously.

"Could you stop that?"

Fia stopped her finger from touching the bar again just barely. She smiled innocently. The pain was worth it.

"My best arrest, hands down, was by the guys in the Mining District. They let me eat donuts in there. Gosh, I want a donut."

"Well Miss, I didn't mean it like that. When I said that this time would stand out from the other times, I was referring to the trap. The trap for your sister. The stakes are much higher now."

"You want to talk stakes? Let me tell ya something. In the Agricultural District, I almost had to sleep on the floor. The *cell floor*, Paulie. Do understand how messed up that is? Those roakers have private lifts to their penthouses. They can't even throw me a blanket? A roacking blanket??? Unbelievable. Can I call you Paulie?"

"Well my name is Ritkao."

"Paulie, let me ask you something—"

"Okay."

"—why would my sister, who just to be clear isn't really my sister. She's my friend. Sure we're orphanage sisters, but that's really more a term of endearment. That's besides the point. The point is, why would she even think about coming to get me from here? I mean what would be the point?"

Fia needed time and privacy. Gem's communicators are limited to only being a single district apart at most. (Or it was the best she could manage to design with the scraps she worked with.) So far Fia had gotten no answer, and she couldn't keep trying with a babysitter. She guessed the ship was in it's usual perching spot: far from the city like it was embarrassed to be associated with it, while still being close enough to remind it who's boss.

To escape, she had to get out of the cell. Then, she had to figure out how to steal and fly a skiff.

Gem is going to be so jealous.

"Well Miss, wouldn't the point be to save you?"

"Save me? Save *me*? *Save*?"

She laughed a laugh so real it was obviously fake

"Paulie Paulie Paulie listen to me. What is she saving me from? I'm not gonna be in here long."

"You're not?"

"Paulie, look at me look at me."

She had both hands pointing at her face to make sure her point was getting across.

"Do I look like I could overpower multiple marshals, multiple times, across the entire colony?"

He shook his head.

"Of course not! I'm fifteen years old! So how come I have never been put in prison once?"

The incepted clarity spread across his face.

"They always let you go."

"Exactly! Because I didn't do anything wrong."

This was not true. Naturally, Fia was guilty of numerous crimes. In times like these, it was hard to survive without circumventing the law at least once in a while. Fia managed to escape every time because, whether the others rescued her or she snuck out herself, the escapes were purposefully carried out during the marshals' meal breaks. That was it, and it worked every single time.

But Fia had convinced him otherwise. He was certain that at any moment, the captain was going to realize he made a mistake taking this child and would order her release. She wasn't even threatening; she couldn't do anything in her cell. He started to wonder what he was even doing guarding her.

Poor Ritk— Poor Paulie. He didn't stand a chance.

"We don't stand a chance!" Amali protested.

The three of them had packed as many supplies as they could from their safe room. They also each had a bag of the few personal items they collected over the years. Chase and Gem had managed to raid Amali and Fia's rooms before fleeing the Green Rabbit. They were all eager to give Fia her books.

At the moment, they were standing on a shady street (literally shady) in the Commercial District, failing at their attempt to look casual as they spied on a landing lot and argued about their next steps.

"Amali you're overthinking it. It's an in and out job. All we gotta do is sneak into the office and figure out who's got a ship here that's gonna be gone a while. They should have records or something, we can figure it out. We use the ship to save Fia, and by the time the sucker realizes his ship has been stolen, we'll be fourteen parsecs away."

"Are you out of your Itarian mind?" Amali asked in the tone of voice of a person who was losing their mind.

"Yeah Chase, fourteen is pushing it. I'd give us twelve though, if we get the right ship."

Gem thought she was agreeing with Amali. She was mistaken.

"Guys, seriously? We can't steal a ship from here. The most powerful criminals in Braroclyn use this lot for a reason. If we don't get killed while trying, they'll certainly kill us when they inevitably track us down."

"That's the beauty of the plan Ames! They're the ships of criminals. They've already been stripped of the official code thingies—"

"Identification Beacons," Gem interjected.

"—because they've already been stolen! Most of the work is done for us. Besides they shouldn't have chosen a lot in this neighborhood if they didn't want people stealing them. Everyone knows ships get stolen here all the time."

"Yes. All the time." Amali's voice started even, but grew more exasperated as she spoke. "*Specifically* not the ones in lots paid for by vicious criminals, *specifically* paid for so that people know that they're going to die if they try to abscond with anything put there!!!"

Gem scrunched her face.

"Huh, I never thought of it that way."

Chase nodded as he pondered this new line of reasoning.

Amali threw her hands up in disbelief. As she turned to walk off some of her frustration, she noticed a ship landing behind them, in a clearing amidst the debris of a partially demolished building.

Amali started moving to go take a closer look, but Chase grabbed her arm and whispered sharply.

"Ames what the roak. You just got done chastising us —"

"Who told you what 'chastising' means?" Gem interrupted.

"—*chastising* us," Chase repeated, throwing Gem a mocking look. "About keeping a low profile and not stealing a ship from here and how we were gonna get killed, and now you just want to walk over to some random ship? With person or persons still on it??"

"Exactly Chase." He gave her a bewildered look. She continued, "It's just a random ship. It's not one of Titch's skiffs—"

"It's definitely not a marshal ship. It's actually not that bad looking to be honest. I could work with it." Gem said, losing herself to her aesthetical thoughts. Her aura slowly churned like far away cosmic dust.

"—which means that it's probably just a random ship from a random guy. The normal kinda random. Someone who's not a pirate, a marshal, and clearly someone who's *specifically* not comfortable parking in the lot for criminals that's right here."

Chase's eyes widened in excitement. His aura flashing briefly.

"You see, this is why you're the leader."

Amali nodded and started walking again, only to abruptly stop of her own volition. "I'm the what?"

"Our leader," he repeated as if that would clear up any confusion she was having. He patted her on the shoulder as he walked past.

Unlike Chase, Gem caught on.

"Sorry, Ames. We've all thought of you like that for a while now. You've kind of naturally acted like it since we all got together. We assumed it was intentional."

Gem gave her a quick, slightly embarrassed, side hug before following Chase. A few milliseconds after processing what her friends had just told her, Amali smiled to herself. All things considered, she felt very lucky.

They slowly worked their way through the debris, they wanted to make sure they wouldn't be spotted, but they were also painfully aware that time was of the essence. Chase led the way, intuitively figuring out a route that would get them eyes on the prize from a safe, hidden distance. This was an art form to him, just as much as painting was.

They settled on an outcropping made from a partially collapsed second floor. They peered down to the ship below, careful not to expose their heads too much. Gem had her multitool in hand, ready to get to work.

Much to all of their surprise, they saw three very official looking Braroclynites. They weren't marshals, but they were obviously wearing some kind of government uniform. Amali wasn't sure who they were, she had only seen district marshals all this time and only the street ones at that. She was sure she'd still be able to tell if it was a higher ranked marshal, so she assumed these people weren't.

Chase whispered, very quietly and slowly, "These guys seem less random to me now."

Amali nodded and replied in the same cadence, "They're not marshals, I'm pretty sure. But that doesn't actually make me feel any better."

Chase pointed at the ship. "And if they're higher up than marshals, why are they flying a worse ship?"

"The ship is perfectly fine," Gem said defensively, and louder than they were talking, "It just needs some love and care."

"Shhhhhhhhhhh," Amali and Chase said in unison.

They sat there for a few moments, not knowing what to do, just watching the people talk to each other. At some point, one of them brought a device out of his pocket and turned it on. They could hear the device beeping.

After an unmeasured amount of time, the official said something to one of the others. The one he spoke to, looked noticeably more fatigued than the other two, even from where the kids were hiding.

The official with the device pointed up to exactly where they were hiding, and the tired official stepped forward.

"Amali Panlost. Chase Westlake. And Kaylagem Laforg."

They didn't move, jarred that they were not only pinpointed but also full-named. Never knowing their parents, that was a new experience that they all decided they didn't like. Amali's mind was racing trying to think of the best way out of this. The device that seemed to reveal their location worried her though.

"Your name is Westlake?" Gem asked in a baffled whisper. Amali kicked her in the foot and shushed them both rather harshly.

"Please come down," the tired official said, "I'm not here to take you. I just want to talk."

They all hesitated. Then, Chase stood up in an ungraceful manner and shouted, "We don't trust you!"

Amali pulled him down harshly and hit him repeatedly on the top of his head.

He turned to the two officials behind him and said something. They looked at each other for a moment, and then started to leave the area.

"My name is Matzin Drexy," the remaining official said, "You don't need to trust me and you don't need to come down. Just listen to what I have to say."

The kids exchanged glances. Gem was nervous, Chase was intrigued, Amali was wary.

What do we think? Amali mouthed.

Whatever you do. Chase mouthed back. Gem gave her a thumbs up.

Amali rolled her eyes. She called down to Drexy, "We're listening." She didn't think that was enough. "But we also have a laser pointed at your head."

This made Drexy grin, just a little. "That sounds fair. Your friend, Fia Cygnet, has been taken to Captain Nequois's ship."

"We already know that," Amali responded, in what she hoped was an intimidating voice.

Drexy nodded. "I can do nothing to release her. Nequois is obsessed with you, whether that's because he's bored and you are eluding targets or because he legitimately thinks you are some kind of threat is beyond me."

"You're wearing some fancy clothes. You can't release her or you don't want to get in trouble with your captain?"

Drexy's face sank a little. "I started working for our government because I thought it would be the fastest way to help Braroclyn. After my parents were killed I had little hope of my own, but I still wanted to try and give hope to our people. My goal was to work my way up the ranks and make changes that would benefit Braroclynites without incurring any additional attention from The All Father. All I wanted to do was help."

Amali's heart softened a little at learning that he was also an orphan.

"But then Nequois came, and almost immediately put to halt things I had been working years on. Things that the public didn't even know were coming, and perhaps that's better. Raising hopes and then dragging them away can be just as damaging. My rank became almost meaningless overnight. And now I am little more than an envoy between the pirate and our government."

"What does that have to do with us or Fia?"

"Because believe it or not Ms. Panlost, you did raise people's hopes. People may not know who you are, but they know of you. They might not even realize you're just children, but they do know how often you've outwitted and embarrassed Titch and his crew. I honestly didn't notice the impact or understand it until I saw someone's face brighten a little just at the sight of that celestial fox of yours painted on the side of a storefront."

Chase looked extremely pleased with himself; Amali and Gem were proud of him too. They both smiled and gave him an approving nod.

"So have you been protecting us this whole time?" Amali asked, "Out of respect for the hope you say we bring to the colony?"

He shook his head. "I honestly couldn't find you. None of my team could. You did very well for yourselves. The only reason I'm here now is because I posted people I trust at all the nearest landing lots and told them to notify me if they saw a group of three approach anywhere near them. I knew you needed a ship if you were going to attempt a rescue." He paused. "I was *very* surprised that you would pick this of all places to try and steal a ship."

Amali gave Chase another look. He just smiled widely.

"So why are you here? To help?" Amali asked, still a little uncertain of what to think of Drexy.

He shook his head again. "I'm very sorry, but I can't help you directly. If I did, it would end badly for all of us. In order to keep the peace, I have to continue to look like I support The All Father. And that means supporting Titch."

He looked around briefly. "I only came to tell you this. I think you've pushed him to his limit. If you all successfully save Ms. Cygnet from his clutches, Titch will go off the roaking rails."

Gem giggled. Chase rolled his eyes. Amali was the only one listening intently.

"If you succeed. It would be best if you were to flee Braroclyn. Not only would that give you the best chance to get safely away from him, but it may be best for Braroclyn. It would save our colony from his wrath as well, because he would surely try to follow you in an attempt to save himself one last humiliation." Drexy swallowed. "This is hardly a fair thing to ask of you. If you don't throw him off your trail completely and he doesn't give up the hunt, you will be in constant danger. And though you have done an admirable job surviving here, the open universe is a much more treacherous place. Even more so since the war began."

He let his posture relax a little and bowed his head slightly. "I'm sorry. I only sought you out to say that to you. I wish you all the luck."

Then, he started to walk away. The speech had taken Amali back a little, but Drexy was right, it wasn't helpful at all. So what was the point?

Chase pulled her out of her thoughts by tapping her repeatedly and pointing at the ship. The open door of the ship. Gem and Chase were giving it puzzled looks. Amali looked back and forth between the door and Drexy walking off.

She stood up and called to him, not caring about keeping a low profile in the moment. "Mr. Drexy!"

He turned to her, faux confusion on his face. Instinctively, Amali looked for his aura, the way she did with her friends. She didn't try it often with strangers, but it's worked before, and it worked this time. His looked dark blue in color, but it was beaming. She saw it swell up and down and up and down, like it was taking quick deep breaths. That usually meant you were excited, or preparing yourself to do something dangerous. Or both.

"You didn't close up your ship."

Drexy shrugged his shoulders. "Everyone knows ships get stolen in this neighborhood all the time. I should've known better. Now me and my team need to walk to the nearest marshal's office for help." He turned again and continued walking. He called back once more without turning his head. "Doubt they can do anything about it though. The IB on it has been busted for years. Hacked or something."

Chase sprang up and matched Amali's astonished expression. Then they noticed that Gem had already run/climbed halfway down the debris. They laughed and followed after her, still processing that they had their own ship now.

Hang on Sis. We're on our way.

They were well on their way. Gem had been running around in the ship familiarizing herself with all of the systems. She was absolutely giddy. She moved so fast she even had time to integrate some of her own contraptions, though the others were clueless as to what they were for. It didn't take long for her to get the ship off the ground and barreling toward the Star Hook.

While Gem was working, Amali and Chase looked through the rest of the ship. For the most part it was pretty bare; a few weeks worth of rations for four people were stocked in storage and there were four laser pistols left out in plain sight. Drexy had been good to them despite his insistence that he couldn't help.

Amali decided that there was no point in keeping a low profile, this time. There was no way they'd be able to sneak a ship so close to Titch without him or his crew noticing. They had no choice but to put all of their hope into Gem's rookie piloting, Chase's ability to navigate inside a pirate ship that he's never been on, and her skill of running circles around people that were unfairly bigger than her.

"One more time Gem," Amali said with her thinking face on, "Tell me why it works please?"

"Ames it doesn't matter why it works." Gem's words were heavy with the burden of being the smartest person in the room. "Just trust me, it's like a force field that keeps air and gravity consistent around the ship. The Star Hook has an open deck, so it has to have one."

"What's the point of an open deck?" Chase asked.

"Well, one example would be star charters. You don't want all that pesky glass getting in the way of your telescopes. That's an older example. A more relevant one would be pirates that want to be able to jump from ship to ship that they don't have permission to access by the regular methods."

"Ah. Yeah that would do it," Chase agreed.

"Gem," Amalie started, failing to stop the concern from entering her tone, "You sure you're going to be okay in here by yourself."

She nodded, her determination clear. "I just got my own ship. I'm not letting it get shot down on the first day."

Amalie nodded back. "Okay. Chase, let's wait by the door. Gem, we jump as soon as you open it."

"You are so cool right now!" It was Chase's turn to be giddy.

Before they left Gem in the pilot's chair, Gem grabbed Amali's hand. "Wait Ames." She pulled out her multitool and held it out to her.

Amali gaped at her.

Gem pulled out two of the extensions. "Use these two and you should be able to open most doors. If she's in a cell, it might be a bit tricky. You'll need to hold the button down in pulses."

"Gem—"

"It's fine. You're bringing it back to me."

Amali nodded, matching her determination, and went to join Chase at the door. For the rest of the commute time, they tried to reach Fia on the communicator to no avail.

They didn't get off to the best start. Gem pulled the ship around and careened to a stop so suddenly, Amali and Chase fell on their asses before the door opened. They only barely stumbled up and out before Gem jetted off away from the Star Hook. Amali and Chase fell to the deck. Gem was right, there was gravity and breathable air. There were also many surprised pirates.

Chase waved like a neighbor on a pleasant afternoon. Amali pulled him into a run.

The next few minutes were chaos. A flurry of commotion likened only to an intense sporting event or a very small battle of a minor war. Chase weaved

between and around pirates charging at him. Amali
jumped over pirates that tried to grab her, using their
arms and faces as springboards, and tripped the ones
that tried to outmaneuver her. The two of them made it
to the starboard door to the lower decks just as the
pirates seemed to remember they have lasers.

Amali heard the laser bolts crash into the door as
she closed it. She worked to lock it with Gem's
multitool. "Chase don't go far but see if you can find
some clue as to where they'd keep her."

Chase nodded and took off down the hallway to the
left. Amali finished locking the door while angry pirates
shouted and banged on it outside. She looked down
both sides of the hallway, considering whether to follow
after Chase or check the other side. Decided it would be
better not to split up, she rushed to the left.

She didn't have to get far before she found Chase,
slumped on the floor with blood streaming out of his
nose. An older looking pirate was standing over him
with his back to Amali. She drew the pistol and was
about to shoot.

The pirate heard her and turned on his heel,
quickly raising his hands in surrender. "Whoa whoa
whoa little lady. No need for that."

Amali kept walking towards him, still having every
intention to shoot. The pirate saw in her eyes she would
have no qualms about killing him. Amali didn't want to,
but she would to protect Chase and save Fia.

"Honest I won't cause you no trouble. I didn't realize this here was a kid. I heard him barreling around the corner and with the alarms on the ship all raised I acted only on instinct. I don't care if you save your friend. Tie me up right here I'll say you knocked me out."

Amali stopped in front of him, jabbing the pistol squarely into his chest. "Why?"

The old pirate sighed. "Miss, if I wanted to keep a tight schedule and sit in one roaking port fer an unbearable amount of time and," he winked, "do well looking after prisoners, I would've joined the military. Believe you me I'm not military material."

Amali still thought she should shoot him. But he continued, "There's rope right there, just tie me up and leave me. I'll take a nap and tell 'em you knocked me out."

He got on his knees and put his wrists together and offered them to her. Amali's expression didn't waver, though she was consciously trying to keep her hand from shaking with the pistol. It was working, this man thought she would surely kill him if he said the wrong thing.

"Where would these prisoners be kept?" Amali asked as she stared daggers at him.

"Down the other side of the corridor. There's a stairway in the wall to the left. Goes right to the brig."

Amali carefully grabbed the rope while keeping the pistol trained on him. Once she had his hands tied well, she worked faster to tie his legs since she was worried about Chase. She went over to him and shook him awake. His poor face looked like a cartoon character that just got hit with a frying pan.

"Ames I dunnothink we should go here."

"Damn it Chase. Are you okay? How many of me do you see?"

He squinted "I know the right answer is one."

"Okay come on, up you go." She helped him up and they started making their way to the other side of the corridor. "Be more careful please?"

Chase smiled, moving faster as they went, "Aye, captain."

"Hush."

"Fia can you hear me? We're on the Star Hook," Amali tried to reach her as the approached the stairway, "We should be getting close to you."

When they got to the stairway, both of their communicators lit up, but Fia's voice didn't come through. They only heard something rustling in the background. Then the communicator switched channels.

"Guys!" Gem's voice came over. "Just wanted you to know they're shooting at me!"

"Get away for now," Amali told her, "We'll let you know when we're back on the deck."

"Aye aye captain!"

Chase was moving normally again, mostly; Fia's lack of transmission and Gem being under fire reminded him of the gravity of the situation. Amali let go of him and they ran down the stairs.

They immediately saw her when they entered the brig. She was outside a cell, laying flat on her face. Her communicator left open. There was a strong smell of smoke in the air.

"Fia!" They shouted in unison.

Amali ran to her side to try and gently rouse her. Chase smartly hung back toward the stairs with his pistol drawn, just in case they were interrupted.

"Fia wake up wake up. What the roak happened?" Amali asked as her gentle rousing turned more into a rough shaking.

Chase looked worried. "I'm sure she's fine let's just carry her out."

Amali didn't hear him. "FIA WAKE UP." Panicking and not sure what to do, she slapped Fia in the face.

Incredibly, that almost worked.

Fia's eyes fluttered weakly, but she smiled when she recognized Amali. "Hey girl." Her voice was scratchy.

"Oh thank the cosmos." She cradled Fia's head in an awkward hug. Fia struggled to move her arms.

"What did they do to you?"

Fia shook her head. "Got rid of him easy. Needed to push that button to open the door." She coughed as she tried to point at a big black button to the side of the cell with the open door. "Bars slightly electrified."

Amali eyes widened. "WHAT?"

"Fia are you roaking kidding me???" Chase shouted from the stairs. "Actually I'm not even mad, that's super impressive."

"Shut up Chase," Amali shouted as she somehow managed to get Fia up. She couldn't really stand, she was relying heavily on Amali's left arm and shoulder.

"We're going."

"Aye aye—"

"Shut up!"

They made their way slowly up the stairway and back to the first hallway. From the other direction of where they entered, they heard the sound of many running footsteps.

"Back out the door?" Chase asked.

"I doubt they all abandoned the deck. Gem!" Amali pulled out her communicator.

"Hi!" Gem said stressfully. "No skiffs to chase me but they sure don't want me coming back."

"What can we do to make it easier for you to get back to us?"

"Are you near stairs? There's an upper deck that's also open. Doesn't look connected, but the force field would be around everything. If you don't find stairs you could try climbing."

Amali heard the footsteps get closer, and the banging on the door to the outside started up again. This time it sounded like it would open.

"We'll meet you there!" she yelled before she closed her communicator. "Chase there were stairs going up where you got knocked out by an old man."

"He's still a pirate!" Chase protested. Fia laughed absently.

Amali and Chase helped Fia move quicker down the hallway to where they left the tied up, napping pirate. They turned the corner and saw stairs to their right. They climbed their way up as fast as they could.

They stumbled through the door onto the top deck. Surprising none of them, there were pirates.

Trying her best to use the open door as a shield, Amali held Fia behind her and started shooting. The pirates shot back. Chase ran around the edge firing off laser blasts without even really aiming in an attempt to take their attention away from Fia. Amali was realizing the extent of her shooting inexperience as it took her four tries to barley land one hit. At least the rapid firing discouraged the pirates from closing the distance between them.

Chase's diversion, plus the fact that they had surprised the pirates, worked. There were only six on the deck, and they had successfully incapacitated all of them. Amali tried not to think about how many were dead, she just took solace in the fact that some of them were moving and some were groaning.

With excellent timing, Gem flew over just in time. Maneuvering a small jump away from where Chase had ended up. Amali started moving toward their ship with Fia. As Chase jumped to the open door of their ship, Captain Nequois jumped up from the side of the deck, laughing maniacally. He had started climbing up after he heard the laser blasts.

He pulled out a pistol and pointed it at Chase.

But Amali realized he was going to do that before he did. She opened her communicator. "GEM BARREL ROLL NOW."

Their ship spun out of the way from Nequois's fire, and poor Chase bounced around inside the ship like it was a pinball machine.

"What was that Ames??? Chase is puking all over my ship now!"

"Keep your distance! Titch is here."

"Roak."

"Can you meet me on the lower deck?"

"I seriously doubt it!"

Captain Nequois was walking confidently towards her and Fia now. Behind him she could see their ship suspended a safe distance away. The Star Hook must not have had lasers on this side because Gem was keeping it perfectly still.

Amali heard more pirates coming up the stairs. Probably more climbing the side of the deck too. "Gem stay right there. I'm coming to you. Keep the door open."

Gem was too flabbergasted to immediately answer that, and she didn't get to at all because Amali closed her communicator.

"Fancy move," Captain Nequois said with a gleam in his eye, "You could've just shot me."

Believe me I wish. But I was worried I'd miss. "I probably should've, but it's just too much fun outwitting you!"

Amali narrowly pushed Fia and herself out of the way before two laser bolts landed right where they were standing, leaving two scorch marks on the deck. Fia fell down and took Amali with her.

Captain Nequois stood over them, fury in his eyes now. "It's been fun, Amali Panlost. But playtime's over."

He reached out to grab her, and Amali didn't bother to aim. She fired as many times as the pistol could handle in his general direction. She must have hit something because he roared out in pain.

She threw her pistol into her coat and scooped Fia up in her arms. She bolted for the edge of the deck, scarcely believing what she was about to do.

"Fia, hold your breath."

Fia's eyes struggled to focus on what was going around her. But she managed to see the edge of the deck rapidly approaching, and the ship in the distance with an open door.

Fia's eyes practically bulged out of her head. "No no no no no no no no—"

Amali heard Captain Nequois scream at his crew to get her. She took a deep breath and leaped into space. She could feel the artificial gravity stop existing once she broke the force field. She flew through open space.

She tried her best not to panic, to convince herself this wasn't the scariest thing she'd ever attempted. She focused on holding onto Fia, onto the feeling of relief that she got her back. She worried about her aim being off, but she pushed it aside. She thought of how happy Gem was that she had a ship to call her own, the ship she was now trying so hard to get to. Her lungs started to burn. She thought of Chase's determination to do crazy, stupid things and how great it would be that she did the craziest stupidest thing.

She kept her eyes on the open door. It was getting closer. Amazingly, she was actually arcing right to it. She couldn't believe she lined it up right. Her vision was starting to blur, her grip on Fia felt weak. Her lungs despised her right now. But then she saw herself fly through the door and felt the gravity return. She passed out before she hit the floor, still clutching her sister.

They were safe.

Braroclyn would be safer now. Matzin Drexy thought to himself.

There was still The All Father, he wasn't going to leave them alone. But at least he didn't make things worse like Nequois did, and the dear captain was gone. Off to hunt down a young girl that apparently "undermined" his authority and shot a giant hole in the palm of his "favorite" hand. Drexy had heard the story in his last call with Captain Nequois, well, heard most of the story. The captain tended to become slightly incomprehensible when he was really angry.

He apparently expected Drexy to still send him money to finance this hunt, and to submit positive reports to The Black Palace so that they would continue to look favorably on him. And Drexy would, because he didn't care. It got The Black Palace and Titch off his back. Now, he and the other genuine public servants could actually get some good work done. And it was all thanks to some lost kids who chose to find their own way.

Drexy wanted them to be able to return home, someday. Hopefully he'd have Braroclyn thriving by then. Until then, he hoped they stayed safe. And he hoped Amali felt good about herself, because she deserved to.

Amali had never felt worse in her life. Her head already hurt when she woke up, and all the rambling that her friends were directing at her was only making it worse. Also, she had bruises all over her body, some of which she had no idea how they came to be. Also also, her skin felt sore. Her actual skin was sore. *All of it.* And Fia wouldn't stop hugging her.

"And you get on to me about the stuff I pull!" Was Chase's contribution to the noise. "YOU FLUNG YOURSELF INTO OPEN SPACE."

"Hey! What are you yelling for?" Amali defended herself. "I mean, you've done that before."

They all stopped and looked at her.

"I've done that before?"

"Yeah the dare. You seriously don't remember?"

Chase couldn't decide whether to laugh or be horrified by this information. "Ames, is that why you thought you could make it?"

"Well I did make it!"

"Sis." Fia got her attention with her disbelieving expression. "I dared him to do that because Itarians can survive in open space. But, they're the only ones."

"Well, dragons," Gem added.

"The only *people*," Fia clarified.

Now Amali's head really hurt. "I- I held my breath."

"Space is a vacuum, Ames," Gem explained nonchalantly, "Holding your breath would make you explode."

Amali reeled back. "But I didn't!?" She looked at Fia. "And neither did you!?!"

"Yeah that's why we're all excited," Fia explained with a huge smile, "Because I figured out that you figured out how to use your Spear Energy."

"What?"

"Here look." She handed Amali the book that they had been practicing with, the one Amali saved for her when she was taken.

Amali read the passage Fia was pointing to. Some of the ink was too ruined to read, but she could make out most of the words.

In essence, flying is an exercise of projecting your aura. Students of the Spear Arts can learn to project the energy within themselves outwards in order to achieve flight. Projecting your aura requires fantastic will and concentration. You will need to concentrate your will to influence your aura to behave differently than its usual nature. Being in touch with yourself and relying on your instincts is key.

Amali looked up, shaking her head. "But, I didn't fly. I just floated."

"How do you think you steered yourself into the door?" Fia pointed out.

"I just aimed good enough."

"You really didn't," Chase said, "I saw you jump off. You were way off course."

Amali was stunned. Fia encouraged her to keep reading.

Most beings' need to breathe is what makes flying in space so perilous. You can replenish your breath with Spear Energy, but that will take maintaining your aura. Maintaining aura and propelling it simultaneously is no small feat. To simplify your tasks, focus on maintaining the aura around your lungs. Think of the sensation of holding onto a good feeling in your chest, that is how you can hold onto enough aura to sustain you while using the rest to fly amongst the stars. But your energy and aura can be exhausted the same as your physical body, so be sure to constantly take in energy from around you. Luckily, space is naturally bountiful with raw Spear Energy.

Amali could not believe it. She didn't know what to say. She just looked at everyone. Chase smiled. "And yet another reason why you're the leader."

Amali returned the smile, but still protested. "This is Gem's ship. She's always wanted one, certainly more than me. I'm fine with her being leader."

"Not how it works," Gem said with a single shake of her head, "I own the ship, I choose the captain. I choose you."

"Are you sure?" Gem nodded.

Amali was starting to feel better. Though her head still pounded. "Thank you." She looked around. "Thanks guys."

They all understood she was saying *I love you guys*.

"I still get final decision on the name though," Gem said quickly, "But I'm willing to hear suggestions."

"The Green Rabbit?" Chase said brightly.

"Not naming my ship after a mall."

"But that was our home for the longest time!"

"Next."

"The Twinkling Bell?" Fia said slowly, clearly just making it up.

"The roak is that?"

"Nothing. I just think it sounds pretty."

"No."

"Rude."

Amali chimed in confidently, "I've recently been made aware that Chase has a lot of practice painting foxes."

Chase gave her a nervous smile that asked her not to hit him.

"Maybe he could paint one on the side of the ship," she continued, "People seem to like it. Like, a lot apparently. And we could call the ship the Gold Fox."

Chase looked elated. Fia nodded approvingly. Gem was delighted. "That's perfect!"

Amali looked at each of her friends. Their auras shone so bright it was almost blinding, and it was wonderful.

They could all feel it. Life was about to get much better, or at least, more exciting. And they couldn't wait to start living it.

What they didn't know: this was the start of a continuous adventure that would turn them into legends. Local legends, but legends all the same.

THE HELL OF SCAV

A man prepares himself, getting dressed in a long red cloak with a yellow trim. He throws a large hood over his face, concealing his identity and heads toward the door of his home.

"Papa," a little boy's voice calls out to him, "Do you have to leave?"

The man turns around and removes his hood. He kneels and puts his hands on the boy's shoulders.

"I'm sorry my son, I must. I go for you, for your future. I will be back."

The man reaches into his pocket and pulls out a silver necklace with a star charm. He puts it on his child.

"This was your mothers. I've kept it on me everyday, but I think it's time for you to have it, to remember both of us by. It's made of special metal found on the surface of Scav that can withstand the heat. I'll see you tonight Taiyo."

The man embraces Taiyo in a long and tight hug before departing.

Four men each wearing the same cloak sit around a table in a tiny, dimly lit room.

"Let's begin," one of the men says.

"I hope you all made it here safely. Satro, I know traveling from Level Four to here on Level Fifteen must've been hard," another says.

"Yes, my son worries for my safety coming here but it must be done. Thank you for asking Lin-Po," Satro replies.

"We came here to discuss business, let's move on," says the final man.

"Eager as always, huh Durge," says the first man.

Durge grunts and the rest of the group chuckles.

"Anyway, has everyone been doing their assignments?" The first man continues.

"Yes Himroc," Satro says, "I have acquired the weapons for next week."

"I have a few other men who are willing to join us," Lin-Po replies.

"The speeders are ready and an escape route is planned," Durge adds in.

"Excellent. Then The Black Palace may finally feel our suffering," Himroc states, "Change is coming, the upper levels may support The All Father but this society is a failure. Our lives on Level Twenty and above are worth just as much. We are kept at the bottom, or should I say, the top of the barrel with restricted access to lower levels to live in filth and heat. Our Fire

Warriors have left to fight for the universe and it's time the rest of us fight back as well. The Occupying Forces will know our voice next week when we attack their supply chain. All the pieces of the puzzle have fallen into place and we are finally ready to fight back!"

"So is everyone ready for the next phase?" Satro asks.

"Yes, no contact until the day of the attack," Lin-Po responds.

"Then we're decided. Safe travels everyone," Durge remarks.

Satro slowly walks back to his home on Level Four. He maneuvers in and out of alleys and between buildings so as not to be seen. He finally arrives outside his home and sees the door is open.

"Taiyo," Satro yells, "TAIYO!"

He calls his name out to no response. He begins panicking and rushes into his home. The inside is messy, messier than normal. The little furniture they had was thrown around. The home was completely in shambles. In the corner, Satro noticed a small amount of blood on the floor.

"TAIYO!" He calls out again and again, each time louder and with more worry in his voice.

He falls to his knees in the middle of the room and begins sobbing. In his tears, he notices a figure standing in the dark of the hallway.

"TAIYO!" He calls out again toward the figure. The figure shuffles around and emerges from the corner revealing itself to be much larger than Satro's son. The figure quickly charges at Satro, growing in size as it knocks him unconscious.

Satro regains consciousness and tries to move his hands, but can't. He looks around to see he is handcuffed to a pipe. He's able to hear several men talking from around the corner. He tries to free himself, but to no avail.

"You won't be able to escape," a familiar voice calls out to him.

Satro looks to the corner to see Durge step out. He motions his hand and a large figure follows from behind him.

"Arboc here is a Fargulkian. Huge huh?"

"Why? What are you planning Durge?" Satro asks.

"What am I planning? Nothing! It's what you were planning that I care about," Dugre replies.

"What do you mean?"

"Your little scheme, the 'liberation' of Scav. I can't allow that to happen."

"Why not? You are a trusted member of the council. We've been friends for a long time. We have been meeting for a year. Letting each other in on our lives. Planning a better future for Scav. You were at the birth of my son," Satro responds. The sound of defeat is painted on his voice.

"Scav is perfect. There is no better plan for our people. The Black Palace keeps things in order. They keep things the way they should be!"

"How could you say that? Life on the upper levels is horrible. We live in poverty, you should know that."

"Yes, you would assume that but you don't truly know me. I don't live on the upper levels. I live on Level 100. Why would I want to ruin the life of luxury I have?"

"What about me, my life, my son's?"

"Oh, you don't have to worry about that anymore!"

Durge nods toward Arboc, prompting Arboc to press a button on the wall. A faint whirring sound could be heard as Satro began to look around at his surroundings. His heart sank when his eyes locked on "*Level One*".

He then shifted his focus toward the elevator in the corner of the room. An elevator to the surface.

"What have you done? What did you do?" Satro screams out.

Durge smiles as the elevator lowers into view. Satro starts to panic as a charred corpse lies against the wall of the elevator. He is unable to tell who it is through the glass.

"WHAT DID YOU DO!"

Satro screams out again.

"Arboc, throw him in," Durge calmly orders.

Arboc slowly walked over to Satro while Satro squirmed and attempted to fight back.

Arboc broke Satro's hand and pulled it through his handcuff. He picked Satro up and carried him to the elevator.

"You won't get away with this Durge," Satro yells, seething with rage. "The rebellion will join The Allegiance and you will lose your power."

"Oh, your little plan. I already told The Black Palace and got a handsome pay. That day is nothing more than a death sentence for Himroc and Lin-Po."

"YOU BASTARD!" Satro yells.

Arboc threw Satro into the elevator and shut the door. Satro banged on the glass, crying and yelling.

"How could you do this? I have a life, a son!"

He looked at Durge who had a faint smile on his face. Durge looked away from Satro and toward the corpse in the elevator with him. Satro, reminded of the body, rushed to the blackened remains. He was still unable to tell who it was. He had a worried look on his face as he noticed a slight sparkle around the neck of the body.

"WHAT HAVE YOU DONE!" Satro screamed.

He turned the body over slowly, afraid of what he's about to find out. All the tension in Satro's body fled as a pit of despair grew inside him. He clutched the star charm on the necklace and pulled Taiyo's remains to his chest.

Satro wept with his child's body as the faint whir started again. Satro looked out the elevator as he began to rise. He watched Durge and Arboc walking away. Satro squeezed Taiyo as the elevator reached the surface. The elevator opened as Satro looked out into the hell-scape of the surface of Scav. An overwhelmingly intense heat immediately washes over him.

He held his son and cried as his tears instantly evaporated into nothing.

BLACK PALACE CORRESPONDENCE

Dearest daughter,

Although I know it has been a long time since I last wrote to you, there is no other way for me to express what I am feeling right now. There is so much that has happened since the last time we wrote to each other and it has been even longer since I have seen or spoken to you.

We may have gone down different paths in life but I want you to know that there was never a moment my love for you was questioned, or waned, and I am proud of the woman you became. Despite my years in the Black Palace military, and my rising to Admiral, you have always been my greatest achievement.

Do you remember those days back on Scav? Who would have thought we would make it so far in life. We didn't have much, but we always had each other and when you developed your flame I was ecstatic. We were poor, but rich in Spear Energy, and those days training you were amongst, if not, the happiest days of my life. Throughout the universe, no star nor sun could compare to the brightness of your smile, for you truly were the light of my life.

But I am indeed a terrible father. As you grew and matured, and we began to see the universe differently. I hardened my heart and eventually, I lost you. We continued to write and that kept me happy, but now even this will be gone from my life.

I should've known. I'm sorry, I'm sorry, I'm so sorry. When a report came to me of an Allegiance warrior with powerful flames, I should've known.
Instead, I sent all my forces out to stop them. Although I may not have pulled the trigger, I aimed the blasters and took your shining spirit from this world. I am so sorry.

When your body was brought aboard my ship words could not describe the feelings of anguish and despair. I know I wasn't the best father, but you were the best daughter. I will join you soon my Phoenix.

Love, Dad

BLACK PALACE INCIDENT REPORT

On the fifth rotation of Scav at 18:03, Admiral Fennik has severely damaged part of his carrier ship, callsign *The Phoenix,* in an apparent suicide. The Admiral's quarters went up in flames and are believed to have been caused by his own Spear Energy abilities. The fire was contained before any other lives were lost, however, the ship must be suspended from duty until a new Admiral is found and repairs are completed. In the remains of the Admiral's quarters was found a letter addressed to his daughter. This led our forensic team, along with an official Black Palace investigation, to rule Admiral Fennik's death a suicide caused by the guilt of killing his daughter in a recent rebel skirmish.

THE SOLDIER AND THE REBEL

"We're pinned down. If you keep moving, the base of this cavern will collapse and we'll die," a young woman said.

"Easy for you to say. Isn't that what all you do? Complain?" A young man replied.

He was wearing standard Black Palace infantry armor. The woman rolled her eyes. Her legs her pinned by boulders. She winced in pain as the Black Palace soldier tried moving again.

"Will you just stop," the woman yelled out.

The Black Palace soldier was also pinned. He yelled out in pain as he tried moving the boulders from his legs. As he did so, the rocks around them began to shake.

"Stop! Stop!" The woman pleaded.

The Black Palace solider stopped. They both held their breath and looked around as the rocks stopped shaking. The soldier slumped onto his back. Blood trickled from his forehead.

"You know, this is all your fault," he mumbled out.

"Excuse me?" The woman replied.

The soldier sat up.

"Yea. It's all your fault. You and these "Allegiance" fighters. Bunch of idiots fighting for a lost cause. Disrupting everything. If it wasn't for you, we wouldn't be here right now!"

The woman snapped back.

"If it wasn't for The Black Palace, none of us would have had to leave our homes and fight for our freedom!"

"Freedom? You were free. You followed a pampered, disgruntled man into war because he had daddy issues. What did The Black Palace ever do to you other than provide safety and security!"

The woman furrowed her brow.

"This war is bigger than Corrin. Or any general. It's bigger than you and me. The Black Palace destroyed my home. Killed my parents because they didn't submit to your "All Father". How dare you ask what The Black Palace has done to me. It's taken everything!"

Silence fell around them. The rocks above were filtering in some light but it was staring to fade. The sun was setting. The soldier swallowed hard and looked around.

"Sun is setting," he said

The woman was still visibly angry.

"What's your name anyways?" The soldier asked.

"Why do you care?" The woman replied.

"I don't really. But if we're going to be stuck here I rather refer to you other than scum."

They both looked at each other. The solider grinned and the woman stabbed him with her eyes.

"My name is Havara!"

"Havara," the soldier said, wincing in pain as he moved a bit, "That's a nice name."

Havara rolled her eyes and sighed, annoyed.

"And what's your name?"

"Hilipp."

"That's a Halvodi name," Havara said, confused.

"And so is Havara," Hilipp replied, looking at her.

"You're from Halvodon? Yet you fight for The Black Palace?" Havara angrily asked.

Hilipp shifted his body, trying to find comfort from the pain shooting from his pinned legs.

"My family left Halvodon when The All Father returned. I was maybe one or two when we moved to The Black Palace. I know nothing of your world!"

"The Black Palace slaughtered our people," Havara responded. She was in disbelief.

"Your people," Hilipp snapped back. "My people are my brothers and sisters in arms. Soldiers being killed and hunted by The Allegiance. Halvodon had its chance to submit. You all will suffer the same if Corrin continues this war."

Hilipp and Havara glared at each other until footsteps were heard above them.

"People," Havara said.

Hilipp eyes widened in excitement.

"Hey! Down here. Down here!" He yelled frantically.

"Help us! We're stuck," Havara yelled.

Voices above them could be heard but were muffled. The sound of rocks being moved made Havara and Hilipp squirm with joy.

"If it's The Black Palace, I'll make sure you aren't harmed," Hilipp said, giving Havara a friendly smile.

Havara nodded slightly, assured by Hilipp she would be safe.

As the rocks were moved, moonlight forced its way down into the rubble.

"Hello, who is down there?" A man's voice echoed.

Havara and Hilipp looked at each other, unsure of who should reply. Havara closed her eyes and spoke.

"Havara. I'm with The Allegiance under Party Leader Acorlius."

Silence took hold for a moment. Havara and Hilipp held their breath. Neither of them knew if their rescuers were affiliated with The Black Palace or The Allegiance.

"We're here to help Havara. I am Jor-San. We are with General Ra-Lins company. Were you in the Battle of Vorath?"

Havara sighed in relief. Hilipp had a hint of fear on his face.

"Yes. Yes I was. Something was hit by a Spearcraft fighter and exploded next to us. I was trapped down here."

"Who else is with you?" Jor-San asked.

Havara looked at Hilipp. He was nervous now.

"A Black Palace soldier. He is injured. We are both pinned down," Havara responded.

Jor-San didn't respond. Quiet chatter could be heard above.

"What're they saying?" Hilipp asked Havara.

"I don't know," Havara responded.

"We are coming down," Jor-San said.

Moments passed as Jor-San and three other people grappled down into the debris. They all were wearing standing military gear with Allegiance patches on their shoulders. The Allegiance fighters glared at Hilipp and gripped their blasters. Jor-San analyzed the situation quickly.

"You three, remove these rocks from her legs. You," Jor-San said pointing at Hilipp "Where is the rest of your squad?"

Hilipp was terrified at this point. The other three were already moving the rocks and un-pinning Havara.

"I- I don't know. Everything happened so fast," Hilipp stuttered out.

"Did he give you any information?" Jor-San asked, turning to Havara.

Hilipp looked at her, pleading for his life with his eyes.

"No," she said.

The Allegiance fighters helped Havara to her feet. Her legs were badly wounded.

"Can you walk?" Jor-San asked.

"I can manage," Havara said, being held up by the fighters.

"We'll head back to camp. This one is no use to us alive," Jor-San said, pulling out his side arm and pointing it at Hilipp.

Hilipp shot his hands up and covered his face, tears filling his eyes.

"Wait, wait please don't. Please," Hilipp cried out.

"Jor-San," Havara said, stumbling forward.

Jor-San looked at her, confused.

"Don't," Havara said, leaning against Jor-San for support. Her legs were almost wobbling.

Hilipp lowered his hands.

"Let me," Havara said, taking the side arm away from Jor-San.

"No, please don't. I- I," Hilipp pleaded right as Havara pulled the trigger.

Hilipp's body slumped to the ground. A hole burned through his head. Havara handed the side arm back to Jor-San as the other Allegiance fighters helped her out of the rubble.

THE MAW

A loud rumble jolted me awake from my exhaustion. The rumble came from a Black Palace carrier ship that I found myself bound to. It looked to be holding myself and about five more suspected criminals on board, however, by the sheer size of it I could guess it could carry more than forty at a time. While my legs were encaged together in Black Palace shackles, it was my wrists that were burning in soreness from their own tightly secured cuff links. Other than the occasional ship rumbles and numbing pain, all I can ponder on is how I found myself here to begin with.

My parents only wanted the best for me, their only daughter. They named me Lira and said my smile burned brighter than the sun on our home world of Pugart. Pugart has such a harsh desert climate, I honestly don't know how my parents survived there. They worked tirelessly to provide for me and maintain a humble living. When I grew older, I wanted to travel star systems, learn a valuable trade, and provide support to my parents who sacrificed so much to raise me.

I was able to reach most of my goals. I've visited countless planets and was able to send money back to my parents on Pugart. How I acquired money, some would say, is a little unconventional. I worked a handful of odd jobs but the job that stuck with me was illegal smuggling. It did feel a little wrong to me at first, but the money was so good. Once it became a true profession for me, all my moral qualms about it faded away. I mean no one was really getting hurt. I just moved products and supplies, and the people I worked for were also very grateful.

I ended up on the planet Itarus, there was a surprising amount of smuggling to be done there. Many Itarians loved their ancient heirlooms and artifacts. These items were tied back to their old empire which was dominated by The Black Palace. To my benefit, many of these items are deemed illegal for civilians to have. I would get these products sourced and move them across the ancient Itarian cities for good pay.

In the city of Var I met a very mysterious client. They wore a complete covering over themselves and a helmet that altered their voice. Whoever this person was they didn't want anyone to know anything about them. They wanted me to move some supplies for them quickly to a checkpoint location they provided. I was curious to know the details on this cargo but then they told me their price. Four million BPUs. I almost tripped over myself hearing that number. Four million BPUs?! I wouldn't have to smuggle anything for the next ten years with that pay. The client seemed more willing to work with me the less I asked about the details, so I accepted their offer and took the cargo.

It was a dark unforgiving night on the way to the checkpoint. This was my only window to move products without notice from the patrols. As I moved in the darkness on one of my usual routes, I could hear a strong hum. The hum grew louder and more powerful, then lights were shining right on me. I thought it was a patrol car, but the model was different, and the decals had a pattern I haven't seen in years. It was a Black Palace military cruiser. The shock and realization hit my body while the soldiers quickly poured out and surrounded me. One of the soldiers seized my cargo container and broke it open. Rations, schematics, and recordings all from The Allegiance poured out. I started to go numb. This is much worse than petty smuggling. I was now an accomplice to Allegiance activities. I was arrested quickly.

The rumbles of the prisoner carrier ship were continuous now. I felt the forces of the ship move whatever part of me that wasn't tightly bound. I think we've reached our destination. A loud static and screech came from the top area of the ship, then a voice.

"B.P. Prisoner load 2-4-7, we're clear for entrance. Delivering the prisoners now."

I couldn't help but laugh at the thought of myself, the smuggler, becoming the cargo that must be delivered. Everyone else looked at me with disgust and tried to move around as we were landing. The leg shackles on me started to whirr and make metallic clicking noises. They morphed into a looser grip. I was able to stand up and move my feet. The ship came to an abrupt landing. All the rumbles dissipated, now I just hear loud bangs and clicks from outside the ship's hull. The cargo door to the ship opened and slowly lowered to reveal our fate.

When the door opened, the air rushed inside like a wave. It was humid and smelled of rot. We were quickly rushed out of the ship into full brunt of the rotting environment. My eyes adjusted to the new area and saw the complex where I would be spending the rest of my days. As we lined up and walked towards it, I could read a sign on one of the security fences.

'BLACK PALACE WAR PRISON 43-7: DI OUTPOST.'

This is horrible. I'm a prisoner on the planet Di, home to the most loyal races to The All Father and The Black Palace. And now to them, I'm a filthy traitor.

We were quickly processed when we entered the complex. The prisoners in front of me were checked in and moved to a corridor on the right of the processing guard. When I approached the processing guard, he didn't say anything, so I decided to speak up.

"Do you need my name or something?"

"We know who you are, Lira Ferzian. Home world planet of Pugart. Illegally smuggling across the systems for over five years. We know all about you, but what you did this time is going to cost you dearly."

The processing guard snickered. He then entered something on his console and continued.

"Let's take her out to holding room B6, the Grand Warden wants to have a little talk."

I couldn't help but think of my parents when that guard talked to me. What did he mean by costing me dearly? I'm already a prisoner, what could be worse? My thoughts kept racing as the prison guards escorted me to a room on the upper level. The room was bare and only had a tall table in the middle. As I was moved close to the table, my arm and leg shackles started to move again. This time I felt a binding force from them. My arms latched onto the table while my legs secured themselves firmly to the floor. I couldn't move an inch and just stared at the wall for what felt like hours. Loud plodding footsteps started to grow closer to the holding room. A figure then entered, their size taking up whatever space was left in the room.

This figure was undoubtedly a male reptilian of Di. Their Black Palace uniform struggled to contain their bulked muscles, enlarged spikes, and long sturdy tail. The figure looked at me straight on with piercing red eyes and flashed their sharp jagged teeth. Their face was a color of a greenish yellow which looked to match the rest of their body from what I could see. The reptilian walked around me like a predator stalking their kill. Then it spoke.

"I am Grand Warden Rodan-Klashik, and welcome to prison 43-7, or what we like to call it, The Maw. I've brought you directly to me to ask some questions about your heinous crime against our government."

"I don't have much to say but go ahead," I replied.

"I doubt that. With what you were providing to rebellious Allegiance forces, you must have more information about this." Rodan then asked. "How long have you been working for them?"

"I wasn't working for them. It was a single job from someone who didn't tell me anything."

"Oh, so just a single job. I find it a little hard to believe that shipping Allegiance supplies would qualify as a one job run."

I can see Rodan is going to keep prodding me, but I was being honest.

"I don't know what to say, the client just told me to move this cargo. They didn't tell me their name or anything."

Rodan's eyes started to sharpen, and his tail whipped around.

"We here at The Maw always get the information we need. We have many methods to do this. Some methods may be a bit cruel, but it's needed to win this war." He glared at me deeper.

"Who was your client for this cargo?"

"I don't know. They were completely covered and anonymous." I tried to be as direct as possible.

"Nonsense!" Rodan roared. "You know I can tell if you're lying. Us reptilians have acute senses. When you answer me, I can sense your heartbeat, eye motions, and breathing patterns to the highest degree. If you lie to me at all I will know, and your punishment will be increased. So I will ask one more time, who is your client?"

"I don't know, they wore a helmet that covered their face."

Rodan looked at me deeply. His eyes moving rapidly in sync with my breath. I knew I told him the truth and I could see him realizing it. Rodan hissed loudly and slammed his fist on the table. The shockwave from his pure strength rattled my wrists that were latched on the table surface. His teeth were now inches away from my face.

"You may be right about this, but this isn't over! I will break you down until you tell us everything. Then we will break you again. Hope you enjoy your stay with us."

Rodan then quickly left the room, his tail slamming into the doorway as he departed. It wasn't long before two prison guards came in and unlatched me from the table. They grabbed me violently and pushed me along an adjacent hallway.

The corridors, chambers, and security lights seemed endless as they dragged me to another floor. Right before entering a new room, one of the guards crouched and scanned my leg shackles. My legs could now move freely as my shackles snapped open, but I'd rather have my arms freed as my wrists still ached and burned.

Before I could take a proper step, I stumbled hard as one of the guards shoved me into the area.

As I was surrounded in this new area, the guard that freed my legs then pointed a device towards me. My arm cuffs sprang open and fell on the ground. My burning wrists now felt a new sting as they were exposed to the hot prison air, but it still felt better than how they were before.

Clothes were thrown at me; it was the official prison uniform, maroon long sleeves, and matching pants.

"Hurry up and change. Your cell is ready," said one of the guards.

I almost forgot I was still wearing my smuggler wardrobe as I started to strip. I ignored the guards' snickering as I changed quickly. Compared to Rodan's piercing eyes, it didn't feel as offensive.

I was then escorted to a lower level and across the prison yard. I could see the guards posted from every viewpoint imaginable; some I could tell were reptilians of Di, while others looked less reptilian-like. Regardless, they were all wearing advanced security helmets, so I couldn't see their faces.

On the other side of the prison from where I entered, I reached my cell. It looked standard—just a wall bed and a bathroom area. When I walked into it, one of the guards commanded me to face them. He toggled his security helmet and scanned my face and body. I was now officially checked in to The Maw; length of stay…who knows.

The cell bars then activated. They were radiating yellow bars of energy that looked like it would definitely hurt if I touched them. The bars also created a loud droning hum that I couldn't tune out, so sleep was not going to welcome me tonight.

The hours passed as I lay in my cell. I couldn't feel much regret or sorrow as the droning hum of the cell bars scattered my thoughts. The prison chamber had no windows; I haven't witnessed daylight since I was locked in. Judging by how my body felt, a day must've passed by now, maybe two. No food was given to me, just water from a rusted fountain in my cell.

Just as I got used to the humming sound, my mind was now overrun with the searing sensation of hunger.

Visions of my parents entered my mind. Josu, my amazing father, and Dufxi, my precious mother. I couldn't see their faces clearly. I can't forget them, not now or ever! My head quickly rose from my metal wall bed; it seemed sleep finally greeted me.

My body was weakened by days of no food, and sitting up felt like gravity had multiplied. I heard a guard approaching. My humming cell bars shut off, and the guard approached me.

"Time to eat. You already look dead. It's too early for that."

I don't know how I could even walk, but I found myself approaching the mess hall. It's the first time I have seen other prisoners since I got here. They kept to themselves and ate their food quietly; conversations, if any, were scattered and short.

I took a tray and was led to a large machine dispenser. It didn't look like anything was made by cooks. A sludge of yellow mush filled my tray, and I quickly sat down to eat. All they gave us was a spoon, which I quickly stuffed myself with. The yellow slop didn't taste like much, but I couldn't stop eating.

My belly started to expand but I couldn't stop myself. A sharp sensation grabbed my neck while I continued to eat. Before I could react, my head was smashed on the hall table. Realizing the sharpness was claws, I was pinned down by a reptilian guard. Pain started to rush to my smushed face as the guard snarled.

"Filthy pig. Who taught you to eat like that? We're not tending animals here."

"That's pretty rich coming from an oversized lizard."

Being fed must've given me some snappy energy as I spat back at him. The guard pressed their claws deeper into my neck, starting to break my skin. My pressed face then began to burn as the guard slid my head across the table.

My head smashed into my tray as I toppled onto the floor. In a daze, I noticed more guards entering the hall. The other prisoners tried to ignore me, taking a quick glance before evading their eyes.

"A little snippy, eh? Rodan ordered us to keep a close watch on you. Although we planned to do this later, sending you to the sting chamber now might fix your attitude."

The reptilian guard shouted. The other guards immediately seized me and brought me to my feet. Some of the prisoners showed more reaction and worry when the sting chamber was mentioned.

As I looked up, all I saw was the end of a rifle hurtling towards my face.

Strands of dark green blocked my vision as I awoke. I recognized that it was my own hair covering my face. As I moved to clear my face, only my thought of it happened. My body was completely paralyzed on the ground. I screamed from the distress of my current state. Okay, I could speak at least, and it also seems like I can move my eyes.

Determining the situation, I scanned the new area I was in; this must be the sting chamber they mentioned. The chamber looked a decent size, but the ceiling was low. Very bare, nothing notable to mark except for a hanging light that covered the chamber in a dark red glow.

Listening deeply, I couldn't hear the usual groaning of pipes and movements of guards like in the other rooms. I screamed again, this time with words.

"Hey! Is anyone here? What is this?!"

"Good to see you awake, Lira. We'll be getting started shortly."

Someone was approaching. I couldn't move to see, but I could tell their voice was Rodan.

"What're you doing to me? Why can't I move?" I was getting more frantic.

"This is the sting chamber. One of our latest developments at The Maw. The room is specialized to remove any outside commotions. This will have you focusing more on your body itself."

"Focus on my body? I can't even feel anything; this isn't making sense."

Rodan walked around my crumpled body.

"You're distressed and don't notice it now, but you can feel everything. Our stinger is currently latched onto the base of your skull and disables any motor function in your body from that point downward."

I could hear Rodan pulling something out.

"That's just the beginning. The stinger will also send the most excruciating pain straight into your nervous system, all with just a push of a button."

Rodan now moved in front of me and kneeled towards my face.

"I don't really have to do this. All you need to do is answer my questions. Who helped you smuggle those supplies?"

Even though I was paralyzed, I still felt my stomach drop before I responded.

"I told you already. I don't know."

The device in Rodan's hand was in view as he pushed it. My vision went flashing white while my brain felt like it was electrified. Pain surged into every part of my being. I could even feel it in my nails and hair. My screams were piercing but subsided quickly, as all I could comprehend was the pain.

"Who did you work for? Did you talk to anyone else for this job?"

Rodan spat.

"No. No one else, just a person with a helmet."

I was shocked at how well I could still speak. With how this technology works, I could assume the stinger doesn't affect my speech. A tortured, paralyzed vegetable wouldn't be useful to The Black Palace.

The pain surged back; it felt even stronger this time. My screams were guttural, and my mouth started to foam. Death flashed into my mind as a way to end the agony.

"Your stubbornness will only make this worse. I won't stop until you give me details. You're only harming yourself!"

"Is that you trying to care? You can already tell if I'm lying. You know that I truly don't know anything, but you still torture me. So, do you just want to keep going? For fun?"

I couldn't tell if the pain helped clear my thoughts or if I was just becoming delusional.

Rodan hissed as he circled me.

"You could be right about what you know. However, there is always something deeper. These 'civilians' act like they're innocent in this war, but I know what they do. Unknowingly aiding our enemy by simply answering questions or providing a form of cooperation. In my eyes, they're all traitors! With what you did, there's no way you know nothing. And I will root it out of you."

The pain kept coming and only took pause when Rodan would interrogate me, like waves in the ocean. I didn't even feel alive, just a vessel for pain. As my torture continued, all I could think about was how to stop it.

I had to give him something, anything, at this point. My mind was scrambling for an answer in between the shocks to my system.

"BPUs! The client paid me in BPUs. Four million total."

I was breathing hard.

"Oh, now that's interesting," Rodan replied.

"Black Palace Units. I'm not surprised The Allegiance used our currency. It holds the most power in all the systems."

I continued in an effort to prolong the next shock.

"Yes! They paid half upfront and I was going to get the rest when the materials were delivered. The delivery area was outside the city of Var on Itarus. You might've known that already, but you can try to see if there is any Allegiance activity in that area."

Part of me felt sick saying this. I felt like a rat doing anything to survive. I didn't care much for The Allegiance, but it didn't take a genius to see that The Black Palace were the oppressors.

The war was a big mess to me, and I just tried to work around it, find a way to survive, and provide for my family. Now I'm in prison, aiding in this war.

Rodan pondered on my answer.

"Itarus is in our control; we are thorough with any enemy activity there. However, The Allegiance using BPUs for smuggling in this system, that is new to us."

He started to face the sting chamber's exit.

"Traitors like you always have something we can use. We have more work to do; this is just the beginning."

The shock hit again like a crashing wave. It always felt worse than the last one. My vision was now flashing in red and white.

My body was jolting now as a reaction to the burning in my muscles. My shrieks hurt my own ears, and tears stung my eyes.

The room was fading. I couldn't see anymore; it felt like I was losing my hold on this world. The pain was still there, but it felt different. Will I die soon? Will I be free?

Water filled coughs shook me back into reality. Looks like I wasn't dead, but I was pretty close. I was face down in dirt and mud. I was finally able to move and found myself in the prison yard.

The guards must've thrown me here after the sting chamber. The air is cold but still uncomfortably muggy. Prisoners are scattered around the yard, they looked more social than before but still carried a sense of hopelessness. I was starting to feel it too.

A voice called out to me. I was shaken at first, the shocks from the stinger made my senses vulnerable.

"They had you there for a while. Usually when someone stays in the sting chamber that long, they don't come back."

It was an inmate, a stringy man wearing matching maroon clothes like I was.

"How long was in there?" I asked.

"Almost a full day, I think. The other prisoners told me what happened in the mess hall. Rookie mistakes are common, but you have the personnel especially interested."

"Why am I so special? Aren't we all prisoners of war? Supporters of The Allegiance?"

The man let out a raggedy laugh.

"Yes! Proud warriors of Corrin we were! They just caught us all on a bad day and whipped our backs red."

His sarcasm didn't amuse me as he continued.

"This prison hasn't had an Allegiance soldier here in months. All the prisoners are here because they're accused of 'helping' the enemy. From what I gathered, we're just civilians, caught in a wrong area or talked to the wrong person."

I wasn't surprised by this. Since being here, none of the inmates really had an appearance of a soldier. I pressed further.

"So, then what did you do?"

The man took a pause and then grunted.

"Not so fast. Why don't we start with names first. You are?"

"Lira Ferzian. I am…was a petty smuggler."

I decided to share more.

"I took a job that was going to set me up for a while. Before I knew it, I was moving Allegiance supplies across zone lines."

"And they caught you. Now that is a serious crime Lira. How could you betray the gracious Black Palace like that?"

The man's mockery was getting annoying.

"What's your name?"

My tone was colder.

"The name I was born with died ages ago. Now everyone just calls me Dek."

Dek raised his arm out to me. I didn't even realize I've been sitting on the ground this entire time. My senses were still scattered from the torture. I grabbed his hand and pulled myself up. Now standing with Dek I got a better look at him.

He was aged but his violet eyes still had some youth in them. Whatever hair he had left on his head was a bright silver. I started to walk with him around the yard.

"Nice to meet you Dek—I think. What did you do to get put here?"

Dek stopped walking.

"That's a story for another time. We should go our own ways now. The guards are setting their sights on us. Just keep to yourself and try not to get in more trouble."

Dek quickly scattered from me. How could he know about the guards' watching when he was focused on me the whole time? I glanced up and around the yard, guards were perched all around and focusing right where I was. Now when I moved to another area of the yard, I could feel their gaze latching onto me.

The Maw was my life now. It didn't feel like a prison but more like a tumor, inevitable and gradually killing me. My buzzing cell kept me from proper rest. The mess hall gave me just enough food to prolong the pain. Visits to the yard were sporadic and Dek was nowhere to be seen.

I thought I was showing good behavior, but I was still sent to the sting chamber. I never got used to that stinging shock. Each time the sting chamber continued to break me. I had no other information to give to Rodan or his guards, but they persisted.

My memory was failing, and my parents' faces were just a blank slate to me. I resented myself for that. It now feels that my spirit is crumbling more than my body. This isn't living, I had to free myself. Death was my only escape. I just needed the right time to truly be free.

My breath was now visible as I drifted around the yard. The cold air was stronger and now piercing deeper into my body. Maybe I can just lay down and freeze to death, just needed to find a good spot.

"Lira," a familiar voice echoed. "What happened to you? You look awful."

"Oh, there you are Dek. I haven't seen you in weeks. I thought the guards were tired of giving you senior care and put you down."

Dek's laugh gave me small comfort.

"Still here for now. I just had to keep my distance. The guards beat me pretty bad after talking to you. Put me in the sting chamber too."

My comfort fleeted as Dek explained himself. All that punishment just for talking to me.

"Why are you talking to me now? Won't they come after you?"

"Possibly, but the guards aren't around right now."

Dek was right. No guards were surrounding the yard like they usually were. Just sentry towers scanning the area for breaches. Something felt very different.

"What's going on Dek?"

"I heard word The Maw is receiving a big transfer today. More new prisoners than usual. Some of the prisoners are rumored to be Allegiance soldiers and commanders."

Dek's voice started to lower as he spoke.

"My guy who told me this is kind of full of it so I'm not sure about the soldier part. But there's definitely a big shipment happening."

"Rodan must be having all guards at the helm for this." I started to hear a soft rumble, which reminded me of the rumble from my carrier ship. "I think they're here. Is there a way to see them?"

"I'd stay away. Anytime you interact with another inmate, Rodan and his lackeys think it's some big conspiracy."

Dek started to walk off towards the yard exit.

"It's getting too cold out, I'm going to see if I can get back to my cell. It's good to see you Lira. You should request more shower time, you need it."

I smirked as Dek headed out. My curiosity was starting to spark. Something is happening here. I might have to find out what it is.

My next few days were spent in my cell. Time was already skewed to me, so they went by quickly. I found myself back in the mess hall with my body begging for food. The hall was much more occupied than it had been. New inmates were littered around the tables causing commotion with conversations and eating, it almost felt lively. I couldn't help but hear a group of them making a lot of noise.

When I went to fill my tray, I subconsciously chose to sit close to them. I wasn't directly facing the group, just in a spot where I could hear them clearly. The guards were also surrounding this area, alerted by all the chattering.

"So you were part of the liberation team on Catovaz?," One of the new prisoners asked. "I heard things got vicious over there."

"Yes, it wasn't easy. But we persisted and freed the people of Tor'vazin. Not without the help of the Ice Warriors, of course," another prisoner replied.

This one seemed to be the center of attention. The group was surrounding him and hanging on every word.

"How did you end up here then Elzander?"

This other prisoner knew his name.

"Catovaz is a whole other star system away."

Elzander smiled. He looked closer to my age. His hair was cut short, and his eyes were a shade of green I haven't seen before on a person. It was hard to tell what planet he originated from. He answered his audience member.

"You are very right. I've been with The Allegiance for a while now, and we've led rebellions all across the universe. My campaign has now brought me here, captured by the enemy. But I will always fight for freedom, no matter where I am!"

While the inmates were enamored by his charming words, one of the guards chuckled. It was one of the reptilians.

"This fool is obviously lying. You idiots can't see though his performance?"

The guard motioned for support.

"I swear each new batch of prisoners we obtain, the dumber they become. If you aren't eating anymore, it's time to wrap it up."

"That's what the enemy wants you to believe," Elzander continued, "They will try to bring us down. We just need to stay strong. We have a lot of potential freedom fighters here. People with talents that will move us forward."

I noticed he was staring at me. Guards were closing in and I got up from my table.

That guard wasn't wrong; his reptilian senses can tell if he's honest. Elzander was so dramatic, even I could tell something didn't feel right. One thing was true however, he knew something about me. How can this be possible when I've never met him?

I felt a grab around my arm. I assumed it was a guard escorting me to my cell.

"You're the smuggler, right?"

It was Elzander. I swung my arm and pushed him aside.

"Wrong person. You should get lost."

"I think you're the right person. My apologies if I was too direct. I should've respected your space."

Elzander started backing away from me.

"Whatever… why are you lying to all these people? Do you hate your life so much that you make up these tales to entertain yourself?"

I snapped at him.

His voice went to a low whisper

"Ok maybe some things might've been dramatized. But I am Allegiance, and I know about what you did. I'm going to need your help soon."

The guards cleared most of the mess hall and were getting closer to us. I answered quickly.

"Help with what?"

"Our liberation!"

Elzander smirked. Then he hunched over his legs while taking a punch to the gut from one of the guards. The other guards grabbed me and led me back to my cell. Is Elzander really serious? I barely know him, and now I'm needed for freedom. He must be truly delusional, maybe his head hasn't adjusted to the swamp air yet.

As I was serving my time, I noticed something. My visits to the sting chamber were less consistent. Rodan must be using it to interrogate the new inmates. I wondered if he had an interest in Elzander. Under all his deception, there could be some truth in there, and Rodan would definitely work to get it out of him.

Whenever I saw Elzander he was either getting pummeled by the guards or telling his tall tales to anyone who would listen.

One night I was in the yard, wearing layered clothes, as the cold air was now freezing. I noticed Dek leaning on the gate wall. I approached him and he didn't move away from me. I guess that I wasn't the focus of the personnel as I was when I first got here.

"Good to see you again Dek."

Dek didn't look at me. He just kept staring up at the open air we all shared. We just stood there for a moment. There was a deep sadness in Dek's voice when he finally replied.

"Do you want to know why I'm here?"

"Sure. What happened?"

Dek sighed as he answered, while still looking up at the night sky.

"When the war started, billions of cities across the systems revolted. So many people were displaced. My wife and I were blessed to keep our home and still live our lives. My wife, Binar, she was a genuine angel, always looking to help those in need."

He swallowed hard.

"An old woman came to our door, needing a meal and a place to stay for the night. They came from a village decimated by Black Palace 'peacekeepers'. Sh-She took her in and cared for this woman like she cared for so many others."

I saw tears in Dek's eyes as he continued. His voice broke a bit but was still clear.

"A few days passed and The Black Palace came to our door. They told us the woman we helped was a spy and accused us of being conspirators against The All Father. We knew this was a lie. Binar called them out; said they just didn't want people knowing about the atrocities they're committing in the name of 'peace'. She was immediately shot in front of me."

I gasped as Dek went on. Tears were falling from his face.

"I've never moved so fast to kill someone. I was ready to die next to her. Before I realized it, I was unconscious and on my way to this forsaken pit."

Dek's sadness turned to anger. I've never seen so much passion in his eyes before.

Dek's story stunned me to my core. The Black Palace has caused so much devastation. They want to blame us, the people, for starting this war and rallying behind Corrin. Regardless of how it started, the boiling point was inevitable.

I felt more enraged now, they want to call me traitor then fine. I'll gladly take that title and actually do something about it. I turned to Dek.

"What if we fought back?"

"I'm not sure how we could. They've broken us. Do you know something going on?"

I looked around. It seemed no guards were surveying us.

"I'm not sure. But I have a feeling things will change."

Dek stood off the wall.

"There was a spark in your eye when you said that. Whatever happens, I'm with you. We can either be liberated or I can see my sweet Binar again. Either way it's a win for me."

Dek's laughter bounced off the yard's walls as he walked away.

As I started to head back to my cell escort area, I heard footsteps pounding towards me. It was Elzander, sporting new bruises and cuts all over his face. I could tell he was trying to be confident, but there was a sense of urgency in him and possibly fear.

He was walking right behind me now as I stayed ahead. I didn't want anyone to see us too close and he knew the optics.

"Things are coming together, but I need you to make it all happen."

I felt my neck stiffen as I answered.

"Make what happen? What do you need me for?"

"I can't say that right now. They're watching us. All I can ask is for you to trust me. You don't have to do this, but I need your answer now. Are you in or out?"

Elzander's vagueness didn't help me at all. I replied.

"Are we going to die for this?"

He lowered his voice.

"We might be dead already just for this conversation. Are you with me?"

I broke off from his path behind me. The guards started to fill in and escort us to our cells. Doubt, fear, and dread filled me as I was taken. Then I looked back, and I could still see Elzander.

His gaze wasn't breaking; it felt like he was starting into my spirit, whatever was left of it. I nodded quickly and mouthed the words.

"I'm in."

I was expecting Rodan to have me put to death or sent to the sting chamber at least, but neither happened. The buzzing from the cells didn't bother me anymore, but I still couldn't sleep.

I laid awake in my cell just accompanied by my thoughts. I wondered about Dek and his suffering. I worried for Elzander, if he was killed by now. The most persistent thought is what I agreed to and what it even was.

The food at the mess hall tasted horrible. Did something change or am I actually tasting my food? I was starving but could barely stomach a few bites. From the corner of my vision, I saw a familiar short haired man sit down at a table.

No mistake, it was Elzander. The wounds on his head were healing, showing more of his face. I took a deep breath and walked to his table and sat in front of him.

"This is it Lira. We're starting!"

Chills dashed through my body as I froze up. I was still able to answer.

"Are you serious? We're out in the open. You still haven't told me what's happening."

"I'm telling you now. It's simple Lira. You're a smuggler and I need you to run a route."

"What are you even saying?!"

I was being too loud but didn't care at this point.

"We're in a cafeteria. How can you even operate from here?"

Elzander stood up from the table.

"I've been operating since I got here."

He then dove right into me, tackling me into the ground. His hands grabbed my shirt tightly as he got close to my face.

"I'm going to make this as clear as possible. As you can already tell I'm making a scene. This scene is a distraction. When the guards pull me off, I'm going to escalate and lure them away from here. While that's going on you're going to the old maintenance walkway right here in the mess hall. It's behind the food station in the corner. At the end of the maintenance walkway there's an old hatch on the ceiling. An Allegiance prisoner put an old transponder on that hatch months ago. Rodan and his team never noticed it, but we need it turned on. That is your route."

The guards started to run to us now. We only had a few seconds left. Elzander got more aggressive.

"When our soldier placed the transponder, he never received the code to activate it. But we have it now, it's 4-2-9-5. Got it?! 4-2-9-5!"

The prison guards quickly pulled him off me. As they lifted us to our feet Elzander moved swiftly. He shoved one of the guards off him then followed up with a quick jab at their helmet. The agitated guard then pulled out their pistol and screamed at Elzander. All those beatings he took must've been useful. He moved quickly again like he knew all the guards' movements and snatched the pistol from their hand. While doing so he spun around and choked the guard from behind while placing the gun on the side of their helmet.

"I'll kill him right now I swear!" Elzander had the rest of the guards shaken.

"He's coming with me and if anyone tries anything I'll blow his head right off!"

Elzander started to move out of the mess hall. The guards were following him with their rifles drawn. As they exited, metallic doors came crashing down on all entrances. We were locked in, but for me it didn't matter.

The maintenance walkway was inside the hall, right in the corner, like Elzander said. I made my move and sprinted towards it.

As I headed to the entrance of the walkway, I heard an alarm ring and the intercom screamed out.

"CODE 8-R. PRISONER HAS TAKEN A HOSTAGE AND IS HEADING TOWARDS CORRIDOR G. ALL UNITS INTERCEPT IMMEDIATELY."

The maintenance walkway was deeper than I thought as I dashed through it. It felt older than the rest of the prison and unkept. I swatted away dust and cobwebs while ducking low hanging pipes. The alarm was still blaring in the mess hall but got quieter as I moved deeper. I finally reached the end and found some climbing bars that lead to the ceiling.

My heart pounded hard as I climbed my way up to the hatch. The height wasn't daunting, but it was very narrow. I would call myself petite and even I barely fit. Maybe this is why Elzander specifically needed me to do it. At last, I made it to the hatch and there it was covered in dust, the transponder.

I frantically blew all the dust off the device until I could see a number pad. It was all right there, our ticket out could really be just a code away. I entered the code exactly like I was told 4-2-9-5. At first it didn't seem to do anything, but then I heard a faint bleep. A small green light flashed repeatedly on the transponder. The flashing green light illuminated my face in the dark narrow space. I couldn't stop smiling as I started to make my way down.

I didn't know what was waiting for me back at the mess hall, but I had to make it back. When I stepped back to the ground from the climbing bars, sparks flew by my head. It came from the ceiling, and I looked up in dread. The transponder light wasn't blinking anymore.

I didn't have time to go back up there. I was already running back to the mess hall while hearing the alarm ring out again. Did the signal work or did it break? Doubts started to pour in as I found myself back in the mess hall. To my surprise no guards were there yet, just inmates standing around confused. The alarm stopped completely. A message came from the intercom.

"PRISONER HAS BEEN ACQUIRED. LOCKDOWN WILL END IN TEN MINUTES. ALL REMAINING PRISONERS WILL BE DETAINED."

My worry rushed in while hearing that message. How far did Elzander go, and how will he pay the price? Suddenly, I heard a low hiss resonate from the walls. Before I could react, a surge of energy spread across the floor we all stood on.

The immediate shock immobilized my body; it felt just like the shock from the stinger. I crumbled onto the floor, motionless but still awake. I heard the lockdown doors rise, and the guards rushed back in. They were yelling at each other loudly while grabbing our limp bodies.

Rodan had all of us chained and grouped together in the yard. It was lightly raining and made the freezing air sting a bit more. Rodan was standing before us with a prisoner next to him. It was Elzander and he was on his knees, bound.

His entire body was battered, and blood dripped from his mouth. It was a horrible sight, but I was relieved he survived. Rodan looked angrier than ever, like a true monster. He scanned the entire yard and hissed before he spoke.

"Treacherous scum! Thanks to our prisoner here, things are going to get a lot worse for all of you!"

He grabbed Elzander by the back of the head and lifted him back. Elzander winced in pain as Rodan continued.

"While this gutter trash was playing suicide by guard, something else happened. We detected a foreign signal coming from an old maintenance hatch."

My body was still as Rodan said this, even though every part of me wanted to hurl. Rodan looked around the group again with his penetrating red eyes.

"That was a clever trick to get this signal out. Unfortunately for all of you, that signal didn't go anywhere. We have disruptors on every tower in The Maw and we quickly snuffed it out. Now we need to snuff out whoever did this."

Rodan turned to Elzander.

"It's not possible to have the signal active while you were in a completely different area. Who helped you with this plan?"

Elzander put on his usual smirk and replied

"Nobody. It was all me sir, I'm just that good."

I wanted to scream but only stood in silence. I needed Elzander to tell the truth. Our plan failed; he didn't have to die for my mistake.

With Rodan grabbing Elzander by the neck he raised his free hand. His sharp claws extended swiftly; they now looked like swords on each of his fingers.

"This is the last time I will ask you. Who helped you?"

This was enough, I was about to say something but felt a nudge on my arm.

It was Dek. He looked right at me and motioned me to be quiet. Just from the expression on his face I can see that he couldn't bear to lose me. Tears blurred my vision as I dreadfully watched on.

Elzander looked at all of us and smiled wider this time.

"It was all me Rodan. I wanted to free everyone in the name of Allegiance but I failed. I'm sorry everyone."

Rodan's red eyes twitched as he listened.

"You're nothing but a liar!"

He then plunged his claws into Elzander's chest. With his blood splashing on the ground his smile started to fade.

The rain soaked Elzander's hair as his eyes started to roll back. Rodan pulled his claws out of him and he collapsed into the ground. I was past my breaking point and screamed.

My screaming was louder than any of the times I was tortured. This pain was deeper somehow. Dek put his head down as I continued to wail.

Rodan reacted to my cries in the crowd.

"It's Lira, she's the other traitor. Why am I not surprised? Guards, bring her to me!"

The guards quickly seized me as I kicked around. I was tired of being moved everywhere, sick of all the subjugation. All I can do is lash out.

"Monsters! Tyrants! That's all you'll ever be! We're not even soldiers. You just want bodies to justify this cursed place!"

"With what you did, you're even worse than a soldier. The only fitting punishment is death."

Rodan flashed his teeth at me before moving his claws towards my neck. As I felt them press deeper something quickly fell from the rainy sky.

Everyone paused to look at it. It was an unknown canister that instantly spewed smoke. The smokescreen spread almost instantly. I couldn't even see Rodan in front of me. Then a massive explosion rattled me to the ground.

Everything happened so quickly I couldn't even remember it fully. There were flashes of moments that I'll never forget. Blaster fire zoomed across the smoke-filled air. I felt more explosions shake The Maw; it felt like the towers were being targeted. The sounds of ships rocketing ripped across the rain filled sky.

I saw guards scramble to pursue the attackers but were dropped dead before even finding their target. Rodan wasn't far from me. I saw him pick up a dead guards' rifle and returned fire towards the hidden invaders. The entire prison started to shake. A ship was starting to descend right into the yard, clearing the smokescreen as it approached.

I sat up, my thoughts became clearer to me. The descending ship was fully visible. Looking at the insignias, there was no mistaking it. The Allegiance is here!

A recognizable hand reached to me like it had before. It was Dek and he frantically pulled me up.

"Can you move? We need to go. Now!"

I responded by running with him while evading blaster shots and flying debris. The ship had now landed in the yard about three hundred feet away from us. The load doors lowered, and Allegiance soldiers poured out; all wearing distinct uniforms from their native planets.

They motioned us to get in while gunning down the remaining guards. As we sprinted toward our freedom, I couldn't help but to look back at Elzander. However, the only figure right behind us was Rodan with his rifle pointed right at me.

"Lira. No!"

Dek pushed me out of the line of fire. He took a direct blast through his back, and he fell back in agony.

The Allegiance soldiers immediately directed their fire at Rodan and decimated him into chunks. I crawled onto Dek's body; smoke was coming out of his mouth. I didn't want to accept that he died right there.

"Dek please no! We were supposed to leave together!"

One of the Allegiance soldiers pulled me off him. They carried me into the Allegiance ship while firing back at the remaining Maw forces.

I woke up to a low hum. My body felt rested, like I slept normally for once. Memories came back to me; I was rescued by The Allegiance and this must be one of their ships.

Fellow prisoners were scattered around me. We were in a large cargo hold of the ship, with most of the inmates laying around. A few of them had bandages covering them. I then noticed I had small bandages on my neck and arms. Based on just the people in the cargo hold it seemed like they saved about eighty of us.

The last prisoner count I remembered at The Maw was two hundred and forty. No one saw Elzander or Dek as I asked around. My worst fears were realized, they didn't make it.

The cargo hold had a large opening into a larger corridor. I couldn't help but head that way while looking around the large new ship. While making my way down the corridor an Allegiance soldier stopped me.

"Lira Ferzian?"

"How do you know my name?" I asked.

"We kept a file on you, ever since you helped with our shipment on Itarus."

"Oh really? Well, that didn't turn out great for anyone."

The soldier laid his rifle on a nearby gun stand. "Yea, our apologies for that mishap. But thanks to your trade lines we were able to move our forces more easily around Itarus. Many people were saved because of you."

He continued.

"Also, without your signal we would've never found The Maw and liberated it."

"How did you find my signal? The warden there told me it was quickly intercepted."

"Well technically yes it was. But we have counter-intercept tracking. We were able to find your location based on the ping of The Maw's disruptors. Courtesy of the planet Myeros' new technologies."

I was stunned by their resourcefulness.

"That's pretty impressive. None of this would've been possible though without Elzander's planning."

I took a deep sigh.

"Did you know him?"

"Oh, you mean the 'great liberator' himself?" the soldier said with patronizing tone. "Yes, Elzander is definitely something. He does pull through when needed. Speaking of that, I think he's healing up in the med bay. Luckily, we had a Wan-Ri healer with us. He was in pretty bad shape."

I immediately started to run to the med bay; almost toppling the soldier as I pushed past him. The med bay rooms were overfilled with injured prisoners and soldiers.

I had no idea which one was his. From one of the rooms a woman exited. She was tall and beautiful, exotic garments covered her body and her hands were lightly glowing. This must be the healer. I went to the medical room she exited from and there he was. I almost cried again when seeing him.

He was in bed with his eyes closed. I held onto his arm tightly. I couldn't believe he made it. I saw Rodan's claws go right through him.

These healers must work miracles. I collapsed to the ground while still holding his arm. It was finally finished. Then I heard a faint voice from the bed

"Stand up Lira, you're a hero now."

THINGS TO COME

Many of The Allegiance forces scattered across the universe received word to rendezvous on Kkooddrraa. Word was there was a Black Palace battalion ravaging the planet. The message being sent out was that Corrin, Morgana, Zhao-Lan, and other Allegiance leaders were already there, meaning the fight must be important.

"Radio to all nearby Allegiance ships, Station One should be a good place to meet up before entering Kkooddrraa's atmosphere. Also, see if we can get word down to the ground. Corrin and the others should be aware that we're coming so we don't get shot out of the sky."

A young man chuckled. His name was Qinto Relm, a native of Taelvum, and a staunch Allegiance supporter. He joined the cause immediately after Corrin's battle for the New Worlds and he assumed command of about nine Allegiance aligned ships located in the Davos System. His tiny, yet fierce, fleet consisted of Allegiance fighters from Taelvum, Vaxlier, and LweeVeer. He even had the respect of Supreme Commander Roan Vallick of Anrach. After joining The Allegiance, Qinto strived to make his mark. He and his crew won vicious dog fights against Black Palace Spearcrafts above Telamor, attacked numerous

Spearcraft Carriers, and even air struck important Black Palace outposts. His name spread fast across Allegiance channels, even though Allegiance leadership hadn't recognized him for his valor or efforts. He told himself he didn't care about that, but deep down he did.

"Relm, nothing yet from the ground. Just static," a radio tech said to Qinto from the communication station.

"Hmm, the battle must be fierce," Qinto replied, his eyes glimmering with excitement.

Qinto's fleet ripped through the Davos System, passing Telamor and Vaxlier on the way to Kkooddraa. The crew on each ship communicated with each other, doing weapons checks and thruster maintenance, making sure the ships were stable at top speed.

"How far out are we from Kkooddrraa?" Qinto asked his pilot.

"Eight minutes," the pilot responded.

"And any word from the ground yet?" Qinto asked, a hint of concern painted his tone.

"None yet," the radio tech replied, turning to Qinto and giving him a worrisome look.

"Keep trying," Qinto said, peering out the ship's windows into open space.

His fleet followed close by, keeping pace. He watched them move as his mind ran with thoughts on why there was no word from the ground. As his mind continued to race, an incoming alert rang from the communication station. The radio tech answered. Qinto turned, eagerly waiting.

"Yes," the radio tech said into her mic, "Of course ma'am. Thank you, ma'am."

The radio tech smiled to herself. Qinto impatiently pulled at his trousers.

"Qinto Relm, ma'am," the radio tech said into her mic.

She turned to Qinto.

"It's General Gaffen of Yres, she asked who is in charge and wants to speak to you."

Qinto's eyes lit up with pride. He jolted to the radio, clearing his throat before he spoke.

"This is Qinto Relm!"

"Relm," Gaffen said on the other end of the radio, "I've heard great things about you."

Qinto tried to hide the smile forming on his face. This was his first time speaking to Allegiance leadership, and getting to speak to General Gaffen almost made him jump out of his boots.

General Gaffen continued. "We received your message. Are you confirming this information about what's happening on Kkooddrraa?"

Qinto spoke fast, this was his moment.

"Yes ma'am! We're currently on route to the planet. We've pinged the ground with no response.

Communication towers must be down so we are going in blind."

There was silence for a moment. Qinto's crew looked him, watching with pride as their leader took control of the situation. Qinto then spoke again.

"With your permission, I'd like to request all Allegiance forces to head to Kkooddrraa to aid Corrin."

There was another moment of silence on the other end. Qinto tightened up as he felt like he might of overstepped his position. He looked around at his crew. Their expressions were frozen as he held his breath. He let out a sigh of relief as General Gaffen finally spoke.

"Commander Qinto, I'll put in word across the other star systems to fulfill your request!"

Qinto punched the air as Gaffen delivered the news. She continued.

"With no update on the status of Corrin and the others on the ground, the situation is dire. With your crew being the first ones arriving, you'll have command of the operation, wether it be an assault or rescue mission, everyone will be informed to follow your lead."

Qinto was shocked. His heart was racing with joy and excitement.

"Yes ma'am. Thank you General. This is an honor of the highest degree."

"Honor is irrelevant right now, Commander. We are urgently awaiting your command! I'll keep this channel open for your updates. We here on Yres have a saying, 'Ride with the tides'. Ride with the tides, Qinto."

Qinto set the mic down and turned to his crew. All the other ships floated nearby. His moment was here. As he geared up to continue on route to Kkooddrraa, one of the pilots called out.

"Qinto…we have multiple objects coming in on us fast."

Qinto rushed to the screen. The objects were racing towards the fleet. As they neared the number grew, and kept growing until the screen was covered in a fast moving blotch.

One of the pilots leaned into the glass as their eyes widened.

"What..what is THAT?" The pilot screamed.

Qinto slowly raised his head as a swarm of creatures zoomed towards his fleet. His mouth slightly dropped as one, two, three ships were engulfed by the creatures. He turned quickly to his radio tech as the swarm reached his ship.

"Get General Gaffen on the line now. This is an emergen——."

GLOSSARY

CHARACTERS

Acorlius, Party Leader - (Aa-core-lee-us)

Amali

Andros, Colonel - (Ann-drose)

Arboc - (Are-bock)

Asher Kells

Benjar

Bi-Zo - (Bye-zohe)

Binar - (Bih-nah-are)

Byeron, Commander - (Bye-run)

Chase

Dagon - (Duh-gone)

Darr, Lieutenant

Darrius, Lieutenant - (Dare-ree-us)

Dek - (Dehk)

Doren - (Door-ren)

Druan - (Druu-on)

Durge - (Durr-jhe)

Elara - (Eh-larr-ah)

Elzander - (Ehl-zan-dur)

Fehir - (Fehh-here)

Fennik, Admiral - (Fehh-nick)

Fia - (Fee-uh)

Gem - (Jeh-em)

Graida - (Gray-duh)

Grock

Gydian, Commander - (Gid-dee-ann)

Havara - (Huh-var-rah)

Heleyna - (He-lay-nuh)

Hilipp - (Hill-upp)

Himroc - (Him-rock)

Horace Va'Rolikun -
(Hoor-russ-vah-role-lee-kunn)

Iinya - (Een-yuh)

Jargus, General - (Jarr-guhs)

Jen

Jessipe - (Jeh-seh-pee)

Jing

Jonli Wirbusing - (Jun-lee-werr-boo-sing)

Jor-San - (Joor-sun)

Kagra Zed - (Kah-gruh-zehd)

Kai-Lung - (Kye-lung)

Kei Yu-Lung - (Kay-yuu-lung)

Kelv

Kreeden Kray

Kurai, Commander - (Kuu-rye)

Lin-Po

Lira Ferzian - (Lee-ruh-fur-zee-ann)

Lycan, President - (Lie-cann)

Lyd'da - (Lid-dee-ah)

Lykard - (Lie-kurd)

Lyle, Commander

Maki - (Mah-kee)

Makisia Bularem -
(Mah-kee-see-uh-Boo-lah-rehmm)

Markovitch, Company Leader - (Marr-cohe-viitch)

Matzin Drexy - (Maht-ziin-dreh-xee)

Mornur - (More-noor)

Niles, Corporal

Odarus Med, Scout Leader - (Oh-darr-us-mehd)

Orkick, Commander - (Ore-kick)

Q, B. Yoring - (Yore-ring)

Qinto Relm, Commander - (Qinn-toe-realm)

Radia - (Ray-dee-uh)

Raito - (Rye-toe)

Rat, The

Reya, Admiral - (Raye-uh)

Roan Vallick, Supreme Commander - (Roahn-vah-lick)

Rodan-Klashik, Grand Warden -
(Rohe-dan-klah-sheek)

Romeo, Ensign

Roxy, Commander

Rylan - (Rye-lan)

Sands, Commander

Satro - (Sah-trohe)

Seben - (Seh-behn)

Sei'yd, Lieutenant - (Sigh-eed)

Sibyl - (Siib-el)

Siphra - (Sii-fra-uh)

Smin, Commander

Suny Havok - (Sun-ee)

Syd Jay

Tai-Elle Anhil - (Tye-el)

Taiyo - (Tye-oh)

Tama - (Tah-muh)

Tan'ya, Captain

Takeshi - (Tah-keh-shee)

Tera

Tilditch Nequois, Captain -
(Till-ditch-Neh-qah)

Troi'tn, Commander - (Troy-ten)

Vander Hox

Venrum, Marshal

PLANETS, PLACES

Academy, The - The Academy is a military officer school located on the planet Anrach. This is where the planet's defense forces mold, forge, and produce Anrach's military leaders.

Anrach - Located in the Davos System, the exo planet Anrach was said by Itarian Scribes to have been formed some time between 310,000-105,000 BTLS(Before The Long Sleep). Isolated by a dense wall of asteroids, Anrach is host to a robust population of over 75 billion. Surrounding the planet is an artificial ring, housing hundreds of shipyards for both civilian and military use.

Black Palace Youth Center - An indoctrination hub located on various planets. The Black Palace Youth Center provides propaganda, resources, and tools for the native youth.

Davos System - After abdicating the Itarian throne and joining the Scribes of Noplia, Davos went on an expedition past the Rayon Prime System, discovering a new planet. From here, the Itarian Empire would conquer Anrach, Halvodon, Kkooddrraa, LweeVeer, Taelvum, Telamor, and Vaxlier. In his honor, the Itarians named this system after the would-be emperor, immortalizing him across the cosmos. The Davos system has two suns.

Dragon's Hoard, The - A large, round orb of smelted Itarian gold and silver. The Dragon's Hoard is the home satellite base of Subspace Underworld crime lord, Vander Hox.

Drexa - A small city located on the planet Rashalon. Drexa is home to Raito, Kurai, Tama, and Siphra. Drexa was known to spark rebellions against The Black Palace in the early days of The All Father's reconquest.

Foryo - A frigid wasteland, the moon Foryo is home to The Network.

Ga-Gadan - A major city on the planet Telamor, Ga-Gadan is a central hub for the centaur-like beings that roam the mountainous planet.

Ge Hinnom - Located on the moon Foryo and inside The Network. Ge Hinnom is where most captives go to be searched, processed, and sometimes executed.

Hanroh - A small planet ravaged by enslavement and colonialism. Hanroh is home to small communities of beings with sharp, long claws for hands. The planet is dry and dusty, with no moon in its orbit. With its low gravity, debris and rocks mask the atmosphere. Hanroh is also home to The Pit, a Black Palace mining facility that forces the natives to dig minerals for The All Father's military.

Jotuun - The first line of defense, Jotuun is a moon of the planet Anrach. Jotuun is used as a forward operation base for the Anarchi fleet.

Kyros VI - Kyros VI is the sister planet of Anrach. Annexed by The Black Palace, Kyros VI became the first military objective for the Anrachi military.

Lumina - Home to weapons maker Rylan, Lumina is a small city on Vaxlier with strong loyalties to The Black Palace.

Maw, The - Located on Di, The Maw is a Black Palace prison. The prison houses political prisoners, dissidents, and dangerous Allegiance members. To meet monthly quotas, The Maw began to arrest anyone suspected to not be 100% loyal to The All Father.

Mehdias JX7 - From Kaasiar to Myero, all the way from Scav to Catovaz, the Mehdias JX7 System is home to some of the most robust planets in the universe. Ice worlds, planets with toxic fumes, and the birthplace of some of the cosmos' greatest fighters, the Mehdias JX7 System is a spectacle. Named after an Itarian emperor's Cosmic Dragon, this system was the last to be discovered by the Itarian Empire.

Mount Ita'r Rus - A large mountain range located on the planet Catovaz, Mount Ita'r Rus was named by the Itarian Empire.

Network, The - Located on the moon Foryo, The Network is an unsanctioned Black Palace site known for its brutal, illegal, and fatal experiments on people with Spear Energy abilities.

New Var - Capital city on the planet Catovaz, New Var was named after the Itarian city of Var when the Itarian Empire invaded in the Seventh Cycle. Known for it's rebellions throughout history, New Var was the first city to completely eradicate its Black Palace presence.

Paradin - The largest city on the small mining planet Gorkon, Paradin is a trading hub for many throughout the universe. Known for its cheap prices, rare items, and Subspace Underworld activity, Paradin provides refueling stations for travelers. The city is also a hotspot for Black Palace prisoner transport. Since Paradin is the largest city on Gorkon, Black Palace command sanctioned it as a docking point for anyone being sent to The Maw, or other prison camps.

Raisa IV - Located in the Mehdias JX7 system, Raisa IV was sanctioned by the Itarian Empire as a dead planet. When the Itarians invaded in the Seventh Cycle, they found remnants of a lost civilization. As the Scribes of Noplia tried to uncover what happened on Raisa IV, many scribes were reported to have lost their minds, and go missing. The Itarian emperor at the time implemented a No Travel Ban on the planet up until the dissolution of the empire. After The All Father woke up from The Long Sleep, Black Palace outposts were set up across the planet, and its small moon. With The Black Palace sealing off access to the planet and its moon, this alerted many within the Subspace Underworld to believe something of importance was found, launching a crusade by many to uncover whatever was being kept a secret.

Rayon Prime System - Host to seven habitable, and inhabitable worlds, the Rayon Prime System belongs to Rashalon, Gorkon, Yres, Pugart, Nyla, Jargun-Ba, and Braroclyn. The name Rayon comes from an Itarian scribe who discovered the system towards the middle of the Fifth Cycle.

Sky-View - An ancient city located on the planet Myero, Sky-View is very lively and keeps its youth by younger generations.

Thrax - Compared to most worlds, Thrax is extremely primitive. Unknown to the Itarians, and discovered by The Black Palace in the Ninth Cycle, Thrax is home to the Thraxians, a small community of beings unaware of who or what The All Father is.

Tor'vazin - A city located on Catovaz, Tor'vazin was liberated by The Allegiance when the War for The Universe started. (Side Note: Elzander during his time at The Maw claims to have been apart of the liberation campaign, but no record has ever been found.)

Vorath - Located on Fargulk, and named after the first Itarian emperor Vorza, Vorath is a large metropolitan city. Plagued by millenniums of massacres, disease, and pillaging, Vorath eventually grew to a heightened status after The All Father woke up from The Long Sleep.

Warin 3 - Warin 3 is the largest moon to the planet Nyla, and fifth largest moon in the known universe.

Xharcos Bay - Liberated from The Black Palace by The Allegiance, Xharcos Bay is a city located on the interconnected planet of LweeVeer.

ITEMS, CREATURES, GROUPS, ABILITIES

Anrachi Republic Combined Forces - Planetary military power of the planet Anrach.

APC - Military term within the Anrachi Defense Force which means Armored Personnel Carrier.

Black Guard - Created by Commander Troi'tn, the Black Guard is a private military unit tasked with protecting The Network. The Black Guard are lobotomized Spear Energy users, repurposed to protect Troi'tn's illegal experimental lab.

BPU - BPU, which stands for Black Palace Unit, is the standard currency for The Black Palace and all the worlds.

Bluepaz - Bluepaz is a nutritious rock used as a food source for the beings on Nyla.

Corvath - Anrachi Destroyer class ship under Admiral Reya's command.

Galefer Collection, The - Galefer was a scientist who looked at Spear Energy from a more biological perspective and connected it to the greater universe. Galefer died under mysterious circumstances before he could complete his third volume.

Gorgoshu Meat - Gorgoshu meat is a native dish on the planet Wan-Ri.

HawkMoon, The - The HawkMoon is the ship of Supreme Commander Roan Vallick.

Ironium Metal - Ironium Metal is a precious resource on the planet Hanroh. Known for its resilience and strong resistance to fire, The Black Palace began using Ironium Metal as a second plating for Spearcraft Carriers.

MagiDa, The - The MagiDa, meaning 'Deliverer' in Telamori, is a large four legged beast with scales, yellow eyes, and a tongue that hisses.

Maven Manufactorum - A military contractor on Anrach, Maven Manufactorum provides the Anrachi Defense Force with state-of-the-art designs to assist in military campaigns.

Of Kings and Fools - A piece of literature from the planet Rashalon. 'Of Kings and Fools' is a satire depicting the ancient houses of Rashalon and the wars that took place in the early Cycles.

OIP - OIP stands for Orbital Insertion Pod and is used by the Anrachi military to bring infantry troops from orbit, to the ground.

Obrah Silentum - The Obrah Silentum is an Anrachi cruiser capable of large troop movement. It was put into effect during Operation Iron Dawn.

S.C.C. Darkstar - Spearcraft Carrier Darkstar is one of the many Spearcraft Carriers located in the Davos system. It was defeated by Admiral Reya and the Anrachi Rapid Reaction Forces.

Sabo Industries - Sabo Industries is a manufacturing conglomerate that builds the warships for the Anrachi military. Sabo Industries is credited with the creation of the famous HawkMoon, ship of Supreme Commander Roan Vallick.

Sylvana's Kiss - The Silvana's Kiss is an Anrachi cruiser and the personal command ship of Admiral Reya.

Subspace Underworld - From Vorza's first interplanetary conquest, through the rise of The Black Palace, a rot dwelled just beneath the surface of of the universe. Drug running, prostitution, trafficking, weapons smuggling, and a myriad of other crimes were taking place--much to the embarrassment of the Itarian empire and, later, The All Father himself. This rot was widely known as the Subspace Underworld. The Subspace Underworld has no rulers or kings. Power flows like an ocean in a storm. Amidst the waves of chaos, gang wars and power struggles are a common occurrence. A crime lord could be at the top of the food chain one day and at the bottom the next. Billions of criminal organizations can be operational at any single moment in the Subspace Underworld's history. The Hox Pirates, The Last Giants, and the Red Suns are just a few of the known organizations that operate in the shadow of the universe.

Surface Chronicler, The - One of the many news outlets across the universe, The Surface Chronicler is considered a reputable source. With billions of readers, there are some who accuse the news outlet of being a mouthpiece for The Black Palace.

Vyruuck - An Anrachi Destroyer class ship under Admiral Reya's command.

The War for the Universe rages on!

Synopsis of 'The Old Universe: Book 2'

The All Father has released a swarm of beings capable of consuming everything in their path. The Allegiance has dispersed, fearing for their individual safety and the security of their home planets. Corrin, son of The All Father, has decided to go find the answers he needs in order to defeat the creatures his father has unleashed. But during his search, Corrin clashes with SPEARHEAD—an elite Black Palace special operations task force created by Corrin in his youth—and with the RAID RIDERS—a vicious outlaw group from the Faoder Sector.

With The Allegiance in shambles, and The All Father doing everything he can to stop his own son, elements of the past resurface. Amongst the Raid Riders lives a descendant of a once powerful and mighty empire, someone who Corrin believes can help shape a better outcome for the universe. However, resentments run thick and deep across the stars, and many are not ready to forgive transgressions so easily. But an unexpected face from Corrin's childhood returns, showing would-be enemies, that the past does not have to represent the future.

Simultaneously, Evrii has been keeping Arcadia stable. With the help of Zhao-Lan, her home has been shielded away from the ongoing war. Evrii begins to feel she needs to do more and with the help of Morgana, Zhao-Lan, and other notable warriors, Evrii attempts to reform The Allegiance in order to aid Corrin. Although she's determined to join the fight, The All Father himself tries to stop her. With rumors of a massive Black Palace assault on Vor Ran'du being prepared, the urgency to reunite and remove any fear moving forward is dire.

As The Allegiance rushes to Vor Ran'du, Corrin begins to understand the creatures unleashed by The All Father. His ability to manipulate Spear Energy will be tested, secrets will be revealed, and kings will be crowned. But… The All Father won't let anyone forget that he yields the Spear of Space, and although armies can be forged, and battles can be fought, there is a reason he is called The All Father.

Fall 2024